THE DRAGON'S TAIL

NIERGEL CHRONICLES
BOOK FOUR

D. I. HENNESSEY

arkHarbor
press
www.arkharbor.press

ISBN 979-8-9859336-6-6 (Paperback Edition)

ISBN 979-8-9859336-7-3 (Hardcover Edition)

Version 004252026

arkHarbor press, www.arkharbor.press

info@arkhsc.com

To special friends who've endured all those revisions to so many stories and offered invaluable advice. Your support is priceless; it's a great blessing to have you in my life's story.

CONTENTS

"Greater love has no man than this, that a man lay down his life for his friends."

~ John 15:13

IMPOSSIBLE VICTORY

Flashback, Earlier today...

A terrible wailing fills the air.
Ghostly black creatures have begun to surround Jeff in a vicious swarm, filling the room and choking the breath from his lungs. He is fighting desperately, dispatching the monsters, one after another, with brilliant flashes of light — but can feel that his dwindling strength will soon be exhausted.

"LEAVE!" he shouts to Genie, "SAVE YOURSELF! I CAN'T HOLD THEM OFF!"

Before she is able to respond, great numbers of the hideous creatures swarm toward her in an overwhelming and brutal attack. Jeff watches helplessly as she is repeatedly stricken and tossed by the violent onslaught; she thrashes at them in vain, but her formidable fighting skills are useless against the murderous ghostly beings. Jeff vainly blasts the creatures off her time and again, only to see more of the beasts quickly take their place.

"NOOOOOOOOOO!" he screams as they smash her against the

floor, crushing the air from her lungs. His last blast is expended, and his heart sinks at the sight of an endless throng of hellish beasts still flying toward them. Hundreds more are swarming across the castle grounds below.

THE IMAGES in Jeff's dream flash in a vivid nightmare, forcing him to relive the terrifying ordeal. He cries out in his sleep, his body shuddering violently.

Hunahpu comes near his great-grandson's hospital bed and places a reassuring hand on his shoulder, breathing a prayer for holy calm to displace the fearful dream. He waits prayerfully as Jeff grows quiet once again while a nurse wipes the beads of sweat from Jeff's forehead.

The old man moves back to his seat, lifting his Bible from the table beside him and reopening it. Before long, however, Hunahpu's eyes grow heavy, and he stares blankly into its open pages, drifting into a dream of his own as he finds himself reliving the momentous day....

"... Join us here as soon as possible; it's best t'be below ground...," he overhears EB urging Jeff from the underground Lab.

He won't be coming... Hunahpu recalls thinking to himself. He already knew that his great-grandson would not heed EB's warning; he had sensed it. The approaching menace bore an evil much more dangerous than mere bombers. Hunahpu knew that it was Jeff's charge to face that evil — it pained him to know that there was nothing he could do to help his young heir.

Except to pray, that is. Quietly retreating to an empty room beside the Lab, he kneels at a chair, using the room's solitude as a makeshift chapel in which to urgently lift Jeff in intercession. In his pocket, a single seed from the ancient Shepherd's Staff suddenly draws his attention — this one was born from the leaf he had claimed from the

Staff on the day Jeff was chosen by it. He feels oddly compelled to reach for it, holding it in his hand as his heart groans in an unction that can only be fathomed by the Spirit of God who inspired it.

He loses track of the time, as is often the case when he loses himself in prayer. The rumble of a gigantic explosion rouses him, so great that it shakes the air violently and echoes in the underground halls. He rushes into the Lab to see what has happened, hearing EB calling for Jeff on the radio.

"...Jeff... Report... What is your status?"

After a tense silence, Jeff's voice is heard, sounding dazed, but offering great relief to the men underground.

While EB and Jeff are still speaking, Hunahpu feels a sudden foreboding of danger as he registers the distant sound of soldiers screaming over the radio.

"I'll call you back!" they hear Jeff say as his comm link disconnects.

Hunahpu senses he must act quickly; slipping into the elevator, he heads straight for the surface. Though he knows that he can not fight the Eljo himself — the Staff's power is Jeff's alone to wield — he still feels a great urgency to go to him.

The elevator doors open to a deserted lobby. Just beyond the castle's front doors, the sounds of a great conflict can be heard. Hunahpu rushes toward the Rotunda, surprised to notice Eugenia dashing across its white marble expanse far ahead of him. She vaults up the circular staircase, taking several steps at a time, and disappears before he has had time to traverse the great Hall behind her. As he ascends the staircase, he can hear the sound of fighting coming from the office suite, mixed with something else — a cacophony of unearthly sounds, like the eerie wailing of monstrous beasts. Bright flashes of light can be seen reflecting off the walls inside.

The sense of overwhelming evil is unmistakable as Hunahpu enters the outer office, and he drops to his knees. With great dismay, he discerns that the flashes of battle have ended, yet the overbearing presence of evil remains, increasing in ever-greater strength. He begins to lift Jeff urgently in prayer, raising his arms in a desperate plea to God.

Barely an instant later, Hunahpu hears Jeff crying out loudly in a voice that is hoarse and strained but nonetheless clear and forceful. It is not a cry of anguish but rather one filled with righteous anger and an immense Heavenly anointing.

"IMPERIUM CHRISTI, VENI VIRGAM DEI[1]! By the POWER OF GOD"

Immediately, the sound of a gigantic rush of wind fills the room where Hunahpu is kneeling, followed by a sudden roar of beastly anguish. It splits the air as hundreds of malevolent shadow creatures cry out in instantaneous unison before being snuffed out a split second later. It is followed by a concussion wave of Shekinah Glory that washes over him like a cleansing wind, completely purging the menacing evil that had filled the air moments before.

Hunahpu opens his eyes and climbs slowly to his feet, listening carefully for sounds of battle... hearing only silence. He anxiously makes his way to Jeff's office and finds a scene that resembles a war zone, with shattered glass, broken furniture, and strewn papers everywhere. Lying in the middle of it all, a few yards apart, are Jeff and Eugenia — appearing nearly lifeless.

He checks them quickly, finding in each of them a weak but steady pulse. Borrowing Jeff's comm link, he quickly calls for help.

"Jeffrey and Eugenia need urgent medical attention — send a team immediately to Jeff's office!"

His request is quickly acknowledged with a promise that EMTs are on their way.

Hunahpu turns back to Jeff, looking at the ancient Staff still clutched in his outstretched arm. He carefully lifts it from his great-grandson's grasp and holds it reverently in his hands; then, thinking quickly, he moves it out of sight before the medical team arrives. Eugenia and Jeff are carefully examined, and then the unconscious pair is lifted onto stretchers while Hunahpu looks on and quietly whispers a grateful prayer.

Once they are safe, Hunahpu looks back to where he has hidden the Staff and retrieves it, studying its smooth surface of young wood in awestruck admiration. He knows what he must do, moving immediately to the Library and boarding the secret elevator to return it to the security of its place in the Secret Chamber.

———

"Jeff is waking up," the nurse announces as she gently nudges Hunahpu, stirring him from his dream.

Hunahpu's replay of the day's events scatters as he opens his eyes, soon recognizing the sound of Jeff's voice as the young man begins to finally awaken. He climbs to his feet and grips Jeff's arm while the attending nurses quickly notify the doctor and check the readings on a myriad of gauges.

After groggily looking around to discern his whereabouts, Jeff's first concern is for Eugenia's condition and then the safety of the Shepherd's Staff. Hunahpu assures him that both are safe, and the Staff, at least, seems no worse for wear; the same cannot be said for Eugenia, nor Jeff, for that matter.

Jeff looks at his great-grandfather with an awestruck expression and confesses that he knows now where the Staff's power comes from. It had only been in his own total surrender that its power was truly revealed.

After a short pause, he looks up with a concerned realization.

"They're not going to stop trying to destroy us, are they." Hunahpu understands that his great-grandson's remark is not a question; he shakes his head in acknowledgment.

"Have they always been this determined?"

"Determined, yes," Hunahpu answers, "but never as desperate as this. They are testing you, I'm afraid."

Jeff sighs. As if the 90-day Challenge and learning to run the world's largest corporation are not tests enough on their own.

Something that Semjaza's ghostly apparition had said on the night it attacked him in the Secret Chamber suddenly strikes him; the words replay in his head...

"...Such a worthless protector you were... proof that the great prophecy of the Tenth Mantle Bearer was but a lie."

It occurs to him that his uncle's letter had also mentioned the fact that he was to be *"the tenth bearer of this great mantle."* He looks at Hunahpu, struggling for a moment with whether he should ask the question that burns in his mind.

"What happens if I fail?" He asks tentatively, "What if I'm not able to complete the Challenge. Why is the Tenth Mantle Bearer different from the others?"

Hunahpu looks at him with an understanding expression and places his hand on Jeff's shoulder reassuringly.

"You will not fail, my son... of that, I am certain."

Jeff studies his Great-Grandfather's gaze questioningly, but the look in the old man's eyes shows no inkling of doubt.

⌘

2

MENDING

~ *10 days later...*

J eff is staring at his office wall as he relives the past week's events for the countless time. Each time they replay in his mind, the scenes become a little more vivid, revealing some new detail he hadn't noticed before.

At the moment, he is considering Hunahpu's words to him at the hospital, wondering how his great-grandfather could be so certain that Jeff will not fail. Granted, it could have been an effort on his great-grandfather's part to encourage him, but something in the old man's eyes told Jeff that his words were based on a great deal more than empty wishes or blind faith.

Once again, the mere thought of faith triggers memories of the Shepherd's Staff and its stunning deliverance, now on two separate occasions. Could that be what Hunahpu saw in him — a special ability of some kind? Was it a hint of some sort of Divine anointing? Could it really be true that he is being called for some remarkable purpose?

He can't help feeling that he is an unlikely candidate for such a role. Barely a month ago, he didn't even believe in God! At least, that was what he had still been telling himself at the time. He realizes in hindsight that he actually had known that God was real all along — he'd only been in denial.

It was pretty remarkable that God had gotten through to him, as a matter of fact. That, in itself, was reason to believe God may have something extraordinary in mind. However, the thought of a special calling makes him nervous. He definitely doesn't see himself as the Old Testament Prophet type.

He quickly stands and walks to the office windows, trying again to clear his head. In the ten days since the attack, the office has been repaired, and its huge windows have been replaced with even stronger, bulletproof glass. He surveys the room gratefully and then lets his gaze fall to the floor as he walks. His eye suddenly catches the reflection of a single bead of tempered glass that was overlooked by the repair crews. He picks it up, rolling it between his fingertips as it triggers memories of the horrendous events.

In his mind's eye, he is once again surrounded by swarming black Eljo as they pour through the shattered windows. Then the image quickly changes, and in an instant, the ghostly fiends are blown away like wisps of smoke in a hurricane. The clean, fresh air that takes their place fills his spirit like a deep cleansing breath. It seems so vivid that it makes him stop where he is and steady himself. The sudden sense of relief reminds him of the way he felt on that astonishing day in the Secret Chamber — when Hunahpu led him to the Lord!

That thought causes another to dawn on him: the only thing he's ever done to qualify for God's favor was that simple act of contrition. It was nothing more than a surrender. He didn't do anything at all except stop resisting. Yet the power that it revealed was so much greater than any he'd ever imagined — it shakes him to the center of his soul as he considers it.

Forgiven… The word resonates within him, sparking near-disbelief at God's capacity to forgive. He thinks of the years he spent

denying God's existence and convincing others to deny Him as well —
years as God's enemy. Yet all he has sensed from God in return has
been unmeasured and unrestrained love.

A KNOCK at his office door prompts him to turn around, finding EB
and Eugenia standing in the open doorway. Eugenia is still nursing
her bruised rib and collarbone, with one arm in a sling. Jeff's sprained
knee forces him to walk with a limp as he waves them in and makes
his way to join them in seats near the fireplace.

EB ignores their injuries as he takes a seat and immediately
launches into the purpose of their meeting — a briefing on the events
they've missed.

"We shot down a Borgia drone just offshore. It was apparently
gatherin' intelligence on damage from the attack. Flight recorders
have been recovered from all o' th' downed bombers, which are bein'
analyzed now."

Jeff nods approvingly. "What about their ships — do we know
where they're being built?"

"Brandish is still tracin' the parts shipments. They've covered their
tracks pretty well."

Genie leans forward, "Anything new from their communications
chatter?"

"It's been especially silent since Dylen's account went dark. Whatever they're workin' on, it likely doesn't involve the rank-and-file.
They must be workin' on it offline — possibly face-to-face."

Genie thinks about that for a moment before commenting soberly.
"That either means they're back to square one or already makin' final
plans for their next attack."

ON MONDAY MORNING, Eugenia insists on continuing Jeff's fight
training. Although neither of them can fight very well in their recov-

ering condition, especially her, she coaches Jeff in basic swordsman-ship and stances. *Slow-motion fighting*, as Jeff begins to call it.

The slower pace doesn't mean the training is less intense, though. Eugenia makes sure that Jeff's movements are precise and measured — making him practice over and over until she is satisfied.

THEY SIT TOGETHER AFTERWARD, exiting the gym to find an empty bench on the castle grounds; it overlooks a stunning view of the ocean. Conversation comes easily to them, having spent a whole week recovering together in the hospital. The parallels between their child-hood stories have formed a deepening bond between them.

"So, I never asked. Were you born here in Loch Harnan?" Jeff asks with genuine interest.

Genie pauses for a moment as a rush of memories washes over her. "Nae. It was in Erskine — back'n Renfrewshire in the Scottish mainland. It was a lovely little place of farms, mostly.

"I remember lovin' to play in the glades an' pretendin' t'be a fairy princess an' whatnot."

Jeff's eyebrows raise, and he looks at her... "You? A Fairy princess?" he jokes. The stone-cold expression she gives him in return prompts a quick apology.

"I suppose I had my share of scrapes as well," she concedes with a sly smile. "Guess I always loved fightin' a bit too much."

Jeff resists the temptation to poke at her last remark. "A farm, you say? Is that where EB is from?"

"Aye, t'was Shan'er's boyhood home. He an' Nanna had moved here t' the castle before I was born. My folks took the farmhouse — mainly fer raisin' me there, I suppose."

"I take it your parents weren't farmers."

"Maw did a bit o' farmin'. It was in her blood, I expect — she'd been livin' there all her life. But it was more of a garden, to be honest; they never sold any produce, as far as I could tell."

Genie falls quiet as her comment triggers other memories too painful to dwell on. Jeff doesn't probe; he's pretty sure he can relate perfectly to what she's feeling. They weren't much different in age when they each lost their parents. He skips ahead to help her past the painful memories.

"Moving here must have been a pretty dramatic adjustment."

"Oh, it wasn't so bad… the movin' part." Jeff watches his own familiar pain flash in her eyes as they share a kindred glance. "It was a big help having Nanna and Shan'er here to see me through the first few years." She looks up from her folded hands with a sympathetic expression… "It must have been so much harder for you… bein' all alone."

Jeff swallows noticeably before answering.

"I wasn't alone. I had my grandmother for that first year; my second parents gave me a loving home — I couldn't ask for more than that."

Genie leans forward, resting her elbows on her knees as she looks over at him, tilting her head curiously.

"She was Hunahpu's daughter — that's so amazing. You never told me what happened… to your grandmother. You don't have to talk about it if it's painful…if you don't want to… It's okay."

Jeff takes a deep breath and lets it out with a sigh.

"There's not much to tell, really. Just that she died in a commercial airline crash. She was on her way home from a visit to Peru.

"I was staying with Mom and Dad Samuels… they took me in and adopted me that same year. That's when we moved to Boston."

"It sounds like they loved you."

"Yeah… I never doubted it."

———

THEIR CASUAL CONVERSATION continues while Jeff walks her back to her apartment. In her eyes, he catches the familiar glint of the swirling emotions that they both share. Neither of them is yet willing to acknowledge the implications of those feelings. She nods to him with an awkward smile before ducking through her door.

Jeff glances at the floor as he smiles, then walks away. Their growing friendship warms his heart... he is feeling closer to her every day.

⌘

3

RUINED CASTLES

Jeff's thoughts are focused on his Quest as he makes his way to the underground hangar for his pilot training session with Corporal Tanner. He continues to struggle with the answers that are eluding him... the location of his uncle's secret vault... the access code... and most importantly, how to destroy the indestructible artifacts. Hunahpu's words of encouragement at breakfast replay in his head, and he draws confidence from the reassurance they instill. Yet he can't help wondering just how God is going to bring about the impossible *this* time.

As the elevator door opens into the Lab, he greets Brandish.

"Anything new from your analysis of those weapon arrays?" he asks as they meet.

"It's much as we expected," Brandish reports. He motions for Jeff to follow him to the test range — a large bunker-like room just off the main Lab where weapons are tested; it was the room where Brandish had demonstrated the new laser cannon after the first anti-gravity attack. He leads Jeff over to a reinforced containment capsule where one of the Borgia ships' weapon arrays is being analyzed.

"The arrays consist of a ring of anti-gravity pulse projectors aiming out in a 360-degree circumference. What's unique is a crude arrangement of power capacitors that amplify the charge in series before releasing it as megawatt bursts to the projectors. It's a highly volatile arrangement — akin to flying a plane with a million tons of nitroglycerin in its belly. It's little wonder they were destroyed so easily with our laser blasts."

"I guess that's good news," Jeff replies, "at least we know their weakness. I don't suppose there's any way to mount a laser cannon in a Dibjet, is there?"

"Bear is already working on it," Brandish replies with a grin.

AFTER A FEW MORE MINUTES OF discussion, Jeff says goodbye to Brandish and continues toward the Dibjet hangar, deep in thought. The mention of weaknesses brings his mind back to the Ring and Scepter. If only he had some clue to go on as to their weakness as well. All he knows is that the Shepherd's Staff had been able to protect his uncle from the Scepter's power, but it hadn't been able to destroy the objects themselves.

He thinks suddenly about CHET's account of the Scepter's discovery. It was recovered from the ocean floor — in the ruins of Semjaza's palace. As he considers it, an idea hits him:

What if a clue to their weakness could be found there as well?

Tanner is waiting beside their usual Dibjet, which has already been prepped for launch.

"Sorry about the break in our training sessions," Jeff says as he shakes Tanner's hand, apologizing for missing a few weeks of lessons.

"No worries. I'm real glad to see you've recovered. It was a true act of bravery, your savin' all of us." Tanner replies admiringly. "And no apologies are required regardless — you're the boss."

Jeff laughs at the comment. He still doesn't feel like much of a boss of anything — especially given the slim likelihood of his actually accomplishing the Challenge, which seems to grow dimmer with each day that passes.

Tanner waits for Jeff to climb aboard, then follows as Jeff climbs into the pilot's seat.

"If you have no objection," Tanner begins, "I thought we'd continue with undersea maneuvers today."

"It's funny you should say that," Jeff quickly answers, "I was hoping the same thing. As a matter of fact, I have a mission in mind."

"A mission, Sir?"

"Yes, but I'll need you to swear to secrecy."

"Yes, Sir. You can count on me, Sir."

"Great," Jeff says as he surveys the ship's controls and begins throwing switches, causing the engines to hum to life. "The name is Jeff, in case you forgot," he reminds Tanner in a friendly voice.

"Sorry, Sir... Jeff. You can count on me, Jeff, Sir."

"O...kay, thanks," Jeff says with a chuckle, dismissing the fact that he hasn't quite made his point; he lets it drop. He taps his radio talk button and speaks into his headset:

"Control, this is DJ-7-1-7 prepared for launch."

"Roger 7-1-7, you are clear for launch."

A short horn blast echoes in the chamber, and the red warning light above the huge hangar doors begins to spin as they split open, welcoming the departing Dibjet into the airlock.

About ten minutes later, Jeff sails out into the open ocean. He switches to an encrypted channel and types a short instruction, then speaks into his headset.

"CHET set a course for Semjaza's palace — or whatever's left of it."

"Plotting a course, heading 236.08 degrees south-southwest," CHET's voice replies over the ship's radio. *"Destination in 542 Nautical Miles. At maximum speed, your arrival is estimated in two hours, thirty-five minutes."*

Jeff looks at Tanner apologetically. "I guess maybe we should have packed a lunch," he admits. He refocuses on his dialogue with CHET, deciding to use the time to prepare a plan for their arrival.

"CHET - What records did my uncle leave of his recovery operations at the site?"

"Transmitting a copy of his ship's log to your screen,"

CHET replies helpfully as the log's pages appear on the screen. Jeff recognizes his uncle's handwriting on some of the entries; they chronicle a series of deep-sea dives over nearly a month's time. As he pages through them, he notices that a few pages are missing.

"Where are pages 6 and 7?" he asks CHET.

"Those pages are not included in the file," CHET explains matter-of-factly.

From what Jeff can see of the included entries, the missing pages must have contained the Scepter's discovery. Jeff glances at Tanner beside him and decides not to probe any further into their whereabouts.

"Are these depth readings accurate?" Jeff asks in surprise as he reads the diving entries. "It says they were searching at a depth of over 13,000 feet!"

"That is correct," CHET confirms. *"Although the palace ruins are located on an elevated peak that is only 12,900 feet deep."*

Jeff looks at Tanner with raised eyebrows. "How deep can this Dibjet dive?" he asks carefully.

"I-I'm not sure, exactly," Tanner replies nervously. He clearly doesn't seem enthusiastic about finding out.

CHET answers for him:

"This ship is rated for a safe diving depth of up to 10,000 feet,

although it is possible that it could sustain as much as 1,000 feet more."

Jeff looks at the log entries more closely, noting that Barry had used a diving bell in his search, which had been lowered from the deck of a large cargo ship. He quickly decides that they are not going to attempt to reach the bottom.

"Could this ship's sensors reach the bottom from a depth of 10,000 feet?" he asks Tanner.

"That should be possible," Tanner allows, "although the image resolution will be diminished at that range."

Tanner aims the sensor array toward the sea floor below them. They are traveling about 1,000 feet beneath the surface, and the scan reveals an accurate depth reading of nearly 7,000 feet for the sea floor at their current position; the scanner poorly defines the sea floor's topography.

"Take us deeper," Jeff instructs.

Tanner warily complies, setting the ship's target depth to 3,000 feet.

Jeff feels them level off as they reach it and carefully examines the scan results. The resolution has improved enough to distinguish objects approximately one foot in diameter, but with poor detail.

"What about the telephoto zoom?" Jeff asks, recalling how the Dibjet's reconnaissance cams had zoomed in on the Eljo pilot's helmet and the boots of those Borgia invaders.

"There's not enough light at these depths," Tanner explains.

"Well, can we do anything to boost the scanner's resolution?" Jeff asks.

After pondering it for a moment, Tanner lowers his eyebrows thoughtfully.

"I have an idea," he says as he opens a computer terminal and begins to type a series of instructions. "If I can direct the scanner to utilize the CCD in the ship's telephoto zoom, then we might be able to create a narrow high-res beam."

"English?" Jeff prods, his grin showing that he loves the idea, whatever it means.

Tanner looks up from the terminal for just a second to register the question, then refocuses on the screen as he continues typing. "The CCD is a charge-coupled device... " You know, like in a digital camera," he explains. It's the digital equivalent of film without the chemical developing part.

Jeff stares at him with an expression that shows he is willing to take Tanner's word for it.

"The Dibjet's long-range camera is much more sophisticated, of course," Tanner continues. "It's really more like a powerful computer that can process billions of bits at a time. That's what gave me the idea; if we can tune the camera's sensor logic...." He opens a command screen and feeds in the instructions he's just created.... "Then it should be able to pick up the long-range sensor's reflected signal." He hits enter, and a window appears on the terminal screen. He flicks his fingers across the screen, pushing the new window over to the ship's large display monitor. It shows a high-resolution close-up of a ten-by-twenty-meter patch of the ocean floor with so much detail that they can make out floating sand particles as they dance across the bottom.

"Not bad detail for total darkness," Tanner brags, congratulating himself as he waves at the screen.

"Whoa... that's awesome!" Jeff agrees enthusiastically.

A sudden shake of the ship unexpectedly sets off its proximity alarm. It reminds Jeff of EB's near-miss with a whale on the day they returned from Boston. It occurs to both of them at the same time that they have all of the ship's sensors aimed at the sea floor and none aimed at what is in front of them.

In a near panic, Tanner quickly redirects the forward sensors, picking up several more whales in their path, a distance away. As soon as they are detected, the ship's autopilot smoothly corrects course to navigate around them.

Phew... both of them intone as they resume breathing. They sit quietly for several minutes as their racing heartbeats return to normal.

"So, where did you learn to hack CCDs?" Jeff finally asks, glancing back at the monitor showing a close-up of the sea floor speeding by below them.

"It's sort of a hobby, I guess," Tanner confesses. "I've made a point of learning as much as I can about our ships — in case I need to make repairs and whatnot, you know? Anyway, a couple of the engineers in the Lab have been helping me in their spare time."

"Nice work," Jeff commends. "Brandish would be impressed — you should show it to him."

"You think so? I don't know if I'm as good as all that."

"Are you kidding? He'd love a guy with your creative abilities. I'll talk to him when we get back."

Tanner nods in thanks, his smile beaming.

For the next hour, the two of them share small talk as Jeff learns about Tanner's time at the military academy and shares stories from his own brief teaching career at MIT. Before they know it, the ship announces its approach to the coordinates CHET had set for their destination.

Jeff nods to Tanner, signaling them to take them deeper. The radio falls silent as they sink beyond the range of communications. Both of them watch nervously as the depth gauge creeps deeper and deeper, passing 6,000... 7,000... 8,000 feet. At 9,000 feet, Tanner slows their descent, bringing them gradually to 10,000 feet.

The ship's navigation display shows that they are nearing the palace ruins, and Tanner slows their pace to a crawl. The sea floor lies shrouded in pitch darkness below them, and they wait for the long-range sensors to aim downward. Jeff gasps as the scene below is suddenly illuminated by the reflected images.

He can see that the palace had been situated on a mountaintop plateau — the mountain's sides appear to drop off steeply into the depths below. Almost nothing remains of the palace itself, only the vague outline of ruined foundations and piles of out-of-place rubble, now covered under eighty centuries of silt and the dead remains of marine life.

Jeff touches the curved, transparent screen hanging in front of him, causing the image to zoom in closer.

"What are we looking for, exactly?" Tanner asks.

"I'm afraid I can't tell you that," Jeff answers distractedly. After a short pause, he confesses, "To be perfectly honest, I have no idea."

He focuses on a section of what appears to be a crumbled wall and zooms in further, filling the screen with piles of collapsed stones that had once been neatly cut.

"If I didn't know better, I'd say that was cut stone... it looks almost man-made," Tanner says incredulously. "But how could anything man-made exist out here at the bottom of the ocean?"

"Remember what I said about swearing to secrecy?" Jeff reminds him. "I meant it. None of this can ever get out. You're ok with that, right?"

"Yes, Sir, you have my word, Sir."

"In that case, take a few pictures of what's in the frame," Jeff requests. Tanner gasps when he sees what Jeff has zoomed in on — a pile of fallen stones scattered like a jigsaw puzzle across the sea floor, and on each stone, there are carvings of strange symbols...

...IT IS WRITING."

⌘

4

ANCIENT CLUE

I t is after 5:00 in the afternoon when Jeff and Tanner return from their undersea mission, and nearly 6:00 by the time Jeff reaches his suite. They have taken hundreds of pictures of the palace ruins, which have all been transferred onto Jeff's O-P, and he is eager to head to the Tower Lab and study them.

"Ah, there you are!" Isabel says, emerging from the kitchen the moment he enters his suite's front door. "Dinner will be on the table in five minutes — you go ahead and wash up."

Her comment makes Jeff smile; it makes him feel as if he is twelve years old, but he can't find it in his heart to be offended by her. He honestly doesn't mind her motherly pampering, thinking how he'd lost his own mother at such a young age. His rush to get to the Tower will have to wait. It is just too hard to pass up one of Isabel's carefully prepared meals, and his stomach is honestly growling from skipping lunch.

EB is in the sitting room with Hunahpu; Jeff joins them after dutifully washing his hands. He looks to EB as he sits down, leaning forward to ask him a question.

"How are things with the special forces team?"

"Genie is more deeply engaged with it now than I am, to be honest," EB replies.

"It was high time for her to learn of it, as a matter of fact," he continues, looking at the two of them. He turns to Jeff in particular, "I'd like to ask her to take command of the secret unit; if you have no objection?"

"Me? ...Objection?" Jeff says, taken a bit by surprise. "No, of course not — that's a great idea."

THEY SIT at the dinner table a while later, and Hunahpu and EB exchange an amused glance, noting the way Jeff is devouring his meal.

"How was your day today?" Hunahpu asks. "From the look of it, you worked up quite an appetite."

"Gwood," Jeff replies with a full mouth, holding up a finger to request a pause as he finishes chewing and then swallows. He takes a sip of water and then apologizes; Hunahpu smiles understandingly.

"It was good," he repeats, more clearly this time. "Genie is teaching me the finer points of swordsmanship. Neither of us is in very good condition for any real fighting at the moment."

After a short pause, Hunahpu interrupts the silence again.

"How was your training with Tanner today?"

Jeff looks at him, immediately sensing that he knows about their undersea explorations.

"Why? What's in his report?" Jeff asks with a cringing brow that looks as if he is regretting his trust in the young corporal.

"Nothing, as a matter of fact," Hunahpu replies. "Just a simple mention of undersea maneuvers, nothing more."

"Oh," Jeff answers awkwardly, realizing that his own reaction has likely given them more cause for suspicion than Tanner had.

"Well, we... that is, he was demonstrating deep-sea procedures. Showing how to use long-range scanners, that sort of thing," Jeff answers unconvincingly. "He's really a genius with the scanners — he developed a hack to use the telephoto zoom for long-range scanning with remarkable clarity; you should have seen it! I showed it to Brandish, and he was quite impressed."

Hunahpu's interested expression does not change. In a friendly voice, he looks at Jeff and comments: "That must have been quite useful in your exploration of Semjaza'a palace." Having rolled that bombshell into Jeff's lap, he calmly takes a bite and awaits Jeff's reply.

Jeff leans back in his chair. "You were tracking our ship?"

"Training ships and fighters are always tracked," Hunahpu explains. "When I realized where you might be headed, I removed your ship from the tracking grid; it was visible only to me." He leans forward reassuringly: "You need not tell us what you found. Simply rest assured that we are here should you wish to discuss it."

Jeff sits, thinking for a long moment, then looks at the others.

"Stones," he says, explaining what they'd found. "There were stones — a collapsed wall, I think. They had writing on them."

Jeff is about to explain that he recognized the same lettering in the Cronicis Niergel but stops as he glances at EB. He looks at Hunahpu intently; "The artifacts were once Semjaza's; I was hoping that something in the palace ruins might hold the clue we need for destroying them."

Hunahpu looks down, considering the idea carefully.

"What led you to this idea?" he asks curiously.

"I don't know, it just came to me," Jeff confesses. "Do you think it was inspired?"

His great-grandfather pauses silently as if seeking an answer to that question from somewhere beyond himself. He looks at Jeff seriously.

"Inspiration comes in many forms… and its fountainhead may spring from many sources," he observes. "Not all of them are divine." He leans closer and places his hand on Jeff's arm; "Be cautious, my son. The incantations of Semjaza are a powerful evil."

EB is not sure who or what Semjaza is, but assumes it has something to do with the Borgia's hideous Eljo forces, noting the ominous look on Jeff's face as he considers the old man's warning.

AN HOUR LATER, Jeff is still feeling shaken by Hunahpu's words, which have stirred memories of that night in the Secret Chamber when the dark prince nearly killed him. It is only the memory of God's amazing deliverance that calms his heart enough to move on. Standing now in the Tower Lab, he debates whether to discuss the pictures from today's exploration with the avatar. How can he be sure they *don't* contain a dangerous incantation?

"Something is troubling you," the avatar observes as he watches Jeff's inner struggle.

"What?" Jeff asks, stirred from his thoughts by the avatar's remark. "No... well, yes, I guess so," he answers uncertainly.
"I explored the ruins of Semjaza's palace today. We found stones with writing — it looked like they had been part of a broken-down wall."

"This was troubling to you?" BE probes.

"Well, not the broken wall, but what was on it — the words. I'm worried that they might be an incantation... something dangerous."

"I see," BE accepts. "You are referring to the image file that you loaded to the O-P?"

"Yes," Jeff replies hesitantly, pulling the device from his pocket.

"Perhaps it would be best if I studied them first, alone," BE suggests.

"Oh... alright... ok, that might be a good idea. You mean, you're not affected by... that kind of thing?"

"In theory, my programming is merely a more sophisticated version of the stones themselves — I am simply a medium in which to store or convey information. It would appear that the stones are not influenced by what is written on them. Likewise, I would expect that I would not be either — provided, of course, that the words are not verbalized."

"Verbalized?" Jeff asks. "Is that what gives them their power?"

"That appears to be what releases their power," BE explains.

Jeff lays his O-P on the countertop in front of him and stretches it larger to make it easier to navigate to the folder that stores the day's photos; a moment later, they are gone as the folder and its contents are moved to the Lab's storage array.

Jeff waits as BE appears to be lost in thought.

"I'm rearranging the stones to determine the most probable sequence," the avatar explains.

Nearly a minute later, Jeff hears a single chime announcing that the sequence has been determined.

"It does not appear to be an incantation," BE soon concludes.

The large wall monitor fills with a reconstructed image of the wall with its stones in the correct order. Jeff draws a breath as the impact of what he sees strikes him — he realizes he is looking at proof of a time before the flood. With its mysterious symbols arranged in the correct order, it appears strangely powerful and ominous.

"What does it say?" Jeff asks carefully. He watches as the image on the screen is translated, morphing into English:

Throne of Semjaza
Heir of the Dragon
Lord of the Gods
Keeper of the Scroll and Portal of Tir Lai

"Tir Lai..." Jeff repeats the words aloud as he reads. "I've seen that name before... in an old manuscript from Maranish," he recalls, "...he wrote that the Ring and Scepter were forged in furnaces there."

The words that Maranish had written flash vividly in Jeff's memory:

They are forged in the furnaces of Tir Lai, infused with powers to enslave and destroy. Semjaza's scepter and ring bring unassailable dominion and might to the one who wields them.

"He wrote that they were called forth from the scroll of the gods," Jeff explains.

"That would appear to confirm our theory that they are not from our dimension," BE observes. "It would explain why they cannot be destroyed."

Jeff sits down in the chair dejectedly. "Then it's true... my Challenge really is impossible."

"Actually, this information makes the destruction of the objects more likely," BE offers surprisingly.

"How... what do you mean?"

"The artifacts cannot be destroyed in our dimension," BE clarifies, "but their destruction may be possible in the dimension of their origin — in the fires that forged them."

"You mean if I can take them back to where they came from...?" Jeff pauses as he considers it, his mind racing. The idea has given him the first spark of hope that he has felt in weeks. He looks back at the image on the screen and stares at the last line of writing in the ancient stones: '...portal of Tir Lai.'

"Do you think the portal is down there... at the bottom of the ocean?" Jeff asks, referring to the ruins of Semjaza's palace.

The avatar seems to be considering the question for a moment, then shakes his head.

"It is more likely that it is not tied to a specific location on the earth. The Dimensions are not aligned in such a way."

"Then how do we find the portal?" Jeff asks anxiously.

"That would, indeed, appear to be the relevant question," BE agrees.

⌘

5

TROUBLED

2,500 Nautical Miles away... Montagne Blanche

The pristine opulence of the evil brothers' Mediterranean estate conveys their access to limitless wealth. It rises like a gleaming palace above the white cliffs of its private island just off the French Riviera. Even in the moonlight, the estate's palatial beauty stands in stark contrast to the hideous specter of a man who is seated alone at the head of its enormous dining table.

Chesed, the eldest son of Maranish, appears corpse-like, with ashen gray skin and thin, bony limbs. The remnants of his white hair hang past his shoulders, thin and scraggly from the sides of his head, which is bald on top and covered with scabs and blotchy dark spots.

His face is clean-shaven, and he wears a regal silken robe. His hands are covered in ancient-looking rings of priceless value, and golden bracelets cover both of his fragile-looking wrists. He sits quietly, staring through the windows at the tranquil Mediterranean scene, with his fingertips pressed together as if in a prayerful gesture. But the thoughts that he contemplates are far from prayers.

As he waits, his brother enters, accompanied by a squad of Eljo soldiers. Eblis appears just as hideous and menacing as his brother. He prefers a long black leather coat; ugly scars crisscross his face and bald head.

"Tell me of our preparations," Chesed implores in a voice that is somehow even more off-putting than his appearance.

"We are nearly ready," Eblis confirms in a slithering voice. "Sea trials have gone as planned, and the ships' systems are being calibrated; munitions and supplies have been readied." He then looks at his brother for reassurance, "What makes you certain that the Heir can be overcome this time? We must not forget the way that he decimated our Eljo invasion force."

"The young heir's downfall will be *his own* doing," Chesed answers, gloating as he considers it. "Our dark lord has other minions through whom to work his purposes — they move unseen among the unsuspecting humans. His dark plan is in motion as we speak; we need only wait for it to run its course; the young Mantle Bearer will soon be in our trap; I can feel it."

It is past midnight when Jeff leaves the Tower Lab. He has searched for answers to the portal's whereabouts until he is exhausted, but still cannot find the slightest clue to its location, let alone the means for opening it.

His frustration mounts as he struggles with it — it seems that the harder he tries to solve the Challenge, the more impossible its solution appears to be. He knows that giving up is not an option, but the urge to quit is becoming intense, nonetheless.

Making matters worse, he realizes that he can feel himself growing impatient with the only one who *can* accomplish it — God. His eye falls to the Bible on his nightstand, and he considers the verse that his uncle Barry had written inside it: '*I know the plans I have for you....*' The words resonate within him just as strongly as the first time he read them, in spite of his doubts.

"How, Lord?" he quietly prays, running his hand over the Bible anxiously.

He changes for bed and lies, tossing and turning for nearly an hour before finally drifting into a restless sleep.

AT BREAKFAST, Jeff looks at his great-grandfather sitting across from him at the table. As Isabel leaves the room, he lowers his voice.

"The message on the stones was a marker for Semjaza's throne room."

"You were able to translate it?" Hunahpu quietly asks in surprise.

Jeff remembers that his great-grandfather still doesn't know about BE or the secret Tower Lab; he carefully backpedals.

"Oh... the O-P helped," he answers in a half-truth, quickly moving past the uncomfortable question. "The message said that Semjaza was the Keeper of a certain portal," he explains in a hushed tone. "I think that may be the clue to destroying the artifacts — if I can find that portal, it may be the key."

"To *Their* dimension — the place of their origin..." Hunahpu says, immediately understanding. He thinks quietly for a moment, seeming to recall something that he doesn't share. "You must exercise extreme caution," he says seriously. "If it is possible, the opening of such a portal must not be taken lightly. Doors can serve both sides."

Jeff considers his great-grandfather's words soberly as their meaning dawns on him. "Do you mean that something else could use it to enter our dimension? I hadn't thought about that. What do you think could be there?"

"If it is, indeed, the place of the artifacts' origin, then I shudder to think."

JEFF REACHES the gym five minutes late, finding Eugenia engrossed in her personal workout. She is getting stronger every day — already nearly back to her condition before the invasion.

Jeff's thoughts are still a distracting jumble; he can't help hearing his great-grandfather's words repeating in his mind — *Doors can serve both sides...*

Genie notices his distraction.

"Still wrestlin'... with your secrets... I see," she notes, surprisingly, between sit-ups. Jeff hadn't even realized she'd seen him enter, seeing that she had her back to the door.

She turns and jumps to her feet, towel in hand as usual, and looks at her watch.

"I haven't needed t' penalize ye fer wearin' late; not a bad record, till now."

Jeff sighs; he'd begun to think that all the talk of her strictness was just a ruse.

"You'll be givin' me ten push-ups fer each minute you're late... THAT'S FIFTY — LET'S GO!"

Her intimidating shout startles him, and he drops to the mat, counting off the push-ups loudly as he does them. The fact that he can complete them at all, let alone as quickly as he does, is a testament to the rigor of his training over the past few months.

When he finishes, Eugenia throws him a padded sparring helmet, telling him to clip it on; she is already wearing one. She waves for him to follow as she breaks into a run toward the boxing ring at the back of the room. As she gets there, she grabs a pair of boxing gloves from the edge of the ring and throws them to him with an instruction to lace them up. She picks up a second pair and does the same, jumping quickly onto the raised platform and through the ropes.

She bounces on her toes as Jeff follows her into the ring.

"Forget whatever you've learned of boxin'," she instructs.

That'll be easy, Jeff thinks to himself silently; he is pretty sure that he doesn't know *anything* about boxing.

"This'll be more like mixed martial arts, but with a few rules relaxed," she explains in introduction. "I don't expect you'll be competin' in any championships, but if you're fightin' fer your life, it'll come in pretty handy.

"The ancient Chinese called it Lei Tai," she expounds. "It was named after the elevated arenas where their tournaments were held; theirs was a brutal sport; they used lethal weapons and bare-knuckle martial arts. You can think of it as no-holds-barred mixed combat usin' martial arts, boxin' and wrestlin' with weapons thrown in."

Her explanation brings to mind a dozen or more of the ways in which he knows she could inflict severe pain, not to mention threaten his life, most of which he has already experienced at least once. This time, he is determined to do all he can to hold his own — not to mention avoid accidentally dying.

They each put in their mouthguards, and Jeff copies Eugenia's fighting stance and hops on his toes, keeping his fists in front of him. She fakes a jab, and he blocks it, then strikes with a follow-through swing of his own, missing her; he notices her kick coming too late as she spins like a blur and connects with her foot in a lightning strike against the side of his head. The blow knocks him off his feet.

He shakes off the dizziness for a moment before getting back up, more determined than ever to hold his own. Climbing back to his feet, he decides to abandon trying to copy her stance, letting his own instincts take over. As soon as he does, he finds himself managing to avoid most of her blows and even connects with a few of his own.

After a furious set lasting several minutes, Eugenia steps away and holds her hands in the air to signal a stop. It isn't until then that he notices her lip is bleeding.

"You're bleeding! Genie - I'm sorry!" he exclaims, immediately feeling terrible.

"There's no need fer apology... You did alright... You did just fine," she insists with a grin as she wipes a smudge of blood from her chin. "But I think maybe we'd best spend the rest o' th' hour on the punchin' bags."

⌘

6

HQ

J eff shakes Tanner's hand as he climbs aboard the Dibjet for the
day's flight session.

"Thanks for yesterday," he says, looking Tanner in the eye,
"...for keeping it off the record, I mean."

"I said you could count on me, Sir, I meant it."

Jeff nods gratefully. He fastens his seatbelt and settles in; "Where
are we headed today?" he asks as he checks the forest of switches and
gauges in front of him.

"To be perfectly honest, I'm out of lessons," Tanner confesses,
slightly embarrassed. "There's nothing else I can teach you — but I'm
happy to keep spending the session time with you until you get the
rest of the flight hours you need for your pilot's license."

"Fair enough," Jeff agrees with a smile. He stops to think for a
moment and then looks over at Tanner: "How would you like to visit
London?"

Tanner's eyes widen, and he flashes a smile; he has only been to the
corporate headquarters once before. "Sure!" he enthusiastically agrees,

quickly catching himself, "I mean... yes, Sir. Plotting a course now, Sir."

Jeff waits until they are out over open ocean before going supersonic — no sense in stirring up the Hastleworth security forces with another unexplained sonic boom. They make the trip in record time, shaving almost ten minutes off his previous London record.

The company's president, Adalwin Brinker, is waiting beside the rooftop landing pad with Cynefrid Arterbury, the COO, as they arrive. Jeff's call had surprised them, but happily interrupted a meeting with the Auditors that they were glad to cut short.

Tanner is impressed by the way Jeff brings their Dibjet in for a smooth rooftop landing despite a stiff crosswind. Jeff discounts the feat, explaining that he was just avoiding the embarrassment of falling off the side of a fifty-story building on his first solo landing at HQ. He breathes a deep sigh of relief as he powers down the ship.

"Thank you for your call; this is a pleasant surprise," Adalwin says as he shakes Jeff's hand.

"Great of you to pay us a visit," Cy agrees with a genuine smile.

"This is Corporal Tanner; he's been my flight instructor," Jeff introduces. "We can't stay the whole day; I just wanted to come to say hello to folks and perhaps join you both for lunch if you don't have plans?"

"Absolutely!" Adalwin agrees as Cy nods.

Jeff stops to say hello to the pair of guards standing inside the rooftop lobby as they enter: "Hi Matthew," he says to the first guard, shaking his hand with a smile, then turns to the second: "Phillip, it's good to see you again." The men both smile back, impressed that Jeff has remembered their names, even without name tags.

The group makes its way down to the penthouse level, and Tanner's eyes grow wide as he takes in the sight of the executive office suite with its impressive gallery of historic photos — many of which are of famous entrepreneurs who he recognizes as multi-billionaires, but taken when their companies were still struggling Startups.

"Is there anyone in particular whom you wanted to see while you're here?" Cy asks.

"I was thinking I'd like to pay Kaerae Mackinzie a visit," he suggests without hesitation. "How is she doing with the renaming of her department?"

"Ah, yes, the Cherished Talent Group," Cy says with a wide smile. "She had the name change completed within a week of your last visit, I believe," he recalls with amusement. "She and her staff even chipped in to have their own shirts imprinted with the new name," he adds.

Jeff is all smiles as they exit the elevator and see a large sign on the elevator lobby wall that reads "Welcome to Cherished Talent" in six-inch letters.

Kaerae catches sight of Jeff and the others entering her department's reception area and waves as she quickly makes her way over to welcome them. Others working nearby smile and wave at Jeff from their cubicles.

"What a nice surprise! It's good to see you again, Mr. Sutherland," she says as she greets him. She looks around for a moment at the people working behind her and then back at him: "The new name that you've given the group has had such a wonderful effect on morale. Our productivity measures are up by more than fifty percent, and I'm getting calls from people all over the company who would like to transfer here."

"It wasn't *my* new name, it was your idea," Jeff reminds her. "And I don't imagine that the name is the only thing responsible for morale; people are drawn to success and to a place where they feel valued. I suspect you have to take credit for those things yourself," he concludes with a smile.

Kaerae blushes as she thanks him, then raises a hand as something occurs to her. "Speaking of ideas, there's a team here that I'd like you to meet; they proposed a truly wonderful idea to me just this week."

She leads the men to the center of the open floor, where a half-dozen college-aged men and women are sitting at a table, working on laptop computers.

"These are our college interns: Dougal Taras, Alina Mendez, Doyle Hallows, Lynette Stuckey, Nareena Lewit, and Cairan Gane," she says, introducing them as they each nod hello.

"They're all working on programs in human resources and business studies," she explains. "Cairan here was kind enough to share with me a paper they're doing on an idea that I think you may find as fascinating as I did," Kaerae explains.

"Cairan, why don't you share your idea with Mr. Sutherland and the others?" she coaxes in a friendly voice, giving him a warm smile.

The young man looks momentarily caught off guard as he is singled out, but then smiles back at Mrs. Mackinzie and stands to his feet.

"Well... <cough>... okay — sure...," he agrees slowly as he nervously clears his throat. He lifts a folder and pulls out a carefully written report, opening it to the table of contents. After scanning it for no more than two seconds, he snaps it closed again and looks Jeff in the eyes.

"It's not just my idea," he says, turning to look at the others around the table, "it's been something we've been working on together. We've been studying businesses — all kinds of businesses; not just today's companies, but throughout history — back to earliest times," Cairan begins. He pauses uncertainly, as if wondering how what he is going to say next will be received.

"Well, the bottom line, as we see it, is that Business is broken," he finally blurts out.

Jeff's smile broadens slightly; he already likes where this is going.

"What I mean is — the way business is done today... in most companies... is obsolete; current technology and today's global marketplace have made the old methods in which companies operate increasingly irrelevant and counter-productive."

Cairan lays the folder back on the table and steps back, using his hands expressively as he continues.

"Since the thirteenth century, there have been four major

economic ages, each of which has been defined by the limiting resources of its day — the key resources that were most in demand and in shortest supply.

In the 1300's, the natural resources derived from *land* were the primary source of wealth; land was the greatest creator of economic power. Monarchs accumulated vast landholdings around the globe because that was what yielded the most economic power. By 1700, the British Empire's land holdings gave it an economic dominance that endured until World War I. That was the first major economic age.

The second began gradually in the 18th and 19th centuries, when a new limiting factor emerged. The need for *capital* became the key fuel for the economy as Institutions and Industry became dominant. Power shifted from Kings to Bankers, and the Industrial Age rose to prominence. By the middle of the 20th Century, banks and industry had become extremely effective at producing capital, but the economy didn't have enough educated workers to continue growing – the limit shifted from capital to knowledge, spawning the Knowledge Economy. This was the third economic age.

"Then, in the late 20th century, an abundance of knowledge, industry, and capital spawned massive investments in *technology* to speed the flow of this knowledge and capital around the globe, leading to the Internet age.

"Now we see knowledge in abundance, along with limitless sources of capital and technology, but economies around the world have begun to see slowing growth – even in the world's wealthiest nations. These declines are not due to global competition from too many businesses; in fact, while invested capital has never been more abundant, there simply aren't enough growing companies to convert this abundance of capital, knowledge, and technical resources into new wealth and jobs for society. Today's limit is the availability of business creators – today, there are not enough *entrepreneurs*."

Jeff watches the enthusiasm and conviction on Cairan's face as he makes his points, impressed by his mastery of the facts.

"Should governments then be doing more to encourage new businesses?" Adalwin asks, following the young man's points with great interest.

"Governments love businesses, but not because they create wealth," Cairan argues. "They love the predictability of corporate employment. It provides neat packaging of revenues and wages into easily reportable and taxable bundles. Governments focus their efforts on corporate oversight, tax audits, tariffs, and regulations, but miss the fact that these very measures are often contributing to the decline of their country's economic strength. The competitive pressures in today's global marketplace have made it more important than ever for businesses to remain nimble and readily adaptable – their very survival depends upon it. Therefore, a government's most effective means of providing a true safety net for its citizens is the creation and protection (from bureaucratic interference) of a robust and independent free market economy."

"I agree with you on that point," Cy says as Adalwin nods his head as well. "But what do you propose should be done to cultivate such a free market?"

"We would argue, Sir, that what is needed is a new business model. One in which the majority of workers become non-employees — in other words, self-employed business owners. The new business model of the entrepreneur economy resembles a shamrock, with each company having a small core organization of knowledge experts — the stem — which is surrounded by a tight network of outsourced services — the leaves — which are provided, in turn, by similarly structured organizations — all interdependent upon one another."

Cairan looks at the executives' faces, sensing that they haven't gotten the point yet.

"That may be quite a mouthful to swallow all at once," he admits, "I'll try to break it down a little. The technological changes that are spawning new ways of working will inevitably change the fundamental structure of tomorrow's companies. As a result, companies will become more decentralized (with more of their functions outsourced) while becoming faster and more adaptable, and thus able to pivot quickly by adopting new skills and capabilities from outside without extensive retraining or complex organizational changes.

"This structure, which has only recently become possible on a wide scale, will allow work to be distributed across a tightly integrated network of partners – providing ready access to new skills and emerging technologies and allowing rapid adaptation to changes in the global business environment. It's the exact opposite of the old centralized command and control model."

"Wouldn't this make companies less self-reliant?" Tanner asks, joining the conversation.

"It's actually the opposite," Cairan explains. "By shifting work to an open marketplace of skills and resources, companies become even more independent and self-reliant. They are less dependent on a limited set of employees and can shift whenever needed from one supplier to another with total freedom."

"That's right," Alina jumps in, "and it will create a lot of new business opportunities for new companies that can provide tools to orchestrate and facilitate the new marketplaces."

"Yeah, we call them MaaS," Cairan says, pronouncing it like '*Mass*' — "it stands for 'Marketplace as a Service.'"

There is silence when Cairan finishes, and his words sink in, making him increasingly nervous as it lasts longer than expected.

Jeff is the first to speak, offering a simple observation:

"It's brilliant."

Adalwin turns to Cy, "I believe you may have found the team of strategists you were looking for," he offers with a smile.

Kaerae Mackinzie stands behind her boss and gives the interns a smiling thumbs-up.

⌘

7

BARRY'S CLUE

Soon after leaving Kaerae's department, the men stop in to see Harti Arenhold, the company's CIO. He is sitting at his desk with his sleeves rolled up and his tie loosened, intently typing away on his computer when they arrive.

Jeff can't resist glancing at his screen, noticing several windows scattered across it containing computer code. "Do you mind my asking what you're working on?" he asks out of genuine interest.

Harti looks back, following Jeff's gaze to the screen. "Not at all," he answers with a smile. "I'm just fine-tuning our latest cybersecurity advancement. This is an artificial intelligence bot that monitors network traffic for signs of suspicious activity. It's extremely good at detecting even the stealthiest virus anywhere on a network by isolating its communications — sooner or later, they *call home*, as it were."

Harti then motions to Tanner, who is standing closest to the door: "Would you mind closing the door, please?" he asks politely. Once it is shut, he types a few commands, and a new schematic design appears on the screen....

"The real purpose of that bot, however, is to test this." He gives Jeff a few seconds to study the on-screen design and then continues: "This is our latest surveillance bot. It's meant to penetrate an enemy network and gather intelligence. But the unique thing about it is the way it transmits that intelligence back — it attaches its packets to the host network's own normal communications. Then, once those data streams are traveling over open internet channels, the surveillance packets are split off from their hosts using a process we've dubbed *evaporation* and make their way back through an infinite number of random pathways to be reconstructed upon arrival."

Jeff considers that for a moment, immediately realizing the usefulness of such a tool for their secret Estonia task force.

"Is EB aware of this?" Jeff asks carefully.

"Yes, he's the one who commissioned the project, in fact," Harti confirms with an acknowledgment that he understands the intent of Jeff's question.

"How soon will it be ready?" Jeff asks, making sure to conceal the real point of his question.

"Within the week," Harti says with a shrug that hints to Jeff it is probably ready now, but he wants to give it a final once-over.

THE MEN MAKE their way back to the top floor for lunch in the executive dining room. Tanner quickly takes a position beside the door and stands at attention, intending to wait there while the executives dine. Jeff slaps him on the back and extends an arm toward the door in invitation.

"You're with us, my friend," he says casually. "The food here isn't bad, as I recall."

"Yes, Sir," Tanner agrees with a nervous smile as he accompanies the others to a table by the window. Jeff takes a seat facing the view of London's skyline, as he had on his previous visit, and invites Tanner to sit beside him.

The men engage in small talk, admiring the view and discussing how long each of them has been with Hastleworth. Eventually, the conversation turns to Jeff's arrival and all that has transpired in recent months, or at least what they knew about it.

"We were so thrilled to hear of your decision to accept Christ," Adalwin shares candidly. "There were many here praying for you."

"I have the feeling that people everywhere were praying for me," Jeff says humbly. "I'm truly grateful. The fact that God got through to me is nothing short of a miracle; I have to admit. In fact, I haven't stopped needing people's prayers;" he pauses with a sigh and adds seriously: "I've definitely been making good use of His miracle-working power, that's for sure."

"Seeing the way your faith has grown strengthens all of us," Cy commends him sincerely.

Tanner shakes his head in agreement and quietly says, "Amen."

"Well, I think faith is something we're going to need a lot of if our enemies keep on the way they have," Jeff notes.

"I must agree with you," Adalwin says seriously. "Their recent attacks on Loch Harnan have shown a new level of intensity that we have not seen before."

"Do you think they could attack here or any of the other sites?" Jeff asks. For some reason, it is the first time that the idea has occurred to him.

"Such an assault in a major city like London would be quite bold. I'm not sure that even Dreyken Sidero would dare it. Nonetheless, all of our locations have remained on high alert," Adalwin confirms. "Eugenia has seen to beefing up our security."

Of course she has, Jeff thinks to himself, not surprised that she would be miles ahead of him in anticipating the threat.

"I have to admit," Jeff thinks aloud, "Loch Harnan is incredibly well protected. I'm sure there are few places on earth with anything like its amazing underground shelter."

"That is true," Adalwin agrees. "Its natural caverns are among the world's great wonders."

"Do you mean the bunkers... with the Lab and Hospital?" Jeff clarifies. "They *are* amazing, but I'm not sure I'd classify them as natural wonders of the world."

"Well, those are impressive, I suppose," Adalwin replies, "but I was thinking of the larger caverns, actually. They bear as close a resemblance to an underground wonderland as I can imagine."

Jeff tilts his head in a signal that he isn't quite following. "Which caverns are you referring to?"

The other three look at one another in surprise.

"The ones surrounding the bunkers? Do you mean to tell me that you've never seen them?"

"Well," Jeff answers uncertainly, "I guess I haven't ventured...."

"I can hardly believe that EB hasn't shown them to you," Adalwin interrupts. "By all means, you need to have a look!"

Jeff looks at Tanner beside him; "...Have you seen them?" he asks timidly, as if fearing the answer.

"Well — yeah, I have, of course," Tanner confirms. "I can show you when we get back if you'd like."

"Thanks, I definitely do," Jeff accepts. He looks down at his plate contemplatively as he quietly considers Adalwin's words: *...I can hardly believe that EB hasn't shown them to you.*

———

BACK AT LOCH HARNAN later that afternoon, Jeff waits for their Dibjet to come to a stop and powers it down, opening the door with a familiar swish.

"You say the caverns are near here?" he asks as he climbs out, still focused on seeing them.

"Yes. The door to the old cave that leads to them is at the end of the main corridor; they're just north of the bunker complex," Tanner explains. "Come on, I'll show you."

Jeff follows the Corporal down the long corridor, past the underground facility's large Mall, and further on past the huge vault door of the Command Center. A dozen yards or so beyond that, the hallway makes a ninety-degree turn and then stretches onward for another fifty meters before finally ending at a lone doorway.

It is more of a hatchway, actually, resembling the thick steel door of a submarine, with a wheel mounted at its center for unlatching it. Tanner spins the wheel counterclockwise, pulls the door open, and steps through. He waits for Jeff to join him and then pulls the door closed behind them and reseals it.

Jeff realizes he is in an airlock — a matching hatchway awaits them a few feet away. He can feel the air pressure adjust slightly before a green light comes on above the second door.

"The caverns are open to the undersea port," Tanner explains. "This airlock preserves the port's natural air pocket and keeps the ocean from flooding the caverns, along with everything else down here.

"Keeping it isolated also protects the caverns' unique biosphere; it's like no other place on earth," Tanner explains. "You'll see what I mean."

Tanner pushes open the second door and invites Jeff to follow him through; he steps into a dark tunnel that appears to have been carved through solid rock — a string of dim lightbulbs along the ceiling provides enough light to see where they are going, but nothing more. Jeff follows the dark passageway for about fifty feet until he reaches its end.

The sight that meets him there takes his breath away! He stands, staring up at the cavernous ceiling in awe of what he sees, over-whelmed by the sudden connection he feels to his family's shared history. The ceiling is covered with millions of glowing specs of light that cast a warm glow throughout the huge cavern's entire expanse.

Drawing his eyes down into the vast cavern itself, he can see mushrooms as tall as Christmas trees and an extraordinary amount of lush growth, including thick, soft moss that covers the floor and roots that hang like vines, loaded with odd-looking potatoes, carrots, and onions. A brook of icy, crystal-clear water flows through it, gurgling in a series of small waterfalls as it traverses the cavern's terrain.

It looks exactly like the description of it that he read in The

Cronicis — it is just as Arubija had described it! The single word that fills his thoughts as he breathlessly takes in the sight is... **Sanctuary**.

Jeff is astonished; he can't help wondering again why no one had told him sooner that this existed. Why hadn't EB or Hunahpu mentioned it even once? Genie had grown up in Loch Harnan! How could she have failed to mention that the Eighth Wonder of the World exists right under their feet?

Jeff runs forward into the cavern a dozen yards further and turns himself around several times to take in the amazing scene. His eye catches sight of what looks like stone foundations. Even though they are covered by an overgrowth of moss, he recognizes them easily as the remains of structures, possibly dwellings; they are extremely old yet well preserved in their sheltered environment.

Looking beyond those, he sees a pedestal of uncut stones that had been piled up to make a table-like platform; Jeff recognizes what it must have been — "An altar," he says to himself quietly.

Everything he sees confirms what he read about the caverns in The Cronicis, right down to the sweet smell of its clean, fresh air.

Tanner waits at the cavern's opening, watching Jeff take in the sight — it's as if he is a child at his first circus. There is no way for Tanner to know the depth of meaning that it holds for Jeff — Tanner is unaware of The Cronicis Niergel with its account of Arubija's rescue from the flood. The rescue that was secured in this very cavern.

Jeff scans the cavern's perimeter, noting how it branches off in several places, then his eye falls on the archway of a large opening. It is at the highest point within the main cavern, and it seems to glow more brightly than the rest. Jeff immediately recognizes it, his mind suddenly flooding with the scene that Arubija described — its words begin to replay with perfect clarity as he starts toward the focus of his ascent:

I looked up and saw in the archway of a large opening... a man standing... his robes were of many colors and his staff was in his hand. ... I approached with shaking knees and shallow breath, knowing of a certainty that the friend who beckoned me was no mere man. He spoke to me softly and his words thrilled my racing heart: "FEAR NOT ARUBIJA, BELOVED OF THE LORD!" I ran to him as I heard those words, falling to one knee before him....

Unexpected tears well in Jeff's eyes as he urgently climbs the cavern slope. He feels a familiar presence surrounding him as he reaches the archway — drawing him to his knees as a wave of emotion sweeps over him. It is the presence he'd first felt on the night he was saved from Semjaza — the same presence he'd felt with Hunahpu on that glorious day in the Secret Chamber. It is overwhelmingly welcoming and forgiving.

Hunahpu's words come flooding to mind as the memory triggers them:

It is a conflict, wonderful and glorious — to sense the grandeur of God's presence, with His power to create life or to destroy, it inspires in any gracious man a solemn awe... a holy fear... yet it is a fear with the terror taken out of it. His presence now carries no charge of judgment... only the love of a father newly reunited with his beloved child.

Jeff's eyes are drawn closed as the flood of tears rains from his soul, a mix of unworthiness and remarkable joy. He basks in the solemn moment as it seems to strengthen and minister to his hurting spirit. When it has finally subsided, Jeff opens his eyes, wiping his face against his sleeve to clear his vision.

It is then that he looks down at the ground in front of him, and his gaze falls on something unexpected — something completely out of place. Jeff knows immediately where it came from — recognizing that it has been left for him by his uncle. It is a single sheet of his uncle's letterhead, turned on its side, with a familiar word scrawled across it in large letters, as if it had been written in a great hurry:

Thuban

JEFF DRAWS a gasping breath and reaches down to lift the paper off the ground. Holding it in his hands, he stares at it while a chill runs all the way up his back and then down again. A blizzard of memories flashes through his mind as he considers the word's meaning, understanding that it is a clue — possibly the key he desperately needs. He carefully folds the paper and slips it into his pocket.

"IS EVERYTHING ALRIGHT?" Tanner asks him as Jeff returns. The traces of Jeff's tears are still visible on his cheeks, a concern about which it is obvious that Jeff couldn't possibly care less.

He looks back at Tanner, considering his question. "I know that it will be," he answers simply. Tanner nods cluelessly in an accepting gesture and then waves toward the way out, letting Jeff walk out ahead of him.

⌘

8

FATEFUL NIGHT

Barrymore wipes a tear from his eye while he watches EB's Dibjet disappear through the hangar's airlock doors for the last time. Pulling his eyes away from the closed-circuit image, he glances nervously down at his watch — realizing that he doesn't have much time.

He has planned for this moment carefully for many years, but now that it is really here, his mind is a chaotic jumble — he has to struggle to focus his thoughts, breathing a desperate prayer for God's help.

TURNING to scan the office around him, the first thing his eyes fall upon is the ornate brass spiral staircase — the one leading to the old observatory. He nods as if agreeing with an unspoken suggestion and makes his way quickly toward it, climbing until he reaches the dusty room above. There is no time to power up the old equipment, but he looks gratefully at the untouched coordinates on the telescope, confirming that they still match those on the old star chart beside it — coinciding with the star he has circled on the chart.

Thinking for a moment, he grabs a nearby pen and scribbles a name beside that star, writing: 'Thuban'. Then, to make doubly certain that his clue will not go unnoticed, he writes the coordinates in large letters at the bottom of the chart:

$$\delta \; 64° \; 20' \; 45.6'',$$
$$RA \; 14h \; 04m \; 33.58s$$

Barry steps back to look at his handiwork, praying it will be enough, and happens to notice the old calendar turned to the date on the matching chart. Using the pen once more, he circles the date repeatedly until it bears a heavy ring around it.

"Surely he will notice his own birth date," he whispers to himself hopefully.

Rushing quickly back down the stairs, he stops at his old desk. Thoughts of the countless hours he has spent here over literally hundreds of years rush through his mind as he is struck with the fact that he is likely seeing it for the last time.

Among a million thoughts running through his mind are countless words of counsel and advice for Jeff that he wishes he could have shared with him face-to-face. They are conversations he has envisioned hundreds of times, and although he has spent years preparing his avatar with answers, it wounds him greatly that he will not be able to share them with Jeff personally.

Seizing a sudden inspiration, he grabs a few sheets of blank paper on his desk and decides to write what is burning on his heart most strongly. He takes a seat and lifts his favorite pen, letting the words pour from his heart.

Dearest Jeffrey,

Events are moving rapidly, there is little time...

He knows that his young heir will be utterly unprepared for the weight of his responsibility as Mantle Bearer and shares his heart's prayer for God's constant help. He warns him of the approaching darkness and the dangers to come, counseling him on the importance of preserving the secrets entrusted to him and informing him of the Challenge he must complete.

He writes with sincere conviction... an urgent admonition flows from his heart onto the paper:

Take courage and doubt not that you are called for this very hour...

As he comes to the end of his letter, he pauses for a moment and considers the task he now faces, feeling moved to share the final thoughts of his heart with Jeff.

I have lived a long life ~ longer than you can yet imagine, and have led countless brave and honorable men into battle, but tonight I embark alone on my final mission.

EB has gone on tonight to warn you of your imminent danger. It pains me only that I shall say goodbye to many dear friends tonight, him most especially, ~ he was my dearest friend. I deeply regret also that I shall not have had the chance to embrace you.

Yet I have no regrets for my own ending; long life is both a blessing and a curse... for I long for the company of many beloved who have gone on before me to their rest; my longing grows deeper with each long year since their departing. Nay, I fear not for my life but truly lament the manner in which I must thrust upon you this great weight.

You have my sincerest, most earnest prayers.

Godspeed, my dear lad!

With enduring love,

Barrymore

With a deep sigh, he rises from the desk and picks up the letter, glancing at his watch. He knows exactly where to leave it, but he will have to hurry. Just as he starts to walk away, he notices his favorite Bible lying at the corner of the desk and picks it up. The feel of its well-worn leather cover and familiar weight is like holding the hand of an old friend. He clutches it to his chest as he takes one more look around the room and then makes his way out.

He moves quickly into the library and latches its thick, ornate doors, then approaches the large table at the center of the room and lays his Bible down on its empty surface, running his fingers over the old book's cover one final time. He rushes to the hidden elevator, opening its secret entrance through the bookcase, and rides it anxiously to the Secret Chamber below.

Barry wastes no time upon entering the Chamber — running to the large Golden Bookstand as quickly as he can and laying his letter down. He holds his hand on it for a brief moment and breathes a prayer for Jeff, then runs back again to the elevator.

JUST AS HE is exiting the library, he stops as a new thought occurs to him. He ducks quickly into his office again and grabs the nearest piece of paper, which happens to be a blank sheet of his own letterhead. With a pen, he scrawls a final clue across it:

Thuban

EXITING THE OFFICE SUITE, Barry takes off, running across the lobby and down the marble staircase to the rotunda, continuing urgently through the Great Hall. He is clearly winded as he reaches the elevator and bends over to catch his breath, placing his hand on the scanner.

"Computer... increase descent to full speed," he requests impatiently while gripping the elevator's nearby support bar. ABBI's voice confirms his request politely, and the elevator immediately accelerates to several times its normal speed, racing toward the underground complex. Brandish's Research Lab is silent as the elevator door opens moments later. Aside from dim lights in the hallways, the underground complex is dark.

He studies his watch anxiously, realizing that nearly twenty minutes have already passed since he said goodbye to EB. Breaking into a run, he races from the Lab and heads down the long main corridor, past the underground Mall and the impenetrable command bunker, around the hallway's ninety-degree turn. He doesn't stop until he reaches the heavy steel hatchway, spinning its handle urgently to open it, and then steps inside. The instant the airlock signals ready, he pushes open the second door and runs into the ancient cavern, knowing exactly where he has to go.

Scrambling up the slope to the prominent archway, he selects a location that would be unnoticed by almost everyone — unless they had read the Cronicis. He kneels to place the single sheet of paper on the floor there, where it can only be seen by someone standing on that spot — at the same time breathing an urgent prayer for Jeff to find it — and to understand!

. . .

MINUTES LATER, Barry is powering up his personal Dibjet, an advanced fighter that has served him well in dozens of battles. It is capable of Mach 9 — more than 6,000 miles per hour. It has the speed he will need to intercept the Borgia fighters, who already have a substantial head start.

As he bursts from the ocean into the night sky, he quickly fires his jet's anti-gravity afterburners, shooting him skyward at supersonic speed. Using an encrypted channel, he raises EB on their private satellite channel as he speeds across the sky.

"Maintain your radio silence and do not respond," he instructs his close friend as he hails him.

He then switches to an open frequency and broadcasts a message for all to hear. "This is BH-1," he deliberately announces himself to anyone listening, using the well-known call letters for his own ship. "I am en route to intercept."

He brings up a satellite view on his screen that shows the telemetry from EB's ship. A squadron of jets matching the Borgia's own Dibjet design can be seen about a thousand miles behind and to the south of his. He sets a direct intercept course toward them.

Barry switches his radio back to an encrypted channel, waiting for their satellite to synchronize with EB's ship before speaking.

"I need to ask you to promise me something," he says to EB.

"You know I will," EB responds without hesitation. "Anything at all; you need only say it," he vows.

"Promise you won't show Jeff the ancient caverns. It's important that he find them on his own — when he's ready. Make sure Eugenia knows as well, and anyone else."

EB thinks the request is a bit strange but readily agrees. "Do you want 'em sealed off?" he asks.

"That's not necessary," Barry confirms. "Just let him discover them on his own when the time is right."

"How will we know when the time is right?"

Barry silently considers the prayer that he prayed in the cavern, finally responding to EB's question after a short pause: "That is in God's hands…. When he discovers them, that will be the right time."

There is another short silence, then EB speaks:

"We can fight 'em together; you don't have t'do this."

"You know that I do," Barry replies. "If just one of them gets through to Jeff..." he stops without finishing his sentence. "Bear's squadron is too far away; they'd never reach us in time. You have to get to the lad first; it's the only way — I'll buy you as much time as I can."

A pair of enemy fighters appears on Barry's radar, heading straight toward him. He locks onto both of them and fires, releasing a matching pair of hypersonic missiles that speed off into the night sky.

"Goodbye, dear friend," he says to EB, clearing his throat emotionally. "I pray that God be with you... For what you do tonight, I am eternally grateful."

EB can't reply; his voice has suddenly left him, and his eyes are filled with tears. He sees Barry's encrypted signal switch off and, a short while later, hears his friend's voice on an open channel.

"Two enemy fighters have been destroyed," Barry announces. "Preparing to engage the enemy squadron."

Barry's console immediately lights up with telemetry warnings as the entire squadron turns toward him like an angry swarm of wasps.

"Bingo," he says as he lets loose four more missiles and then pulls the nose of his ship upward, launching his plane straight up into the sky. Explosions shake the air as four more enemy fighters erupt in flames, and the entire angry swarm follows him upward in hot pursuit.

He sees one of them break away to continue toward its original heading and quickly runs it down, destroying it in a blizzard of fire. After that, there is no shaking the rest of them; they chase him with vengeance.

Barry leads them southeast as he spins and fights, and fights and spins, taking out a dozen of their finest pilots before his ordinance is exhausted. He knows he could outrun them, but chooses to remain in range to keep them engaged for as long as possible, leading them further away from EB and Jeff.

EB listens anxiously as Barry provides a blow-by-blow report until their ships are nearly out of radio range. He suddenly hears a loud crack, and Barry's radio goes dead, leaving only silence.

TEARS RUN down EB's cheeks as he struggles to maintain his focus. In the distance, the lights of Boston and the Massachusetts coastline can now be seen through the rainy night sky.

⌘

9

STRONGHOLD

M orning light peeks over the eastern horizon as Jeff sits on the Tower's secluded balcony high atop the castle. He is watching the breathtaking sight of a new day just breaking over the distant Scottish cliffs.

The sight is all too apropos. This particular daybreak marks the dawning of the final week of his quest; he has only seven days left to find the Ring and Scepter and destroy them.

He has been up all night, poring over the data from his uncle's analysis of the objects and combing the Tower's recorded archives for clues... again. It has been more than three weeks since Hunahpu showed him the *Book of the End* and a dozen hours since he discovered his uncle's clue in the ancient cavern. He has been searching endlessly for their meanings ...to the point of exhaustion. By now, he has been through all of the data a half-dozen times, from beginning to end, and has read every volume that the Secret Chamber has shown him, yet the means for destroying the objects still eludes him.

He goes over in his mind his repeated daylight visits to the Vault of Archives, searching for any references that mentioned the objects. He has studied the accounts in Cornelius' diary that recounted how he fatefully gave the ring to his young wife, Katkeruus, as a gift. Unfortunately, Cornelius never mentioned in his diary where he found the Ring, a clue that might have revealed its weakness.

He suddenly leans forward on the bench as he zeros in on that thought. Cornelius may not have known of the Ring's dangers, but his father, Cerdic, certainly did... he had been there, after all, when it was wrested away from Maranish. Jeff recalls Cerdic's portrait in the main hall of Cornelius' suite, remembering how he was dressed in a soldier's armor with a nameplate that read: *Cerdic of Hastleworth*. As a man who had known the bloody thousand-year conflict with the Dyfarniad firsthand, he surely would have understood the Ring's tragic power and secured it safely — in a way that ensured that its power would be contained. If Jeff could find where it was secured, he might learn something about the objects' weaknesses.

Jeff considers whether Cerdic would have hidden the Ring in the Vault of Archives, but quickly decides that he would not likely have risked it falling into the hands of that fearsome demoness, Leanan Sidhe. No... it had to have been hidden somewhere else. The Secret Chamber was not exactly a well-kept secret in Cerdic's day; given its recent history at that time, Jeff guesses that he was not likely to have hidden it there either. Eliminating both of those possibilities actually made the puzzle much harder... There are countless places to hide things in the old castle...

...Jeff's last thought is interrupted as he suddenly realizes that he is wrong about that ...most of the current castle structure had not even been built yet at that time; the drawing in Maranish's manuscript showed no castle at all!

Jeff urgently returns to the Tower Lab. "BE," he calls as he enters... "When was this castle built ...who built it?"

"The main castle, consisting of the three towers and their rings, was built by Cerdic after the Thousand Year War," the avatar quickly answers.

Part of what BE has just said repeats in Jeff's mind like a bell ringing ...*the three towers and their rings*. A sudden inspiration strikes him; he can hardly believe he hasn't seen it before! The castle's amazing symmetry ...the scenes depicted in the stained glass dome and on the door of Cornelius' suite ...even the three-shaped key that opens the Secret Chamber ...it all suddenly comes into focus.

All at once, he understands what the scenes depict: their three parts constitute the exact opposite of eternity — opposing the power of the Ring. They represent *Energy, Time,* and *Matter* ...the antithesis of the Ring's innate nature. The castle was built as a stronghold, but not only against outside attacks. It was built not just to keep enemies out but also to keep something *in*. The castle itself is a restraint — meant to contain the power of the Ring! But how?

"SHOW ME A BLUEPRINT OF THE CASTLE!" Jeff nearly shouts to BE.

The castle's 3D CAD image appears on his screen, and Jeff immediately begins rotating it and removing layers until he has uncovered what looks like a gigantic Venn diagram ...three huge circles overlapping one another in the center.

"What are these rings made of?" he asks the avatar.

"They are the purest silver ... each one made in a single pour without joint or seam," BE explains.

Jeff considers that silently; silver is the best-known conductor of electricity. He spins the 3D image, examining it from every angle. He can see that the towers are positioned at the outer edges of each silver ring and that each tower contains a series of copper 'collars' that rise their entire height. The collars are all connected with copper rods that come together at each tower's base, and then a single rod extends downward from each tower, deep into the mountain. Jeff remembers something that CHET said about the mountain beneath them when he was describing how his family retained their unique traits: '*This mountain...contains enormous strata of lead buried within the rock.*'

"...It's a battery!" Jeff says to himself in amazement as he understands what he is seeing.

"It is very much like a battery in its basic design," BE elaborates, "however, it does not store energy ...rather, it absorbs it, directing it into the earth — somewhat like a lightning rod."

"It's brilliant!" Jeff says in astonishment. "How was such a thing conceived in the eleventh century?"

"Perhaps a more appropriate question would be, how are we unable to replicate the advancements of Arubija's time?" the avatar replies.

Jeff nods, humbly admitting that BE is right about that. He turns his attention back to the castle diagram, avoiding the distraction posed by that thought.

"Where did Cornelius find the Ring?"

"That detail is not recorded, unfortunately," the avatar answers.

Jeff doesn't really need the answer; the likely location is staring him in the face. It had to have been directly in the center of the castle — surrounded by the interlocking silver rings, somewhere beneath the floor of the rotunda. He remembers the underground tunnels leading to a subterranean version of the dome ...that has to have been it. He is certain that if he searches that underground dome, he will find the place where it had been secured.

Why would Cornelius have removed it from there? He wonders to himself silently.

The avatar's voice interrupts Jeff's unspoken thought:

"All that is known is that it was given to Katkeruus in a unique wooden box. She kept it on her dresser, at least at first."

Jeff stops and looks at BE, "Do you know where the box is now?" The avatar appears to be thinking for a moment before answering,

"I have just reviewed all of the castle's security cameras …a possible match has been detected in your grandfather's private office, in his quarters."

The screen in front of Jeff shows the identified video feed; he leans closer to examine it.

"Zoom in on the box," Jeff instructs, watching as the image closes in on a cylindrical-looking wooden canister with a hinged lid. He quickly forms a theory of what it is.

It demands a closer inspection; Jeff immediately turns to the elevator to go check it out. A few minutes later, he is running down his suite's main staircase — Isabel sees him heading for the front door and protests his obvious intention to skip breakfast, but he doesn't stop… or wait for her to notice that he is still wearing yesterday's clothes. Dashing out the front door, he ducks quickly into the doorway of his grandfather's suite, narrowly avoiding EB's notice as his older friend comes up the rotunda stairs.

Jeff locates his Grandfather's large private office, getting his bearings, then quickly finds the bookshelf that he had seen in the video feed. After lifting the small wooden box in his hands, his suspicions are confirmed. It is extremely old… ancient, in fact. It has been handcrafted and carefully polished, but Jeff can tell what it is… There is no doubt that it has been cut from the Shepherd's Staff. He slowly opens the lid and notices how it has been carved to serve as a secure holder for the ring. The inside has been carved to create a post from the heart of the Staff upon which the ring would have been placed.

He turns it over to examine the bottom and notices an inscription: *Secure Manu Deorum* …Secure in God's hand. The words bring to mind the familiar commands that Jeff himself had uttered when calling upon the Staff's power, now on several occasions.

The box's discovery confirms what Jeff already knew about the power of the Staff to restrain the Ring, but it doesn't get him any closer to finding a way to destroy it. It confirms, in fact, that Cerdic couldn't destroy it either... settling, instead, on a means to limit its power.

Jeff carefully sets the ancient box down in the center of the large office desk and half-collapses into the desk chair. He sits staring at it as if hoping that it will suddenly reveal to him the answer he desperately seeks. He picks up the box again and turns it over, reading and rereading the ancient inscription. It is written in Latin, ...ancient Roman, actually. Ironically, it is the same language and dialect as the inscription on the door of Vault Degli Archivi.

It is also the same language that came to him when calling the Staff....

JEFF IS SUDDENLY SEIZED with a new idea; ...*words* ...*language...* can express more than mere thoughts. They are *commands...* they convey *power.*

As he considers the thought, other memories begin to come to mind ...of the way that Nuevel's timepiece mysteriously activates the Secret Chamber's retrieval system with commands in this same language ...and the way the Staff and its seeds have responded to his words.

Just as significantly, Jeff recalls Maranish's description of the means by which the Ring and Scepter originally came into existence ...they were *CALLED forth* from the Scroll of the gods!

"That has to be it!" he says to himself, instantly wondering if it could really be that easy. *Words* have to be the answer... the objects are *controlled* with verbal commands... with *WORDS*. Perhaps, he reasons, they can also be ***destroyed*** with words in the same way!

· · ·

JEFF PULLS his O-P from his pocket and expands it on the desk in front of him.

"CHET - open the manuscript from Maranish," he requests urgently.

As soon as it opens, Jeff turns quickly to the heading he had located earlier for Q*uod Virgam et Cylch o Awydd* …the Staff and Ring of Desire, reading the account of their origin again:

'…these implements fantastic were conceived by Semjaza's mighty will. Called forth from the scroll of the gods, they draw their power from a realm unseen. They were forged in the furnaces of Tir Lai, infused with powers to enslave and destroy.'

Jeff considers what the avatar said to him when Jeff inquired about the alternate dimension that the objects came from — *"You will need to seek for that answer …it is the key to your quest."*

Jeff has been searching the Secret Chamber's volumes exhaustively for every mention of the *Ring and Scepter,* and he guesses that his uncle Barrymore had done the same, yet the secret to their destruction has eluded them both. As he looks down at the O-P screen, it dawns on him that Barrymore never had the benefit of seeing the ancient manuscript of Maranish …the one now right in front of him. Barry never knew that the Ring and Scepter had come from the Scroll of the gods …he never knew about Tir Lai.

"CHET - What's the translation of Tir Lai," Jeff asks curiously.

"Tir Lai has no known translation," CHET answers unhelpfully.

Jeff reaches for his timepiece as the idea forms; until now, he never thought to ask the Chamber about Tir Lai! He distractedly squeezes the timepiece in his hand as he urgently stands and then drops it back into his pocket. He collects the O-P and starts toward the office doorway with a renewed resolve.

HE IS JUST MAKING his way through the door when his phone rings — it's Eugenia. Glancing at his watch, he remembers his fight training session with a sigh of regret.

"I'm so sorry!" He quickly apologizes as he answers, "...I've been studying something... all night, actually, and completely lost track of time."

"Is everything all right? I was worried about you," Genie says sincerely. "It's not like you to miss our session." You didn't even call." Jeff can sense the hurt in her voice.

"Genie, I'm really sorry; it was wrong of me — don't be worried, I'm fine." He looks at his wrinkled suit and dress shoes; "I think we'll have to skip training today. I'm kind of in the middle of something I need to do ...it's important."

"It doesn't have anything to do with finding your uncle's secret vault, does it?" she asks suspiciously.

"Don't worry," he assures her, "I'm not going to do anything stupid."

"Jeff, please!" she pleads with concern, "it's too dangerous ... promise you'll stay away from it!"

Once again, Jeff wants to explain to her that he has only days left in the Challenge... he wants to tell her everything he has discovered ... about Tir Lai and the objects' origin, but he knows he can't. He can't tell anyone.

"Look, please don't worry," he repeats as reassuringly as possible, although he realizes he is evading a direct answer to her request. "I'm sorry..." he says uncomfortably, "...I'm not able to talk now... I need to go."

"Wait! Where are y...?" he hears her trying to ask him as he hangs up the call.

⌘

10

TIR LAI

J eff quickly makes his way into the main hallway and begins toward the front door of his grandfather's suite, then stops and looks instead toward the large staircase behind him leading down to the Vault of Archives. He is thinking about Maranish's ancient manuscript, with its depiction of a hidden tunnel leading from just outside the Vault of Archives to the Secret Chamber. The instructions for its entrance replay in his photographic memory:

'Seek entry in the south face of Fortress Rock... where first light makes its arrow mark. There you will find the entry stone....'

He doesn't know if the old landmarks can still be seen or even if the old tunnel still exists, but he knows that he needs to get to the Secret Chamber as fast as possible. Entering through the office library is risky at this time of day, and EB and Genie are likely to be searching for him. If the old tunnel still exists, then it is worth a try.

. . .

HE QUICKLY MAKES his way down the sunlit staircase, intently scanning the ancient walls at their base the entire way. Whatever natural formation existed, Jeff realizes, was covered over with the castle's stone walls centuries ago. He also knows, however, that the stone walls in this castle aren't necessarily impassable.

First light has passed some time ago, but Jeff rapidly scans his surroundings for every possible way in which a beam of early sunrise might be cast in the area. The castle now encloses what had once been an open-air setting, but he can estimate the direction of sunrise, along with his knowledge of the Secret Chamber's location, guessing which wall is most likely to hide the tunnel's opening.

He pulls out the O-P again and opens the manuscript, quickly reviewing the ancient blueprint. He can see in it the location of the Vault's door, using that as a reference to try to locate the position of Fortress Rock. The drawing contains a small 'X' at the spot where the entry stone should be found; from its position relative to the Vault door's size, he estimates the stone should be located about half the door's height from the floor — roughly four feet off the ground. That gives him a swath of wall area to search, no more than a dozen feet long and about a foot high, with its center about four feet off the floor.

He remembers his discovery from weeks earlier of the O-P's sonar scanning abilities and decides to see if it will work here. He holds it against the wall to scan inside, starting about 4 feet from the floor, then slowly moves it sideways. The screen shows nothing but dense black stone as he drags it across the surface.

He has examined more than half the length when he notices that the stone's depth suddenly grows thinner. Moving ahead a little further, he sees something in the image; it looks like a small slotted opening …a keyhole.

Removing the O-P from the wall, Jeff can see that there is an almost imperceptible gap between two of the stones directly over the hidden slot. The gap is barely wide enough for a knife blade.

That gives him an idea. At the time this was built, it would have been common for travelers to carry a weapon for protection... a sword. He remembers seeing several ceremonial swords hanging in the upstairs hallway, but they are too broad and don't seem old enough. Then he remembers a lone sword hanging just above the door inside the Archive Vault, which seems extremely old.

Deciding it is worth a try, he opens the Vault of Archives, watches it flood with sunlight, then steps inside. Quickly grabbing the ancient sword, he examines it carefully, marveling at its shine — it shows almost no sign of tarnish in spite of its great age. An inscription runs along the blade's length, and Jeff uses the O-P to interpret it: *Guardian of the Mysteries.*

Jeff carries it back with him into the stairwell, resealing the Vault's door behind him. Standing then in front of the hidden slot, he prays that he isn't destroying the priceless artifact and slowly begins pushing it into the gap in the wall. It slides in smoothly, with no resistance at all, continuing until it is buried all the way to the hilt of the handle.

Nothing happens.

Jeff looks all around for some other lever or keystone that needs to be pressed or moved in combination with the sword, searching the wall from top to bottom, but can't find anything. Finally, he reluctantly surrenders and slowly pulls the sword out again, conceding that he will have to use the Library entrance after all.

No sooner has he removed the sword completely, however, than he hears a rumbling sound and then watches a section of the wall sink inward several feet, looking like a puzzle piece with its jagged interlocking edges. When it stops moving, Jeff can see gaps on either side that open into a dark passageway.

He instinctively holds the sword in front of him as he cautiously enters, moving around the section of the wall and into the tunnel behind it. The wall slides closed again with a rumble as he passes; he stands still, letting his eyes adjust to the darkness. Once again, using his phone as a flashlight, he holds it up to examine the ancient tunnel. The walls appear to have been chiseled through solid rock, and he can see that the tunnel slopes gradually downward. Thick spiderwebs crisscross the tunnel, and a deep layer of dust covers the floor, suggesting that it hasn't been used in many years... probably centuries. The air inside is surprisingly fresh, hinting that he was right about its intersecting with the Secret Chamber's ventilation shaft.

He uses the sword in his hand to clear the webs and slowly moves forward. After twenty meters or so, he comes to the first of several sets of stairs that have been carved into the rock, leading downward. Even at a cautious pace, it doesn't take him long to reach the tunnel's lower opening; it exits into a large vertical column that Jeff realizes also serves as the elevator's shaft. It is far larger than he had guessed — nearly ten meters across and stretching upward as far as he can see. It must have been a massive undertaking to carve it by hand from solid rock.

Using the light of his phone to look straight across the dark shaft, he can see the opening and hallway where the elevator ordinarily stops; when the elevator is present, it completely blocks the tunnel entrance, explaining why he never noticed the shaft's huge size before now. A whistling sound of moving air can be heard, hinting at an efficient ventilation system somewhere high above.

Jeff carefully makes his way across the base of the open shaft and steps into the familiar hallway, then uses the hidden combination to enter the Secret Chamber.

———

HE LOOKS AGAIN at the ancient sword in his hand, wiping it clean of dust and spiderwebs before gently laying it down on a table, just beside a small urn that is full of the seeds that he collected from the Chamber floor. He quickly turns his attention to the bookcase and makes his way immediately to the imposing golden bookstand, reaching into his pocket for his timepiece.

"Lego Tir Lai," he instructs as he speaks to it, then attaches the timepiece to the golden pedestal.

It stands completely still for more than a minute; Jeff feels a sense of deep disappointment growing within him as he begins to concede another defeat. Then suddenly, it jolts to life, moving a dozen long strides away; a single book is unlatched from its place …Jeff's heart sinks as he realizes what it is.

It lowers to the pedestal as he approaches it warily, eying its ornate gilding and elaborate inscription: *Liberatricem Commemorans* ~ Thaliard's compendium of evil incantations. Jeff looks upward at the place where the Shepherd's Staff is stored, wishing that he had thought to retrieve it first. He then remembers the urn of seeds and makes his way back to it, picking up a small cluster and dropping it into his pocket. He keeps a single seed in one fist as he carefully opens the book's heavy cover.

The familiar-looking title page sends an eerie chill up his spine as he reads its translated text again: *Inscribed by the hand of Thaliard ~ Prince of Eljo and Lord of the Niergel.*

The ancient book does not contain anything as convenient as a table of contents. With his O-P reduced to the size of a credit card, Jeff holds it in the air above the pages; "Search for Tir Lai," he instructs. Then he begins paging forward with his other hand, letting the O-P rapidly scan each page. He is a little more than halfway through the thick volume when the O-P chimes urgently.

Jeff lays it down on the open pages, letting the device expand to cover them from edge to edge. He begins to read the translated pages:

The Mysteries of Tir Lai… the Forging of the Ring of Desire

He who was brightest of the angels of light, even that archangel Lucifer, son of the morning, the Dragon. It was he whose rebellion ignited the flames of Tir Lai. From its smelting furnace were forged weapons of power, and with them a ring, mighty to wield destruction and to enslave. It bore within it a stone of enchantment, the Eye of the Dragon, and together with the dragon's scepter, it was made to hold unassailable power.

The Ring and its Scepter were made eternal, and thus they remain untouched by time — for no earthly power can destroy them. Naught, but the fires of Tir Lai itself could threaten them; no eternal fire is stronger than its own flame.

These implements of power were given by the Dragon to Semjaza, prince of the gods, so that he would wield the Dragon's power on the earth. They were commanded by the word of the Dragon, in secret oracles that held power to break natural laws ...even to cross between time and the eternal realm. The Dragon's secret oracles were written in the eternal scroll ...the Scroll of the gods.

THALIARD WENT on to write that he believed the Scepter and Scroll had been lost forever on the night of the flood when they were swept away with Atlan's gleaming palaces. He described the way that Semjaza himself was destroyed that night by the Dragon's mortal enemy, referring to the Dragon's fearsome foe as *'the Shepherd with great power'* and as *'the Ancient of Days.'* Jeff realizes that Thaliard's writing was the obvious source of the story recounted by Maranish, who had, no doubt, heard it told to him by his father.

He stops reading and steps back, dejectedly taking a seat on the bench. He is feeling more convinced than ever that it is likely to be *impossible* to destroy the Ring and Scepter. While he sits there, however, his eye catches sight again of the miraculous writing on the golden volumes above ...a reminder that Jeff's strength has nothing to do with it. It occurs to him that if this challenge is truly from God, then a way will, in fact, be found — or made — to destroy them.

Even... he thinks nervously... if the objects have to be cast into Hell itself.

This all sounds crazy, he has to admit, but a few months ago, most of what surrounds him would have seemed to him like someone's insane delusion ...yet it is all perilously real.

HE LEANS FORWARD and rests his elbows on his knees. In the quiet solitude of the amazing Chamber, he can't help remembering the way Hunahpu led him to Christ — in this very spot. Jeff closes his eyes and breathes a desperate prayer, asking for God's help.

Soon, feeling some renewed courage, he stands and returns to Thaliard's huge book, using the O-P to scan the rest of its pages, but finds no other mention of Tir Lai. Thaliard must have assumed that the Ring's birthplace could never be reached; after all, the Scepter and Scroll had been lost for thousands of years, as far as he had known.

It is nearly noontime when Jeff completes his painstaking search of Thaliard's writings, finally sending the book back to its place. As disappointed as he is about his findings, he is even more relieved to be done with the evil tome.

He tries asking the timepiece again for other references to Tir Lai, but realizes after what feels to him like an endless wait that there are no others. He stifles a yawn that reminds him he hasn't slept in almost thirty hours and steadies himself against the bookstand. So many thoughts swirl through his mind ...of the prophecy and the Beast, of Cerdic and the castle's amazing construction, of Tir Lai and the supernatural nature of the Ring and Scepter ...and the impossible quest of his Challenge. He feels dizzy from it all!

Finally, with an escaping yawn, he drops the Timepiece into his pocket. Carefully picking up the ancient sword, he slowly makes his way back to the tunnel.

⌘

11

TAKE DOWN

J eff is sound asleep in one of his Grandfather's stuffed armchairs when EB nudges him on the shoulder.

"Are ye all right, Lad?" he hears him saying.

It takes a moment for Jeff to get his bearings as he looks around, slowly recognizing Cornelius' study.

"Ye've got Genie a fair bit worried about ye," EB confides. He looks at what Jeff is holding loosely in his hand and nods toward it; "Found that, did ya? I must say, yer sleuthin' skills are impressive, me-lad."

Jeff sits up straight and looks at the Ring's wooden case in his hand; "You recognize this?"

"Sure, I do. It was Neil's, that is… old Mr. Hastleworth's, greatest regret. The poor soul tortured himself by staring at it for hours."

"Do you know where he found it?" Jeff asks hopefully.

"Never would say," EB answers, "…just that it had been the greatest mistake he'd ever made. I suppose he would've done nearly anything for a chance to reverse it …anything at all."

"Did Uncle Barry know where his father found it?"

"If he did, he never let on," EB confirms.

Jeff looks around the room, trying to guess the time; "Guess I dozed off ...What time is it?"

"Near dinner time. I've been searchin' for y' half the afternoon. Should've looked here first, I suppose," EB glances around him. "Were y' studyin' here all night?"

"No, just the afternoon...," Jeff begins to answer, then corrects, "... or.... slept the afternoon, that is; came in the morning, I guess."

"Well, from the look o' things, y' didn't sleep last night. I'm not surprised t' find y' nappin'."

Jeff looks at his older friend with a discouraged expression: "There are only six days left for my challenge," he says, leaning forward and running both his hands through his disheveled hair. "I'll be honest with you; I'm not sure I can do it ...complete it in time. I'm not even sure that it *can* be completed — if it's even possible. Maybe you'd better warn the Board — there must be something else that can be done...some other way to change the bylaws...."

EB cuts him off: "Let's not be havin' any o' that talk." He places a hand on Jeff's shoulder and looks him in the eyes: "There's nobody I know who has a better chance of it than ye have, my boy. I'd put all I have at risk bettin' on you."

Jeff stares at him for a moment, an ominous thought crossing his mind. "...I think you already have," he answers nervously.

EB shrugs off the comment and holds out a hand to help Jeff up, then gives him a friendly slap on the back as they head for the door.

EB AND HUNAHPU are having a casual conversation at the dinner table with Jeff. As worried as he's been, Jeff hadn't realized just how starved he was — he hadn't eaten anything since dinner the night before. He is on second helpings by the time he slows down enough to speak.

"How much do you know about this castle?" he asks the two of them, wiping the corner of his mouth with his napkin, "About its design and construction, I mean."

The men look at him and then back at each other as they ponder the question. Before they can answer, Jeff has another question…

"The images in the stained glass dome, for instance, what do they represent?"

EB has the distinction of calling the castle his home the longest, at least among those present in the room; he is the first to venture an answer.

"Well, now, that's a story with a fair bit of local folklore. It surely has to do with the castle's three parts …the cloverleaf wings and their towers …although there are some different theories about the actual meanings. If y' look right up at it, the first thing y' see is its clock face, but then if y' study it, there are other images in the glass …earth and ocean, mountains and lightning bolts."

"So how does that equate to the castle's three wings?" Jeff asks, prodding him to continue.

"Well, as I see it," EB explains, "It's metaphorical — it's about time and history …about the three aspects of it. There's Time, of course; then there's the earth …this island — Loch Harnan. And the third aspect points to the forces of nature with their cycles — to storms and the sun and seasons."

Jeff nods as he accepts his friend's interpretation. "Which wing of the castle is which?" he asks curiously.

"Well, I dare say I couldn't tell y'. At least, there's nothin' that points the symbols to any one of 'em in particular. It's more like all of 'em are parts o' one thing — like somethin' that's unified but with complimentary traits, a sort o' Trinity."

"Alright," Jeff says as he engages EB with a look of understanding. "You mean, like the three dimensions of the universe …**Energy, Time, and Matter.**"

EB pauses and considers Jeff's answer… "Aye, I'd say that's an excellent description… that's exactly what it is!"

Hunahpu has been quietly listening. He catches Jeff's eye with a discerning gaze: "You had that deciphered before asking your question …what was the real reason for asking?"

Jeff humbly admits that he is right with a nod and a glance down at the table. "There's more to this castle than meets the eye," he says without elaborating, looking back at both of them with a searching expression: "Did uncle Barry or my Grandfather ever talk about the castle's design or its construction?"

"Hmmph..." EB intones, leaning back in his chair as he considers the question. "Barry knew this castle well, that I can say for sure. Seemed he was always building or changing something or other ...like this suite of yours here. He was always careful to keep the main castle's original layout as it was, though. He never interfered with the castle structure that was built by his grandfather."

Jeff thinks about what EB has just said, looking around him. "What was here before this suite?" he asks curiously.

"Barry had his private workshop here," EB answers with an air of nostalgia. "Some great inventions were born here ...the means to harness anti-gravity, for one." EB chuckles as he thinks about it — "We had to repair the roof after that one."

Jeff shakes his head in amazed disbelief. "What about the towers ... were they ever used for anything?"

"The southern towers are open for anyone to climb, but don't get used much," EB offers, "...these days they're mostly for show." He pauses briefly in thought before continuing... "The north tower is another story; there was a tragedy there that caused Cornelius to have it sealed off. That was more than ninety years ago — y' won't find an entrance to it from anywhere in the castle."

"Do you remember what happened?" Jeff asks him.

"I'm afraid I wasn't living here in those days," EB explains. "It's said that one of Barry's brothers died in that tower ...fell to his death, as the story goes.

Jeff looks to Hunahpu, who is sitting quietly, "Do you remember what happened?" he asks his great-grandfather.

"Hmm ...Hunahpu answers, stroking his chin. "I recall hearing of the tragedy. His name was David ...the son who died, that is. Barry seldom spoke of him and never discussed the accident."

Jeff decides to let the question go, determining to ask the avatar instead. He looks up to see Isabel refilling their glasses....

"Dinner was excellent, Isabel," Jeff says sincerely. "I could hardly get enough!"

"I'm not in the least surprised, seeing how you've been starving yourself the past two days," she retorts with a sly smile. "You'll not want to miss my warm apple pie," she adds, making certain he doesn't run off before dessert.

As she leaves the room, Jeff turns back to his mentors, lowering his voice.

"Has our ...surveillance... detected anything new?" It is clear that he is asking for news about the mysterious Estonian organization.

It has been a few weeks since Hunahpu revealed to Jeff the special espionage team that had been under Barry's direction.

"I'm sorry to say that nothing has changed; things have been quiet lately," EB replies, "...Ominously so."

He considers EB's answer: "Do you think they've detected our code in their systems? Could they have learned to block it?"

"That's possible, of course," EB says, considering Jeff's remark, "although they'd have to out-think CHET to do it."

Jeff nods his head in an admission that doing that would be no mean feat.

ISABEL RETURNS with a tray of generously sized slices of her warm apple pie, each with a dish of ice cream. Jeff manages to finish his in record time, and then Hunahpu offers Jeff his as well, watching with a hearty laugh as Jeff eagerly accepts it.

The three of them retire to the sitting room afterward, where Jeff quickly succumbs to exhaustion and dozes off in his chair.

Thursday morning...

EUGENIA IS WAITING for him in the gym when he arrives on time the next morning. She doesn't look him in the eye as he enters, and he can

tell she is still annoyed with him about missing their last session —
not to mention hanging up on her.

"We'll be goin' a bit longer this mornin', to make up for lost time,"
she announces in an especially strict tone of voice as she grabs a pair
of broadswords from the rack.

Jeff knows he is in for it. She throws him a sword and immediately
attacks, spinning and swinging with a controlled fury that he hasn't
seen from her in a while. He does his best to fend her off, finding high
ground wherever he can, but her attack is overwhelming, eventually
knocking his sword from his hand, disarming him.

To his surprise, rather than ending the skirmish at that point, she
throws her own sword down and attacks him hand-to-hand, kicking,
punching, and chopping with amazing speed — she isn't holding
anything back. Jeff catches a glimpse of her heel speeding toward him
overhead as she flips in the air, and he manages to catch it between his
open palms, throwing her backward. She instantly flips backward,
spins free, then attacks again.

Jeff has no time to think as he fends off her relentless strikes,
reacting purely on instinct. He suddenly finds himself anticipating her
moves ...things begin slowing down around him — he can see her
facial expressions, the way her eyes blaze, and her lips stretch tightly
as she strikes. It reminds him of that first day in the flight simulator —
when it was spinning out of control.

Without a thought, he instinctively ducks aside, dodging her kick
with lightning speed as he grabs her ankle with one hand and twists
her around in mid-air. Then his elbow strikes her hard between her
shoulder blades, sending her to the mat face-first. The entire set of
moves has happened in under a second — the shock of it surprises
him, and he quickly steps back as he looks at her apologetically and
tries to figure out what has just happened.

Genie is clearly dazed, looking as though the wind has been
knocked out of her. As she slowly recovers, he offers a hand to help
her sit up.

· · ·

"I've been waitin' for y' t'do that," she says mysteriously as she dusts herself off, panting heavily. "Guess I've been goin' too easy on ya."

"What just happened? You expected me to do that?" Jeff asks with a confused look.

"I thought ye might," she says, using a towel to wipe the sweat from her forehead. "I remember the first time Nanna downed me like that. She felt terrible about it, but I was elated …it meant that I'd finally become good enough to pose a real threat.

"The two o' ye are so much alike," she confides to him; "Yer moves, the way y' learn …it's almost uncanny."

Jeff doesn't know how much Genie knows about his heritage or her grandmother's, but her comments reveal that she already understands there is a connection.

"How long have you known?" he asks quietly.

"What? About yer superpowers?" She half-jokes. "A person doesn't have t' be a genius t' see what's right in front of 'em. She drapes the towel over her shoulders as she grabs a water bottle… "I could see it in ya when y' first got here… but it was also pretty clear that y' didn't know it, …did ya."

"That I had superpowers?" he asks in a joking tone, "No, I can't say that I did."

"Well, it was pretty obvious that ye didn't know what you were in for when y' got here, but I knew y' were different …that y' were like them; I could see it in ye right away."

Jeff flinches uncomfortably, rubbing the back of his neck.

"So… my family has some distinctive traits, I guess. I can't claim credit for any of that."

"I know," she says in an understanding voice, "it must all be a big adjustment for ye. I'm fairly impressed by the way ye've handled it; it hasn't gone to your head."

Jeff imagines that she would understand his humility if she knew about the Challenge … especially how close he is to failing it. He bites his tongue as he wishes he could tell her about it.

"I have t' admit I'm a little jealous," she confesses, "Your family is so amazin'!"

Jeff just looks at her, feeling confused about what he can reveal. She seems to understand his hesitation and explains further...

"I started t' realize your family was different at a pretty young age ...look where I grew up, after all. When I moved here after my parents died, it didn't take long fer me t' start askin' questions. By the time I was in my teens, it was pretty obvious t' me that Nanna was unnaturally young for her age ...she also had these amazin' reflexes and was so smart ...she could learn anythin' just by hearin' it once." She looks at Jeff: "just like I've seen ye do.

"After Nanna died, it was just Shan'er and me," she adds quietly. "It wasn't until then that he finally confided to me how old she really was and why she looked so young. Then he revealed his own age and told me how Barry's son had saved him durin' World War One. That's how I learned Barry's age... he made me swear t' secrecy as he told me how the Hastleworth lineage has had their special traits all the way back through history.

"I'd already known that Barry was different — like Nanna. Bein' so close to him, I could see it easily; he still seemed t' have the reflexes of a man in his forties or fifties, even though he was so much older. I've never met a more brilliant man than he was." There is a distinct sadness in her voice as she thinks about him.

"Shan'er also explained the origin of the Niergel and your family's history ...what he knew of it, anyway..." She looks at Jeff with a sad expression, "...and that ye're the last."

"Did he tell you anything else?" Jeff questions, trying to see if she knows about the Challenge.

She doesn't answer his question but gives him a knowing stare as she drops her hand towel and picks up the sword. "He believes in ye," she simply says, "...aside from yer uncle Barry himself, he's never believed in anyone as much as he does in ye."

With that, she jumps to her feet and assumes a defensive stance with her sword, signaling that their break is over. Jeff picks up his own sword from the mat and prepares to defend himself; given what she has just said, he feels like he has no choice but to prepare as hard as possible. He suddenly feels a new determination to give it his all, even if the cause feels hopeless.

⌘

12

CASTLE SECRETS

Jeff's clothes are drenched as he makes his way back to his suite; he can't remember having a more strenuous workout in any of their morning sessions, but it makes him feel good. It occurs to him that there is no better cure for stress than a good hour or two of kicking, punching, and sword fighting. After showering, he decides to make a quick visit to the Tower Lab.

"BE," he requests as soon as he enters, "search your archives for everything you have about the castle's construction, especially this tower — the north one.

BE materializes, and the lab's screens soon fill with drawings, diagrams, and photographs of various parts of the castle from throughout its history.

"What can you tell me about Cornelius' son David?" Jeff asks.

"From the context of your question, I discern that you are asking about David's unfortunate death. It happened ninety years ago, in this very tower, when the boy was fifteen years of age."

"Only fifteen?" Jeff asks in surprise, "Was he a half-brother to Barry …like my father?"

"He was the son of Cornelius' fourth wife …her only child. The boy's death destroyed her; she lived only a year longer before succumbing to pneumonia. It was widely understood that she lost her will to live."

"So, Cornelius had the tower sealed after David's death?" Jeff asks.

"That's right. He had all of its doors and windows filled in with thick stone," BE confirms. "It was as a memorial to his son."

"I take it then that it was Uncle Barry who built this lab?"

"Yes. It was begun in the year after the tragic deaths of Cornelius and Aeden…."

"…and of my parents," Jeff adds quietly. The avatar nods sympathetically.

"…When you were eight years old," BE confirms. "Barry built it as a monument to their bravery, dedicating it to the search for a means to destroy the Ring and its Scepter …and as a classroom for you," BE adds. "He converted his former laboratory into the suite you occupy today, using your suite's remodeling to cover for this Lab's secret construction."

"Who else knew about it …who built it?" Jeff wonders.

"Angus Baird supervised the construction crews — all of the workmen were brought in from distant countries for short work assignments of a month at a time. Barry recruited many of the workers personally."

Jeff sits back and considers what he is hearing. It doesn't surprise him that his uncle had coordinated such a massive undertaking; the fact that he was able to keep it completely secret, however, was pretty astonishing.

He switches his attention to the rest of the castle. "Where did these CAD images come from?" he questions as he studies the screen, "they must have been converted to CAD files from old blueprints ...where are the originals?"

"Many of the source prints are in the office library," BE replies. "Others are stored securely in the Vault of Archives."

Jeff notices, as he carefully examines the floor plans, that the secret passages and connecting tunnels beneath the castle are not included, nor is the underground domed chamber beneath the rotunda, with its secret stairways.

"These floor plans are not complete; where are the passageways beneath the castle's foundation?"

The screen immediately refreshes to display the missing tunnels.

"You understand why your uncle instructed that this level must only be displayed upon its specific request," BE explains.

Jeff nods, agreeing that Barry's safeguard had been a wise precaution. He can see that the tunnels radiate from the domed central chamber to each tower in a spoke pattern, confirming his suspicion about where the other chamber tunnels lead. In addition to those, a large circular tunnel connects each tower to the others. Jeff locates the section of tunnel he had first explored, wondering what lies behind the steel door he had discovered there. To his disappointment, the plan has no record of a door or connecting passage anywhere along its length.

"BE, display the passages connecting with these," he requests.

"I'm afraid that will require further authorization," BE replies mysteriously.

The monitor displays a login screen for entering the requested Authorization Code.

Jeff sits back in his chair, frustrated. He tries a few combinations using his uncle's birth date and other snippets of information, but is unable to guess the password. He even tries using the shapes that open the other secret places, saying and typing derivations of: "Circle - Square - Triangle" in various languages, but nothing happens.

Jeff finally remembers what BE said a few minutes earlier about the whereabouts of the original blueprints:

'Others are stored securely in the Vault of Archives.'

"I have to go," he says quickly without explaining his intentions to BE.

Quickly entering the elevator, he takes it back to his room, exiting with a single-minded purpose. He is deep in thought as he makes his way into the upstairs hallway of his suite and down the staircase.

ISABEL'S cheerful voice greets him as he comes down the stairs. "Ah, there you are. Will you be at home for lunch today?" Her question interrupts Jeff's focus, stumping him momentarily.

"Well ...I ...I'm not ...maybe," he stammers.

"No worries," she says happily, "I can see that you've got important business on your mind; apologies for interrupting."

"No, please don't feel sorry ...I'm the one who should be apologizing," Jeff says quickly. "Lunch sounds great," he agrees with a nod.

"I'll have sandwiches prepared if you can pull yourself away. I know it's a busy job you've got — running such a large company."

Her comment makes him feel guilty about the fact that he has actually been paying very little attention to the company lately. With genuine thanks and an impatient glance at his watch, he quickly excuses himself.

MINUTES LATER, he enters the dusty Vault of Archives, scanning its endless rows of bookcases and file cabinets. Finding anything here seems like a monumental task. He considers asking CHET to direct him to the castle blueprints, but quickly decides against it — recalling the way the avatar had been stubbornly awaiting a password before revealing the prints' electronic versions.

Instead, he makes his way to the old handwritten volumes that serve as the library's directory, pulling out the first volume and flipping its pages until he finds a reference for 'Blueprints.'

'Section three, Row three,' he repeats to himself as he searches for the section indicated. It is in a dusty area of the library, far in the back, where the aged wooden file drawers are ornately carved. A good indication that they date from the time of the castle's original construction.

The first drawer in Row Three is heavy as he struggles to pull it open, revealing a deep stack of sketches and blueprints inside. He quickly thumbs through them, looking for any that depict the castle's foundations and ancient tunnels, but reaches the bottom without success.

The other drawers in row three yield the same results; there are plenty of blueprints of the ancient castle, but none for the secret passageways. He is just about to go back to search the Archives' directory again when he stumbles across a small group of prints that have been misfiled among unrelated papers. The small stack is pinned together, and the top sheet catches his eye immediately — it features a fascinating sketch of the stained-glass dome. It is part of a series that depicts the castle's main rotunda. Sliding them from the drawer, he carefully removes the pin and spreads them across the top of the file cabinets.

His attention is drawn at first to the dome's plans; he can see clearly in the black-and-white sketch that its original design reveals more images than are obvious to a casual observer of the real thing. Jeff can see a clear depiction of the Shepherd's Staff, which blends with the huge minute hand in the actual dome. He takes note that the long minute hand points to *Five* on the clock face, which is due north in the rotunda's dome; he hadn't noticed that before.

He can also make out that the three lightning bolts, which are visible in the stained glass emanating from the center of the clock, are actually shooting toward images of the three towers that are hidden in the stained glass. The towers are embedded within depictions of mountains of the same color, which hide their presence.

As he studies it, Jeff is surprised to see an image of a Ring at the exact center of the dome. In the real dome, its golden shape is virtually invisible against a circle of golden glass, but its outline is clearly visible in the black-and-white blueprint. It also clearly shows three large rings that overlap one another like a Venn diagram — each ring surrounds one of the three towers. It's an intriguing detail hidden within the dome, among the many leaded lines of its stained-glass relief.

He looks again at the plan's depiction of the Shepherd's Staff, noting that it points with its tip toward the Ring, rising upward from the number five in the clock face. It is then that he notices lettering in the outer ring of the clock, just beneath the number five; he rotates the blueprint to read it: *'Thuban.'*

Jeff is taken aback. Granted, the dome's large minute hand points north, but even at the time that the ancient castle was built, Thuban had not been the star at true north for thousands of years. While he stares at the prints, pondering that point, another realization strikes him …the hour hand is pointing to the number ten.

In all the times that he has glanced at the dome, he has never given much thought to the time it depicts. Ten twenty-five didn't suggest any meaning; it was not like 11:59, a time steeped in symbolism, or even ten o'clock, which could at least suggest a *position* …like pointing west-northwest. Ten twenty-five, on the other hand, is about as random a time as there could be.

He can make out three small letters in ornate script, etched in the outer ring just above the number ten: *'TMB.'* Jeff can't help recognizing the initials for the Tenth Mantle Bearer. He gulps slightly.

He notices one more detail in the thousand-year-old document. Written, almost imperceptibly, along the length of the hour hand is a short Latin phrase: *De Tribus Una.*

"Of Three One," Jeff whispers, translating the phrase. He guesses at what it could mean — perhaps referring to the three towers. His eye catches the initials *TMB* once again, and a thought suddenly strikes him: it could refer to the joining of the three bloodlines. If true, that would be an especially odd thing to find in Cerdic's design; at the time the castle was built, it should have seemed inconceivable that the three lines could ever be joined again.

Jeff carefully lays the blueprint of the dome aside to review the next page and finds himself looking at a diagram of the rotunda structure, with its complete multi-level floor plan and intricate details of the compass-shaped pattern in the marble floor. A small architect's notation in the center of the compass catches his eye, and he leans closer to read it. It appears to be a reference to another blueprint: R~1.5.

"Rotunda, one point five," Jeff says to himself distractedly as he interprets it. He begins to thumb through the small stack of blueprints that were pinned together and locates one about halfway down in the pile with the matching reference in its corner. He carefully places it on top of the stack and is quickly frozen in place as he realizes what he has found.

THE IMAGE CONTAINS a detailed schematic of an elaborate mechanical device. It is in the shape of a large cylinder, about three feet in diameter and four feet tall. There is a door on one side. The schematic shows a small shelf suspended in the center of the cylinder. Most interesting of all, the cylinder is attached to a mechanized lift that is shown rising from the center of the rotunda floor. Jeff recognizes its smooth top to be the circular slab of marble at the exact center of the rotunda's compass pattern.

Notes throughout the page appear to be written in a combination of Gaelic and Old English. Jeff has to use the O-P to translate, confirming his suspicion that they point out the instructions for a series of controls that provide the means to raise and lower the cylinder.

Jeff ponders what he is looking at. It is obvious to him that it was created as a secret storage compartment — but for what, exactly? Bending to look more carefully at the small shelf in the cylinder's center, it suddenly dawns on him... the cylinder was created by Cerdic to be the secure storage place for the Ring!

It was designed to remain secret, yet the intricate drawings clearly show the means for retrieving it while giving no warning about the Ring's power. It's possible that Cerdic intended for this print to be destroyed. Cornelius must have stumbled upon it while perusing the Archives. He would not have known of the Ring's dangers.

Jeff guesses that the secrets of the Ring were likely kept from Cornelius by his father in order to protect him. Perhaps Cerdic had hoped to pass along its secrets to his successor — the next Mantle Bearer. Unfortunately, he died before Barrymore was selected. Maybe that was the reason why Barry did so much to prepare Jeff — his own successor... to spare him some of the pain that he had no doubt experienced himself.

Jeff's thoughts return to the drawings in front of him, and he ponders the strange design, wondering how it could have protected the ring or possibly even neutralized its power somehow. One thing is certain; it no longer contains the Ring, unfortunately. Jeff sighs at that thought and then tucks the mechanical drawing back into the stack of prints and returns it to the drawer.

⌘

13

THE DRAGON'S TAIL

By the time Jeff finishes his lunch, guilt about the way he has been neglecting his CEO duties has gotten the best of him. He decides to spend some time in his office while he still can — he may only have a few more days in the job, after all.

The office suite is empty, as usual. Its eerie quiet makes him wish there were staff working here. He recalls EB saying there had once been a small team, but the help was no longer needed, thanks to ABBI's prowess and the ease with which employees in London or other offices could be engaged. Jeff understands the reasons but can't help feeling painfully lonely in the grandiose suite all alone.

EB has been spending most days in the London office. Jeff feels bad that his older friend has had to take on many of the duties Jeff should be assuming himself, especially at EB's age. He sits at the huge desk and opens his email, calling on CHET for help with several thousand unread messages once again.

. . .

WHEN IT IS FINALLY time to sign off, Jeff spins his chair around and looks out at the ocean and distant horizon. He imagines himself speeding over the sea in search of his impossible quest, only to tumble off the edge of the world in inevitable failure as he runs out of time.

His eye catches a flash of late afternoon sunlight reflecting off the polished brass railing of the old spiral staircase. It draws his thoughts back to his uncle's observatory, making him think of what he had found there. About eighty days have already passed since that strange discovery, he notes, glancing at today's date on his computer screen.

"Thuban," he whispers to himself. It ignites memories of his uncle's handwritten clue in the cavern… and of seeing the star's name in the blueprint for the castle dome. The combination of clues makes his hair stand on end. His mind races as he attempts to see the connections between the dome and his uncle's clue. The hour hand pointing to Ten, with its Latin inscription of *De Tribus Una*, clearly signifying the Tenth Mantle Bearer — it signifies *him*, he reminds himself. The dome's minute hand, in turn, connects him to Thuban … his uncle's clues in the observatory also used his birth date to do the same thing — connecting him to Thuban. He can see the message clearly …but has no idea what it all means.

JEFF BARELY TOUCHES his dinner as he wrestles with the puzzle that has seized his thoughts. Isabel has learned that there is no use in talking to him when he looks this way. His distracted nods and grunts mean absolutely nothing, aside from confirming that he hasn't heard a word. After twenty minutes, he silently gets up from the table and heads upstairs to his room.

Isabel shares a concerned glance with Hunahpu, and they each breathe a silent prayer as they watch him go.

THE LATE AFTERNOON sun has turned the midsummer sky a golden hue as Jeff walks out onto the Tower's balcony. He finds that the breathtaking view and crisp, clean air up here help him think more clearly. The lessons of the past two days stream through his mind, yet despite all he has learned, he is no closer to finding a way to fulfill his quest. If anything, it now seems more impossible than ever.

Being in the tower has reminded him of why he had gone to visit the Vault of Archives earlier in the day, forcing him to admit that his search had not turned up any blueprints for the missing underground tunnel sections in the vast Archives. He decides to temper his curiosity about them for now and refocuses on the thing that is clearly the most urgent …destroying the Ring and Scepter.

He drops himself onto the balcony's bench and takes a deep breath of fresh air, recounting what he has learned so far. He knows that if there is any possibility of destroying the objects, it has something to do with Tir Lai… it is evident that somehow a portal will have to be opened to the place where they were created. The thought of it sounds insane, he admits, but more than that, it terrifies him!

As he considers what he knows of the Ring's origin — of the way it was called forth — it makes him despair. Even if it is true that words could send the objects back to where they came from, the odds of guessing those words are beyond impossibility. He has searched every page of the Cronicis Niergel, along with every other book and scroll that the Secret Chamber has shown him, and none of them offered the slightest hint of the actual words contained in the Scroll of the gods.

He leans back against the tower's bench with a deep sigh, looking up to stare into the open sky. It is a crisp, clear evening, and the sky has begun to fade from light blue to deep purple, letting a single bright star peek through — hinting at the approaching night.

Once again, the thought of Thuban's dim star fills his mind. He wrestles again with the puzzle …why would the dome's image connect the Tenth Mantle Bearer to Thuban… and why did his uncle do the same with his clues?

He sits watching the sun slowly melt into the horizon as he

ponders it. He eventually looks up, realizing that night has fallen around him, and catches sight of the Big Dipper in the northern sky. He locates Thuban's dim light … just beneath Mizar in the crook of the Dipper's long handle — just where his grandmother had shown him. He can practically hear her voice in the way that she used to point it out to him: *'See it there …the Dragon's Tail,'* she would say to him in a half-whisper — her voice full of mystery.

The memory of his grandmother's voice suddenly brings to mind Hunahpu's words as he spoke of it: *"The Dragon's Tail, in the constellation Draco —*

In ancient times, the pole star was believed to be the doorway between the mortal world and eternity."

"The doorway… a portal to eternity…" Jeff repeats the words aloud.

It's all connected — *The Dragon…* the words in the stones from Samjaza's palace: *Keeper of the Scroll and Portal of Tir Lai.* Thuban is the key!

The Dome's complete image hangs before Jeff's eyes as his photographic memory recalls it… The connections now seem obvious. The Dome's clock hands are naturally connected by a central hub — and that hub contains the Ring …*the Eye of the Dragon*. The ancient ring is the central purpose of the castle's design, and Thuban represents the portal that must be used to destroy it.

Jeff feels astonished that the dome's secret message has been encoded and hidden in plain sight for more than a thousand years!

There is one more mystery in the dome's image. The clock hands also contain something else: the Shepherd's Staff. A connection between the Staff and the Tenth Mantle Bearer does not surprise him, but what does it have to do with opening a portal to Tir Lai …and destroying the Ring?

Friday Morning...

JEFF IS NOTICEABLY DISTRACTED as he sits at breakfast, pondering the night's puzzles. He still has not said good morning to anyone when EB arrives, joining Hunahpu at the table; the two older men share a nod, then a silent prayer for their young friend as they consider the extent to which his quest has burdened him. The weight of it must be truly great, having consumed his thoughts so completely.

Isabel comes alongside with the coffee pot, noticing that Jeff's mug has barely been touched. She looks at the others with concern as she slowly turns away.

Jeff suddenly speaks, catching their surprised attention. He fixes his gaze on Hunahpu. "Do you remember the conversation we had a few months ago about Thuban?"

"Thuban...," Hunahpu repeats thoughtfully. "Yes, I believe I do."

Jeff shifts his gaze between Hunahpu and EB, including them both in his questioning. "Did Uncle Barry ever talk about that star? Did he use the name Thuban for anything else? Was it a name for anyplace in the castle?"

It is EB's turn to repeat the name thoughtfully as he considers it... "Thuban...." He looks at Jeff regretfully, "I'm afraid not. I can't say that I recall him ever mentioning it."

Jeff's gaze returns to Hunahpu, focused like a detective in pursuit of a dangerous mystery. "You said before that it was considered by the Egyptians to be a doorway..., a portal to eternity."

"Well, yes. Its position as the pole star meant that all the heavens appeared to orbit around it. This gave it special significance for the Egyptian priests."

"What about the constellation Draco?" Jeff questions. "Did it have significance for the Egyptians?"

Hunahpu searches his thoughts briefly. "The Egyptians depicted the Draco constellation as a hippopotamus or crocodile, represented by gods and goddesses who appeared in the forms of those animals.

"The most significant of these was their god Sobek, one of the oldest deities named in the Pyramid Texts. Egyptian sects believed that Sobek arose from the "Dark Water" — the chaotic universe. He was revered for his ferocity and quick movements; however, he was an unpredictable deity associated with chaos."

Jeff's head bobs back momentarily as he takes this in. He nods as he considers it, "That figures," he says simply without explaining.

GENIE STOPS her warmup to look at Jeff as he enters the gym. The bags under his eyes hint at how little sleep he has had. The normal spring in his step is barely a step as his feet shuffle against the mat.

"What's this? Ye're lookin' particularly horrid this mornin'."

He looks up at her as if catching only part of her words. "Ah... sorry. Guess I didn't sleep much."

His tired appearance is a sharp contrast to Jeff's energy yesterday when he surprised both of them by flattening her to the mat with lightning-fast reflexes.

"I'm probably not going to be much use as a workout partner today," he apologizes.

Genie doesn't argue. The turmoil and exhaustion in Jeff's eyes are a pretty clear indication of his inner struggles. She speaks softly as she steps nearer. "Whatever i' tis ye're wrestlin' with, it's wearin' on y'; that's easy t' see. Maybe we should take a pause for today."

Jeff looks at the sharp broadsword in her hand and agrees — he's not in the clearest state of mind. He's not even in a suitable condition to operate a moving vehicle, let alone a deadly weapon.

THEY TAKE a seat together on a nearby bench while Jeff sits back and scans the large gym, eying it fondly. "We've had some great memories here," he notes with an obvious air of nostalgia.

"I suppose so," Genie agrees. "What's it been, about three months?"

"Today makes 85 days since I arrived," Jeff informs her. There's no guessing on his part — the count looms prominently in his mind.

Genie registers the information and gives him a sympathetic look. "The time limit for yer quest... was that...?"

"...90 days," Jeff interrupts, finishing her sentence.

Genie sits silently. She knows she cannot ask him about it. Everything about his quest must remain a secret until it is completed. She can only infer from the look of him that it's not going especially well.

Jeff leans forward, resting his elbows on his knees as he stares at the floor. When he speaks, she gets the feeling he's deliberately changing the subject.

"How's the communications chatter from Estonia? Has there been any change since the last attack?"

"It's been bloody quiet — a bit too quiet. Harti's new surveillance bot is workin' its way into their network," she reveals, referring to the artificial intelligence program developed by Harti Arenhold, their CIO. "It will take another week or so for anythin' meaningful t' find its way back."

"Why do you suppose they haven't launched any other Space Planes?" Jeff wonders.

"Could be that they don't have any others built yet," she suggests.

"Have we learned anything about where they're being built?" Jeff wonders.

"It looks as though some o' the materials are bein' shipped to an island off the Riviera coast. Our satellites don't detect any manufacturing there; it's just some old medieval castle."

"Underground, maybe?" Jeff posits.

"Certainly possible," Genie agrees.

"What about Uncle Barry's secret vault?" Jeff asks, changing the subject again. "Have you had any luck with the access code?"

Genie glances at him like a mother scolding an unruly child. "Y' know I can't talk about it. There's not much t' say, in any event. Whatever knowledge Dylen had about it died with him."

Jeff lets out a sigh and sits back, looking again at their surroundings with a quiet resolve that seems a little like surrender. It's as if he's memorizing the sight for the last time.

⌘

14

APPROACHING STORM

Sunday morning...

Jeff has to admit Sunday chapel services have become his favorite time of the week. He has come to genuinely understand EB's fondness for saying, *'Nothing calms the troubled mind like a Sunday worship service.'*

Genie and Jeff are seated beside one another again in an arrangement that no longer needs to be choreographed by EB; they wouldn't have it any other way. Jeff releases a contented sigh as he takes in the Chapel's comfortable atmosphere and breathes a thankful prayer for the company of his friends. This is one part of the week that would be perfect no matter what happens with his Challenge.

Rev. Colby Abbott, the Chapel's Pastor, is speaking today. As is his habit, the kindly Pastor is kneeling among the choir pews as the service begins; he soon rises, makes his way to the pulpit, invites the choir onto the platform, and welcomes everyone.

Jeff senses right away that something is different about today's service. Not that he has a long history of church experiences to draw from, but he can feel that the mood is distinctly different from any he has felt before. The atmosphere seems strangely electric with anticipation.

Pastor Abbott gives Jeff a friendly nod as he begins the service, and Jeff notices Genie glancing over at him at the same time, giving him a feeling that she and the Pastor are in cahoots on something; he can't help suspecting that it has something to do with their shared prayers over the approaching deadline for his Challenge. In fact, Jeff senses that each of his closest friends has been praying about that.

Following several songs from the hymnal and a moving selection by the impressive choir, Pastor Abbott steps to the dais.

"In my preparations for today's message, I have felt a strong leading to the subject I want to share with you. I would dare say, in fact, that I have never felt a stronger conviction of God's direction for any message in my life."

His glance turns to Jeff as he says this, triggering a feeling of focused anticipation in Jeff's soul. It's almost as if Jeff has felt God suddenly tap him on the shoulder to pay attention.

"Today's passage will be familiar to most believers. Turn with me, if you'd like, to the fourteenth chapter of Matthew, beginning at verse twenty-eight."

> *"And Peter answered him and said, Lord, if it be you, bid me come unto you on the water. And he said, Come. And when Peter was come down out of the ship, he walked on the water. But when he saw the wind boisterous, he was afraid, and beginning to sink, he cried, saying Lord, save me."[1]*

"We are talking about faith this morning. There are several important lessons in this familiar text that God is calling our attention to. We see in Peter a spark of that great faith that our Lord said would form the foundation of His church. It is based on an unquestioning trust in the absolute lordship of Christ.

"In this case, it was a trust in His lordship over winds and waves. Yet Peter's faith was not yet complete; he still had lessons to learn and setbacks and failures by which to learn them. Disasters and defeats are constantly occurring on our path to triumph. Our trophies are never won without troubles.

"Peter was an impulsive man, a man more often moved by emotion than by intellect. He did not waste precious time calculating the merits of faith or determining the odds of success. Faith does not concern itself with natural laws. If Peter had considered these for the briefest moment, he would never have gotten out of the boat.

"This is the first rule of great faith. Anybody can walk on the land, but *faith is a water walker*. She can do, act, and work where others fail. Remember, Jesus did not say that faith would merely lift mustard seeds or remove molehills. These little things are not the sphere for faith. He said, "You will say to this mountain, Be removed; or to this sycamore tree, Be plucked up by the roots." Faith loves to deal in great things, in marvelous adventures, in projects beyond human power. There is no room for the exercise of faith where reason and human strength will suffice. Faith is a vessel expressly built for the deep seas.

"If you have faith in God and that faith is in active exercise, I am persuaded you will feel an instinct within you prompting you to dare something more than others have ventured to attempt.

"Yet, venturesome as Peter's faith was, he would not make a

move without first having the Master's permission. He first called out: 'If it is you, bid me.' We must not fondly imagine that we can do whatever we choose.

"Walking on the sea without divine permission would be a presumption to attempt and an impossibility to perform. But Peter, with Christ's approval, could have walked across the Atlantic itself if his faith had not failed.

"So it is with you. If your Lord has called you to a work, rely upon Him for the power to achieve it. He will not forsake you. But if it is merely your own whim or caprice that has thrust you into a position for which you are not prepared, then you have no right to reckon upon the divine aid to speed your false steps. Blessed is he who goes to his Father and asks His counsel.

"It is true for all believers that we must attempt some things which look like impossibilities. This is indeed our duty as true soldiers of the cross.

"Yet, we see another lesson in Peter's bold act. He was not immune to fear - that great enemy of faith.

"We can imagine that the first two or three steps on the water must have exhilarated him and made him feel what wonders he was doing, but there came a rough blast which threatened to overthrow him, and as he could scarcely stand against so rude a wind upon so slippery a floor, he began to be afraid. Some threat occurred that he had not foreseen, and he yielded to unbelief.

"Be forewarned and prepared, for such fear of our own weakness is common to all humanity. When it seizes us, we must do what Peter did — Cry out to God for rescue! We must cry out instantly!

"I am sure Peter did not stop to think of ways to make his prayer sound eloquent on that occasion. I am quite certain that he did not search for music to which to set that prayer. It just came up from the depths of his soul. These are indeed the very best prayers — those that well up from the heart in our times of desperation.

"Here is God's most urgent admonition to us this morning. When you find yourself in that same condition — and most certainly you will one day- tell your Savior of the grief that distracts you, of the woe that overwhelms you. Confess your sins, acknowledge your inability to rescue yourself, and cast yourself immediately upon the gracious promise of the loving God[2]!

"Know that in that hour, He will hear you. Consider the encouragement of Isaiah 40:28, 'Have you not known? Have you not heard? The Lord is the everlasting God, the Creator of the ends of the earth. He does not faint or grow weary; his understanding is unsearchable.'

"Remember that He has not forsaken you in your falling. Hold to what He has said in Joshua 1:9, 'Have I not commanded you? Be strong and courageous. Do not be frightened, and do not be dismayed, for the Lord your God is with you wherever you go.'

"Finally, do not forget His great purpose in your most severe test of faith. It is to prove to you what you are worth to Him — to reveal His ultimate plans for your good. As He has declared in Jeremiah 29:11, 'For I know the plans I have for you, plans to prosper you and not to harm you, plans to give you hope and a future.'

"Never forget — it is when we are weak in ourselves that we are strongest!"

Jeff sits thunderstruck as Colby's words reverberate in his mind — especially his last two comments. Most importantly, they carry the weight of an urgent charge along with a stern warning. He must move with caution — caution to keep focused on the source of his strength — but **move** nonetheless.

THE TIME for waiting is nearing its end.

IT IS late afternoon as Jeff sits alone once again on the open balcony above the Tower Lab. The approaching sunset has begun to turn the sky golden, with beams of sunlight bursting from the distant clouds along the horizon, yet Jeff barely notices the spectacular scene. He is too busy replaying Colby's words. He can't help sensing that his message was as much a warning as an encouragement.

Jeff considers Colby's charge: *We see a lesson in Peter's bold act... he was not immune to fear. Be forewarned and prepared, for such fear of our own weakness is common to all humanity.*

Jeff already understood what it meant to learn from failure. In his scientific training, he knew that failed experiments were as valuable a teacher as successful ones. But his quest is something altogether different. Failure at any stage could be deadly — or catastrophic!

He also senses that something important has changed. He can't say exactly how he knows it, but there is a strong sense that events are now in motion that will soon change everything. It is a sobering feeling.

Colby's words flash through his mind once again: *faith is a water walker... There is no room for the exercise of faith where reason and human strength will suffice. Faith is a vessel expressly built for the deep seas.*

He has no idea what it all means in his case. The point about faith overcoming natural laws made sense. If there was one thing he knew for sure about his Challenge, it was the fact that nothing on earth could accomplish it. The memory of his battle with the smoky Eljo armies fills his mind in vivid detail. There was nothing natural about that.

"...It is when we are weak in ourselves that we are strongest!" Colby's words echo like an urgent reminder as Jeff recalls his own unlikely victory on that day.

———

THE SIGHT of stars emerging overhead draws his thoughts back to the greater puzzle he's been struggling with for weeks. In the open sky, he locates the star called Thuban once again and sits staring at it while an image of the castle's stained glass dome comes into focus. Once again, he can't help but conclude that Thuban points to the portal that must be used to destroy the ancient objects.

If only he could piece together what he needs to do in order to open it!

⌘

15

UNSETTLING WORDS

The treacherous Maranish brothers sit in silence on one of the elegant terrace patios of their palatial estate, admiring a glorious full moon. Its silver light is reflected in the peaceful waters of a seasonally calm Mediterranean sea, and a warm breeze adds to the image of paradise that engulfs the scene. There is no peace, however, in the evil brothers' tormented souls.

"Are the preparations complete?" Chesed asks his brother in his hideous-sounding voice, "How soon will all be ready?"

"Soon, brother," Eblis assures him. "Our Eljo troops are anxious for vengeance against the young heir who slew their brothers."

"Good," Chesed notes, "vengeance is a potent motivator; we can use it to our advantage. What is the status of our ships?" he probes further.

"They are nearly ready," Eblis confirms in a slithering voice. "Nothing prevents us from making our departure on the appointed day. We will leave at first light; the young one will never suspect it."

"You're sure they will not detect our coming?" Chesed challenges.

"The young Mantle Bearer has proved himself a troublesome adversary."

"Yes, but we have seen his weakness …his affection for her will be quite useful," Eblis answers with gloating anticipation.

"And you're certain they know nothing of the secret tunnel?" Chesed probes.

"Our scout confirmed it," Eblis answers, "it has been undisturbed since our father's expulsion."

"What of the demoness Leanan Sidhe? Can we be sure she will not awake?"

"We have timed our incursion for high noon …even within the depths of her crypt, she will not be stirred in that hour," Eblis assures him.

Chesed nods approvingly. "Soon we will be home, my brother," he gloats. "Our father's dream for us is nearly fulfilled… very soon, we will again be the masters of the ancient mysteries.

"You have done well, brother." He turns to the Eljo commanders standing nearby: "Make ready! You dare not fail me again!"

Sunday Night...

IT IS after nine o'clock when Jeff makes his way from the Tower Lab's balcony back to his room. His head is still spinning from trying to solve the Dome's mysteries. He instinctively breathes a prayer — something that would never have occurred to him to do a few months earlier, but now has become a common response whenever he feels troubled. It is not frequently enough, he admits to himself; he has a great deal of growing to do before he is as wise and godly as his great-grandfather.

The rumbling in his stomach reminds him that he missed dinner; he decides to head down to the kitchen for a late snack. As he makes his way into the upstairs hallway, he notices Hunahpu's light on; he stops and knocks gently.

"Yaykuy" ...*enter*, Hunahpu answers quickly.

Jeff pushes open the door and sees his great-grandfather reading his Bible.

"I was just on my way to the kitchen for a snack and saw your light on," he explains unnecessarily.

Hunahpu nods politely and waves toward a nearby chair, inviting him to sit down. Jeff gratefully accepts, leaning forward anxiously as he sits.

"Your mind is troubled," Hunahpu says observantly.

Jeff shakes in a nervous laugh, "Yeah, that's for sure."

"Has worry been a help to you in your quest?" Hunahpu asks, letting the question lead Jeff to the answer he already knows.

"I need to trust God, I know," Jeff admits to the wise old man, "I just don't know how ...this is too hard." He leans further forward with a forlorn expression: "There are only three days left; I don't think I can do it ...I don't see how it can be done."

Hunahpu doesn't answer right away, taking his time as he removes his reading glasses and slowly closes the Bible in his lap.

"YOU ARE RIGHT ABOUT THAT," he finally says, "...you cannot do it." He looks at Jeff with a kind expression: "You were never meant to do it."

Jeff feels a swell of despair as he hears his great-grandfather's words; he stares into Hunahpu's face, trying to fathom what he is saying.

"That is the true lesson of the Mantle Bearer's Quest," Hunahpu continues, "it is the lesson that, once grasped, changes a man forever."

Jeff struggles... "I don't understand ...do you mean the quest is not really meant to be completed? What, it's all symbolic? ...it doesn't have to be actually achieved?"

"Oh no, it most certainly does ...and complete it you must," Hunahpu affirms dauntingly.

"Then I don't get it," Jeff laments, "If I was never meant to complete it, then how...?"

"I did not say you were not meant to complete it," Hunahpu clarifies patiently, "...I said you were not meant to *do* it."

Jeff's head is in his hands as he struggles with Hunahpu's imperceptible distinction. Hunahpu sits quietly, breathing a silent prayer for Jeff's help — knowing that he needs more than counsel at this hour.

Jeff soon straightens and lifts his face as he remembers the Secret Chamber's handwritten message: *'My strength...'* he whispers to himself.

"He's the one who will do it," Jeff finally acknowledges as he yields again to the idea. "But doesn't He need me to do something? There must be a part in it that I have to play - how will I know what to do?

"When the time comes, you will know," Hunahpu states simply. He then looks down at his hands for a moment, and Jeff sees the old man's eyes reveal a look of deep sadness.

"Events are moving rapidly now," he reveals to Jeff, "I'm afraid that I must leave you soon."

"Leave? Why? Is there something wrong back in Peru?" Jeff questions anxiously.

"You are not the only one holding secrets that he cannot reveal," Hunahpu says mysteriously. "Your quest will be done soon," he adds reassuringly.

"Wait ...how do you know? ...What's going to happen?"

"Great things often require great sacrifice," Hunahpu says, avoiding a direct answer to Jeff's question.

"Sacrifice? What kind of sacrifice?" Jeff studies Hunahpu's eyes... "It's you... You're the sacrifice," he says, discerning the truth that Hunahpu will not reveal. "I won't let that happen! You have to stay out of this ...it's not your fight; it's mine!"

Hunahpu stands and walks toward the door; Jeff follows him closely, continuing his impassioned pleas. His great-grandfather simply looks at him, the wisdom of long years reflected in his face.

"Qam ruru munay Dyus, churi ...*You must yield to His will, my son. To allow or not allow is neither yours nor mine to choose.*" He looks at Jeff with a gentle expression, "Do not worry for me. What I shall do is easy... it is what you must do that is hard."

With that, he closes his eyes and places a hand on Jeff's shoulder, leading them in a prayer together. The old man's prayer stirs Jeff to the center of his soul, replacing his anxious turmoil with a great calm but also a deep sorrow. Jeff's eyes are filled with tears when they finish, and he instinctively embraces his great-grandfather. Hunahpu hugs him back, holding him until the flood of his emotion subsides. Jeff makes his way out the door and turns to look back.

"Allin tuta, churi ...*Good night, my son*," Hunahpu says in a slightly broken voice. Jeff notices a tear on the old man's cheek as he closes his door.

JEFF TOSSES and turns restlessly throughout the night as Hunahpu's unsettling words replay in his mind. He struggles with the enormous burden of his seemingly insurmountable challenge and the impossibly short time frame left to solve it. After several hours, he finally drifts off to sleep from pure exhaustion, but his mind is a chaotic swirl of troubling dreams.

Eventually, however, the chaos begins to fade. In its place, a startlingly clear thread of thought emerges in his dream; its clarity is because it is actually a memory, ...he finds himself reliving an experience from a few months earlier — in his uncle Barry's observatory.

He can see himself approaching the base of the room's iron and brass spiral staircase, looking upward at the place where it disappears into the ceiling. He feels himself climbing until he emerges into the small observatory above, with its ancient-looking telescope and paper charts; the memory brings to mind how strangely comfortable it made him feel. He watches the old lighted gauges and vacuum tubes glow as they slowly warm, and he can smell the old electronics, feeling again as if he has stepped back in time.

The image of the worn-looking star chart comes into focus, and he sees the old desk calendar beside it, turned to August... Once again, a chill runs up his spine as he stares at the date that is circled — August 25th, in the year he was born. The circled date is his birth date. His mind replays again the sight of the same date scrawled at the top of the star chart in his uncle's handwriting beside a single star in the chart that is circled, with the name *Thuban* written beside it.

Jeff's dream suddenly shifts to memories of his grandmother pointing out the stars to him — he can hear her voice telling him colorful stories of how this exact star lived in the constellation *Draco...* *The Dragon*; she called the star *the Dragon's tail*. He smiles peacefully at the memory of her voice.

Then his dream suddenly changes again — in a flash, he is in the Vault of Archives looking at the Blueprint for the Stained Glass Dome. He is studying its depiction of the large minute hand containing the Shepherd's Staff; it points to the number *Five...* it points north, he recalls. He studies the image of the castle's three towers connected by lightning bolts, noticing the Ring at the exact center of them all.

His dream flashes from scene to scene, like the frames in an edited movie. A close-up view of the detailed lettering that is written, almost imperceptibly, along the length of the clock's hour hand: *De Tribus Una;* "Of Three One." Then to the outer ring of the clock, just above the number ten, seeing the three small letters etched there in an ornate script: *'TMB'* — *the Tenth Mantle Bearer*. Finally, the lettering just beneath the number five as it grows to fill his entire field of vision:

THUBAN

He sees himself lifting the handwritten word, scrawled on his uncle's letterhead, from the floor of the ancient cavern.

SUDDENLY HE IS BACK AGAIN in the old observatory, focused on the set of coordinates that his uncle had written at the bottom of the old paper star chart:

..

Declination 64° 20' 45.6", RA (Right Ascension) 14h 04m 33.58s.

All of the clues suddenly come together, arranging themselves in his mind like gears in a clock that has assembled itself and begun to tick before his eyes. He stares at it — the realization that suddenly strikes him is like the jolt of an electric shock!

⌘

16

THE SECRET VAULT

T he first hint of daylight is beginning to show through the stained glass windows in Jeff's room when he awakes with a start, bolting upright. With his heart racing, he draws in a sudden gasp of breath, and his eyes snap open.

Throwing off the covers, he grabs his phone from the nightstand and swings his feet to the floor as he urgently swipes through photos until he comes to the one he is looking for — the snapshot that he had taken in Barry's observatory ...Thuban's coordinates on the day Jeff was born.

He runs a hand through his hair in shocked realization as its meaning dawns on him, staring at the picture of his uncle's handwriting.

Declination 64° 20' 45.6", RA (Right Ascension) 14h 04m 33.58s.

He is certain of it — his uncle's clue is a combination ...an access code! As he is pondering this, another thought suddenly strikes him; in his mind's eye, the pieces of a vast puzzle seem to be falling into place. He looks over at the Bible on his nightstand, recalling his uncle's handwritten note as this new inspiration comes into focus. He pulls the Bible's cover open and rereads the scripture reference: 'Jeremiah 29:13,' jumping to his feet.

Quickly grabbing the nearest thing he can find to wear, he is still fastening buttons as he enters the hall and runs toward his suite's stairway, pressing speed dial. He nearly yells into his phone the second Genie answers.

"Meet me in Barry's suite …it's urgent!" he says.

"Why? What's wrong?" she questions.

"No time to explain. I'm on my way there now! Come alone." Jeff says, hanging up the call.

FROM HIS BEDROOM, Hunahpu hears Jeff's voice on the stairs and nods to himself in acceptance. Then he quietly makes his way to the side of his bed and kneels to pray.

EUGENIA HAD JUST BEEN on her way out the door to the gym for her morning warmup. She apprehensively pulls a pair of black assault trousers over her sweats, straps on a small holster, and places a security comm earpiece in her ear. She pauses, wanting to call EB, but then remembers that he has already left for London, where he will be staying for the week.

Jeff is waiting for her in Barry's suite when she arrives — her heart is racing in concern as she runs in looking for him. She finds him pacing back and forth in Barry's study, in front of the wall of bookcases that Jeff has already opened to reveal a passageway to his uncle's secret vault.

"How'd you find it?" she says, looking at the open passage in surprise.

He stands back and looks at the bookcase, confiding in her: "It was a note that my uncle left me …it had a verse in it that's been a real comfort to me since I arrived here, Jeremiah 29:13:'*You will seek Me and find Me when you search for Me with all your heart.*' I didn't realize until this morning that it was also a clue."

Jeff explains what he means, pointing to the small brass plate at the top of the bookcase with '*Jeremiah*' engraved on it, then he demonstrates, tapping the shelves as he counts top-down — first one shelf, then three more. "One and then three, that's the thirteen," he explains. Then he counts across from right to left — "Two," he notes as he touches the first two books, then he counts nine more, speaking the count aloud. The sequence leads him to the book that he has already tilted forward, displaying the title on its worn leather cover: '*All That Your Heart Desires.*'

"May you find here all that your heart desires …

That was literally what he wrote," Jeff reveals with a chuckle. "Talk about mysteries being hidden in plain sight!"

Genie steps in front of him, blocking access to the secret passageway with both her hands on Jeff's chest, forcing him to look her in the eyes.

"You can't do this! You can't go down there!" she insists forcefully.

"Genie, I have to…" he says, determined to explain. "That's my challenge … it's the Quest that I've been given."

She stands back, carefully studying his eyes. "You have the access code, then?" she asks carefully; "Your uncle left it for you?"

"I think so; at least, that's what I think it is," he answers honestly. "That's why I need you here, just in case there's a problem; you can… You know… call for help."

She shakes her head 'no' and begins to object, but he gently puts his hands on her shoulders and looks closely into her eyes.

"I have to do this; there's more at stake than just …*us* …more even than Hastleworth, or the Niergel. You know it's true."

. . .

GENIE GROWS QUIET. She knows he is right about all that, but what reverberates in her mind is how he said the word 'us.' She feels a tear form in the corner of her eye as the bottled-up admission of her own deep feelings for him crashes against her fear of losing him. With an impulsive surge of emotion, she suddenly takes hold of his face with both hands — and then kisses him.

The shock of it makes both of them gasp for breath. They look at each other in stunned realization, then Jeff anxiously returns her kiss, taking her into his arms.

When it ends, their hearts are beating wildly ...so wildly, in Jeff's case, that he can't speak. He stares into her eyes and then hugs her close, looking over her shoulder at the open passageway behind her with a sudden reluctance. He holds her tightly as he fights for the courage to continue.

FINALLY, Genie gently pushes away, looking at him with wet eyes.

"Ye need t' go... finish the Challenge," she says as she nods toward the opening.

"Genie... I..." he starts to say — but she touches his lips with her fingertips, stopping him. She can't bear to hear him say that he loves her ...only to lose him.

"Ye can tell me when y' get back," she answers with a forced smile. "I'll be right here ...waitin'."

He studies her eyes and nods awkwardly, then turns toward the passageway.

"Wait! Take this," she says, handing him an earpiece. "It's just linked t' mine; no one else will hear."

"Thanks," he says, slipping it on. "Wish me luck."

She nods and puts her hands together in a praying gesture.

. . .

THIS TIME, Jeff has come prepared to explore with a flashlight. He switches it on and slowly begins making his way downward; the narrow staircase is made of neatly cut stone, like the rest of the original castle structure. It winds downward in an odd corkscrew pattern without landings, continuing for about four or five stories — it is hard to tell exactly.

At the bottom, he comes to a small room, only large enough for one person to stand in comfortably. He recognizes the Niergel crest on a round-shaped stone halfway up the wall and presses on it. As he expected, it sinks inward an inch or so. He scans the wall, looking for a square-shaped stone to press next, trying several, but none budge. Looking at the floor, he notes that the stones beneath his feet are all square; he picks out a stone near the corner, three blocks from each wall, and tests it with his foot — it sinks an inch. He finally looks for the expected triangle, finding it at eye level on the wall directly ahead; his press causes one of the wall's large stones to draw back, exposing an opening with three shallow holes: one cylindrical, one square, and one a triangle. Quickly retrieving his key, he lowers it into place.

It immediately triggers a rumbling sound as the wall rolls aside.

"IS EVERYTHING ALL RIGHT? What was that noise?" Genie asked him over the comm, sounding uncharacteristically nervous.

"Just the wall opening," he explains, "it's fine." An overhead light comes on in front of him, revealing a long, narrow hallway with walls and a floor made of shiny metal. Sprawled there on the floor in the center of the metallic hallway is a charred corpse. The enclosed space smells foul inside, causing Jeff to raise the front of his shirt over his nose and mouth.

"I found our missing guard, Seamus Gill," he announces to Genie as he confirms the name on the body's partly melted nameplate. "It looks like Dylen was right about the security measures."

"Jeff — be careful!" Genie reminds him as if the sight of a blackened corpse wasn't warning enough.

Jeff examines the hallway carefully, looking for a security keypad or anything that might serve as a security scanner. There is only one; it's a terminal on the wall just beside the door at the far end of the hall. He cautiously steps around Seamus' body and slowly approaches it.

The display screen flashes to life and silently presents a warning:

!! DANGER !!

This compartment employs lethal security measures. Any unauthorized access attempt will result in certain death. Do you wish to continue? Y_ N_

It sounds just like Barry to warn intruders of the danger they are in, Jeff thinks to himself. He holds his breath and types, 'Y'.

The screen immediately displays an unusual prompt: the letter 'D' is followed by three blank fields.

$$D: \_\_ \ \_\_ \ \_\_$$

As much as Jeff trusts his memory, he decides that if there was ever a time when he ought to rely on notes, this is probably it. He pulls out his phone and opens the picture with Thuban's coordinates, comparing it against the terminal display:

Declination 64° 20' 45.6"

"Here goes..." he says over his comm as he begins to type: ...64 ... 20 ...45.6 — he pauses to triple check his answer and then presses the *'Enter'* key.

The terminal offers a single beep as it accepts his entry, and then it immediately displays a new prompt:

$$RA: \_\_ \ \_\_ \ \_\_$$

"What happened?" Genie asks anxiously.

"It accepted the first entry ...so far, so good," he answers as he concentrates. He looks again at the picture on his phone's screen:

RA (Right Ascension) *14h 04m 33.58s.*

"I'm typing in the second sequence now..." he announces, as he begins entering the second half of the coordinates: ...14 ...04 ...33.58 — then he presses 'Enter.'

Another single beep registers his entry, still with no confirmation that it is correct. The terminal begins to show a third entry screen — causing Jeff's heart to drop; he has nothing more to provide! He watches as it types its third challenge question across the screen:

THE DRAGON'S TAIL: _____

"THERE'S A THIRD CHALLENGE QUESTION," he announces to Genie. "... I'm entering an answer now." He silently prays as he types the answer that he hopes is correct: ...Thuban — and presses 'Enter'.

The terminal beeps once more and displays a final instruction to place his hand on the attached palm scanner. "That seemed to work... It's doing a palm scan now," he informs Genie as he nervously watches it scan his hand.

For a long moment, nothing happens — Genie and Jeff both hold their breath, not wanting to miss any audible queue that could signal a need to run. Suddenly, Jeff hears the rumble of the wall behind him closing — cutting him off from the stairs. He yells into his comm, but can only hear static as Genie's panicked voice can be heard breaking up.

⌘

17

ETERNAL THINGS

J eff is frantically scanning the interior for a way to reopen the stone passage when he hears another chime from the terminal and turns to see the screen flash green, and then the Secret Vault's solid steel door slides upward. The code has worked ... He is in!

Jeff stands for a moment in its open doorway, wondering whether there are any other security measures inside. The vault is made entirely of some kind of smooth metal with a surface that is pure white. In combination with the brightness of the room's lighting, the entire vault glows intensely. He notices another door in the opposite corner across the room to his right with a palm scanner beside it. A thorough examination of the rest of the vault's blank walls reveals an identical scanner inside the vault beside the door where he stands. He cautiously places his hand on the scanner nearest him and sees it flash green — it apparently recognizes him. Feeling safe for the moment, he slowly steps inside.

Directly in front of him, he sees a long, thin box lying on the floor;

he guesses that it holds the Scepter. Its case appears to be made of the same metal that covers the walls; it is solid all around, except for a small lid at one end that is clamped shut with a dozen latches, three on each of its four sides.

Looking to his right, he finds a small box that he guesses contains the Ring. It is made of the same metal and has an equal number of latches.

JEFF IS MOST INTRIGUED, however, by a third case directly in the center of the room. It appears to be lying on its side, about three feet long by two feet square, and is constructed of two halves hinged on one side and latched on the other, like an oddly shaped trunk. Jeff approaches it warily; there is no telling what it contains — Jeff has not come across anything in his uncle's records hinting of another dangerous artifact, certainly nothing else requiring equal treatment with the Ring and Scepter.

He kneels down and slowly releases one latch on its large case, then nervously stops and reaches into his pocket, grasping the lone seed he is carrying and squeezing it in his fist. He opens the rest of the latches in a slow, methodical cadence until he has unlatched them all. With his heart beating wildly, he lifts it open, letting its open lid lie back against the floor. The sight that meets his eye confuses him at first, and then it takes his breath away as he realizes what he is looking at.

It is a scroll, but nothing like any scroll he has ever seen. The two long poles around which the scroll is wound are like gold, but Jeff can tell that it is not gold. Even pure gold could not be as brilliant as its ancient surface. More incredibly, however, the scroll's parchment appears as if it has just been made — there is no hint of aging in it at all.

Jeff immediately thinks of the words in Thaliard's description of the Ring and Scepter: '...*made to exist untouched by time, and thus they remain eternal.*'

His heart races wildly as he considers the rest of Thaliard's account....

'...secret oracles that held power to break natural laws ...even to cross between time and the eternal realm; these oracles were written in the eternal scroll ...the Scroll of the gods.'

Could this really be the lost Scroll of the gods? He is trembling as he considers it. That would explain why Barry had hidden it here — just like the Ring and Scepter, it would be impossible to destroy.

Jeff notices a folder mounted inside the open case and carefully retrieves it. It contains a topographic map of the ocean floor—Jeff recognizes the terrain. A pair of 'x' markings has been added to the map by hand, each with a handwritten notation: the first reads 'Scepter' and the second 'sotg'.

Jeff swallows hard. It hadn't been just the Scepter that Barry found on that deep-sea expedition! He sits back, staring at the scroll as he considers it; his uncle had been wise to conceal it, Jeff agrees. He wonders if EB and Hunahpu know it's here — maybe this is why they didn't want the vault opened.

HE HEARS Genie's voice in his earpiece, suddenly breaking the silence....

"Jeff, can y' hear me? Are you in there? Please answer... please answer me!"

He touches his comm and quickly answers, "I'm here... I'm alright; how did you get through?"

"I'm at the bottom o' the stairs, on the other side o' this wall. How does it open?"

"I'm not sure," Jeff says, quickly closing the case and latching it. "At least, I mean, I'm not sure if it can be opened while the vault is open."

"Did you find them?" she asks him, "Did y' find the Ring and Scepter? Are they secure?"

"Yes, I think so," he answers as he stands to his feet. "They're in special cases... I need to open them to be sure."

"Please be careful," she pleads, "Do you know how t' destroy them?"

Jeff stops and looks at the Scroll's case, feeling hopeful for the first time. "I think so; I think I know how," he answers. He makes his way to the Ring first: "I'm opening the Ring's case now."

As he lifts off the lid, the Ring's beauty takes him by surprise. In the room's bright light, it seems to glow and sparkle magnificently, and its large stone, the Dragon's Eye, almost seems to call out to him. It gives him an uneasy feeling — he snaps the lid closed quickly and shakes himself.

"It's here…" he reports, "It's secure." He turns toward the Scepter's case, "I'll check the Scepter, too," he says as he makes his way to it.

A minute or two later, he has removed the lid from that case as well, reaching in to pull the Scepter up by its top. When he touches the Ring's sister stone, a strange, sickening feeling comes over him, and he lets it drop back inside. He shakes himself again to clear his head.

"The Scepter is here… it's safe," he reports, shaking the sudden dizziness from his head. He slowly stands and looks once more at the large case containing the Scroll, but decides not to mention it to her.

"Hurry out o' there," he hears Genie coaxing him, "…this gives me the creeps."

"All right, I'm resealing the vault now," he says, admitting to himself that his head is beginning to hurt and his heart is pounding. He staggers slightly as he returns to the terminal and confirms the command to re-lock the vault.

As soon as the vault's door is firmly sealed, the stone wall reopens. Genie covers her nose as she sees Seamus Gill's corpse.

"I'll get a crew t' come remove him and clean this up," she offers, "There's a team I know we can trust."

Jeff looks down at the macabre sight and nods in agreement. He is feeling increasingly shaky, but it isn't from that.

"Y' don't look so good, are y' feelin' OK?" she asks.

Jeff nods that he is fine, but he is visibly staggering as he makes his way out. "M-maybe I am a little dizzy," he admits, slurring his words "...the lights, I think."

Genie catches him and pulls his arm over her shoulders to steady him.

"We need t' get y' to some fresh air," she advises.

When they get to the bottom of the stairs, Jeff looks up, trying to focus his eyes. "W-we should take the elev... evlev... evlavat... evata-tor," he stammers, then collapses to the floor unconscious.

WHEN HE COMES TO, he is stretched out on the couch in Barry's study with one of the Medics from Eugenia's hand-picked security team checking his pulse.

"How did you...?" he tries to ask her as he realizes where he is.

"Reinforcements," she answers, pointing toward the hidden passage where a pair of burly-looking agents are just emerging carrying a body bag with Seamus' remains. A few others in hazmat suits are waiting for the men to pass before heading down to finish the cleanup.

The Medic finishes checking Jeff and nods to them both that everything looks normal.

"The doc says it was probably a state of asphyxia from bein' down there so long with no ventilation. I'm sure the burnt corpse didn't help any," she says, watching them carry it out the door.

Jeff slides his feet off the couch and sits up; his head is still swimming, and he can feel a bad headache coming on. "I guess my super-powers don't include breathing without oxygen," he wisecracks. Adding more seriously: "Maybe the high voltage discharge that killed Seamus damaged the ventilation system."

"I'll have my team look at it," Eugenia offers.

"No ...maybe you'd better not," Jeff cautions, "we wouldn't want the vault's security system to think it was being threatened."

"Yeah, …good point," she agrees.

"So now what?" she asks him, "Can y' destroy those things where they are …there in the vault?"

"Well," Jeff hesitates, "…it's a little more complicated than that. They're sort of …eternal."

"You mean, like forever and ever — that kind of eternal?" Genie probes.

"Yeah, pretty much," Jeff acknowledges, "nothing created can harm them."

"Nothin' …created," she repeats, "Y' mean, nothin' man-made?"

"No, actually nothing *made* …by God or man. There's nothing in our *universe* that can harm them."

Genie sits down in the chair beside him; "So, help me with this," she says, clearly perplexed. "Ye've had a lot o' time t' think about it, and I'm sure it seems really simple t' ye." She looks at him with narrowed eyes, "I… don't get it."

"I've probably already said too much," Jeff apologizes, "I'm really sorry, but I can't tell you anything else right now. It has to be; I can't let you get involved …I have to do it alone."

"Right," Genie says, sounding a little annoyed. "It's yer …*Quest.* Fine."

After a short pause, she adds through gritted teeth: "Try not t' pass out again as ye're doing whatever it is ye have to do, …ALONE."

Jeff looks at her for a moment before answering sheepishly: "Good advice …thanks."

GENIE'S EXPRESSION softens as she looks at him, realizing he is right about what he has to do; it just kills her that she can't help. "I'm sorry," she apologizes, "I know it's what y' have t' do. Be careful, will ya?"

Jeff nods his agreement. Neither of them wants to talk about their earlier encounter, but it hangs in the air between them. The buzz of activity from the security team all around them doesn't help. Genie finally gives his hand a gentle squeeze and stands to her feet.

"I'm goin' t' check on how the cleanup is goin'."

She turns and makes her way to the passageway stairs, stopping to look back over her shoulder at him before she descends.

Jeff watches her go, trying to process the complex mix of feelings swirling inside. Soon, however, the aching in his head becomes his primary focus; he closes his eyes and leans his head back against the sofa.

⌘

18

CARGO LOGS

When Genie emerges from the underground chamber, she finds Jeff holding his head, obviously in pain.

"Come on, I'll help y' get back home," she offers.

"HE JUST NEEDS some clear air and a bit o' rest," Genie explains to Isabel, who greets them with a concerned look.

"I'll be fine," Jeff objects, feeling embarrassed by the attention.

Isabel gets something for his headache as Genie helps him sit down. With her usual efficiency, Isabel has returned before the two of them have time alone to talk. Genie takes Jeff's hand briefly as she says goodbye.

"I need t' get back to the team," she explains, studying Jeff's eyes. He squints back at her with a nod of thanks.

As soon as Genie leaves, he uses his headache as an excuse to go to his room. Despite his throbbing headache, he quickly makes his way up to the tower. He desperately wants to study the ancient scroll, but doesn't dare go near it now with all the activity still going on outside the vault. In the meantime, he has to see what the Avatar knows about it.

"BE," he calls as he enters the Lab. "What records are there from the expedition that retrieved the Scepter?"

Log entries from his uncle's trip appear on the screen. They detail the Scepter's discovery but make no mention of the Scroll. Jeff notes their date: June 18th, forty years ago.

"Was anything else discovered on that expedition besides the Scepter?" Jeff asks more specifically.

"The logs do not mention any other discoveries during that mission," BE responds.

"What about the cargo?" Jeff probes. "Was anything else unloaded when the ship returned?"

"The cargo logs do indicate that another unmarked crate was also unloaded."

"That has to have been it," Jeff comments aloud distractedly.

"I'm sorry," BE asks, "to what are you referring?"

Jeff doesn't answer, asking a question of his own instead: "What information do you have on the Scroll of the Gods?"
The avatar appears to consider the question for a moment.

"It was an ancient artifact mentioned in the Cronicis Niergel and other ancient texts."

"Did my uncle examine it?" Jeff challenges. "Did he run the same analysis on it as on the Ring and Scepter?"

BE pauses; "I cannot access that information."

Jeff carefully interprets the avatar's reply ... it didn't say the information didn't exist, only that it could not be *accessed*.

"Did Barry find the Scroll on his expedition to the Atlan site?" Jeff asks directly.

"That information is not accessible," BE repeats.

Jeff decides to take a different tack. "From what you know of the Scroll, what would you assume of its origin?"

"The writings that describe it do not reveal its origin," BE states.

"Yes, but what would you assume it to be?" Jeff presses, "Where did it come from?"

"Based on mentions of its abilities, it was likely an extra-dimensional object," the avatar postulates.

"You mean, from another dimension ...like the Ring and Scepter?" Jeff probes.

"Yes."

"How did it get here?" Jeff asks, not really expecting an answer.

"The only logical explanation is that it was placed here," BE replies, surprisingly.

"Placed here? Why do you say that?" Jeff wonders.

"Since it is an inanimate object with no mention of a beginning," BE reasons, "it could not have been created in our dimension and could not have initiated its own transport here."

"Fair enough," Jeff concedes, agreeing with the avatar's logic. "The Cronicis mentions that the Scroll was used to *call forth* the Ring and Scepter — is it possible that the Scroll contains instructions for accessing that other dimension?"

"Yes, there is a high probability that it could have been used to establish a portal to that dimension."

Jeff leads the questioning further: "If a way could be found to reopen such a portal, what would it take to destroy them there? Could a man survive in that alternate dimension long enough to destroy the Ring and Scepter?"

"Survival would be impossible," BE answers matter-of-factly.

Great, Jeff thinks to himself, *this challenge just keeps getting better and better.* He thinks for a moment about other ways that the objects might be sent back and destroyed. "Could the artifacts be carried through such a portal mechanically?"

"Anything containing matter from our dimension would be obliterated the moment it touches the portal, preventing it from passing through," BE explains.

"What if they were sent through at high speed — like with a rocket?" Jeff wonders.

"I'm afraid that is not possible either," BE determines. "Such a portal would generate enormous friction at the point where matter and antimatter interact. Even an object moving at high speed would be easily destroyed by it."

"Then what could be a means for sending them through?" Jeff asks, feeling exasperated.

"No means would be required," BE answers mysteriously.

Jeff struggles with the avatar's answer... "Do you mean there is no possible way ... they can't be sent back, ever?"

"I mean that no method of transport would be needed," BE clarifies. "The artifacts would be irresistibly drawn to the portal ...in the same way that objects in our dimension are attracted by gravity."

"So we only need to open it near the objects, and they'll be pulled in," Jeff repeats as he grasps what BE is saying. "That's brilliant! Is that possible?"

"All of these are hypothetical scenarios," BE concedes, "No means exist for creating such a portal."

"Actually, there might be," Jeff reveals. "The Scroll exists... It's here ...in the secret vault with the Ring and Scepter. I've been inside the vault — I've seen it."
The avatar looks surprised, an expression that Jeff would never have expected from an AI program.

"You took a great risk in using the access code without first consulting me," BE states sternly. "It was meant for me to verify the code first and provide further instructions. You are fortunate to have survived."

"Verify it?" Jeff questions. A realization quickly dawns on him. "You mean the coded password you asked me for yesterday was supposed to be the vault's access code?"
He remembers that BE asked for the password when he tried to

view the castle's hidden passages. "What else were you going to show me? Is that the password to open the remaining areas of the castle blueprints?"

Jeff doesn't wait for the avatar to answer, immediately reciting the code from memory: "It's *Declination 64, 20, 45.6, Right Ascension 14, 04, 33.58.*"

The screen in front of him instantly switches to a display of the 3D castle floorplan and then zooms in to show the underground tunnels that connect the towers and central chamber.

As Jeff watches, the screen begins to render another set of chambers and tunnels that intersect those. His eyes are immediately drawn to the mysterious metal door he had discovered weeks earlier, and his eyebrows raise in surprise. The door is connected to a short tunnel, the opposite end of which opens directly into his uncle's secret vault!

"How does this open?" he asks the avatar, pointing to the door.

"That is an emergency regress," BE explains, "it can only be opened from inside the vault."

Jeff remembers the palm scanner and door inside the vault, opposite its entrance, and nods in realization. On the floor plan, he can also see the vault's metallic hallway where Seamus' body was found. It includes electrical schematics with specifications for delivering a ten-megavolt blast into the hallway's metal interior, enough to turn the air inside into a thick forest of lightning bolts. No wonder the oxygen in the chamber had been so depleted.

"The vault's ventilation system is not working," Jeff tells the avatar.

BE quickly runs a diagnostic on the system, and one of its components turns red on the screen, then after flashing several times, turns green.

"The blower has been restarted," BE confirms.

Jeff spends a moment studying the computer's 3D floor plans. They contain no record of Cerdic's elaborate storage container in the center of the rotunda floor; its absence adds to Jeff's suspicion that Barry never knew it existed.

After puzzling over that silently, his attention finally switches back to his Challenge.

"If you had the scroll, do you think you could find the means for opening a portal?" Jeff asks as he studies the underground passages.

"If the Scroll, in fact, contains such knowledge, then I should be able to locate it," BE confirms.

⌘

19

SCROLL OF THE GODS

A short time later, Jeff descends the stairs in his suite and meets Isabel in the main hallway. He can tell the moment he sees her that no excuse for skipping lunch will be tolerated, not that he wants one; his stomach is growling. He had forgotten how hungry he was. He barely touched last night's dinner and skipped breakfast altogether. He is soon seated in the kitchen, gratefully accepting the meal she places in front of him.

"Have you seen Hunahpu this morning?" He asks Isabel as he takes a bite. Jeff has been concerned about him ever since their last discussion the previous evening.

"Yes, he said he was going to the chapel for some time alone," she answers. "He is a deeply spiritual man; such a dear man of God."

Jeff fights back an uneasy feeling in the pit of his stomach. He is refusing to accept that his great-grandfather's worrisome premonition could, in fact, be true.

"I know it is not my place to mention it," Isabel begins as she fills his water glass, "but you should try to spend more time with him ...

he's not getting any younger, you know. Jeff nods his agreement and thanks her for the refill.

"All of this running around at all hours..." she continues in a motherly tone, "...you really must take better care of yourself. Going without sleep or nourishment will catch up with you; you will likely fall ill if you keep up this pace."

Jeff can't help thinking to himself that he'll be a lot worse than sick if he *doesn't* keep up his current pace or even accelerate it. He keeps the thought to himself, however, thanking her for the well-intended advice.

As much as he enjoys the meal, he is soon fidgeting in his seat again, eager to get back to the business at hand — almost to the point of desperation. He gets up quickly from his empty plate the instant he finishes and distractedly thanks Isabel as he darts for the door without looking back. His abrupt departure leaves her holding the slice of apple pie she was about to serve him.

JEFF RUSHES from his suite's front door back to Barry's suite, covering the short distance in seconds, and is soon back in his uncle's study. The security team has done a good job cleaning things up, leaving behind no sign of the morning's events.

He quickly opens the hidden passage, letting it close again behind him. Moments later, he is inside the Vault's entrance hallway and enters the access codes, watching the stone wall close, and then the vault's door rises open.

The air is noticeably fresher as he steps inside, sensing a slight breeze as the air pressure equalizes. He wastes no time using the vault's second palm scanner to open the emergency door and then grabs the case containing the ancient Scroll and pulls it toward the door. He was thinking that his plan had been well devised until he realizes how heavy it is. Nonetheless, he is not about to abandon it. He grabs the handle with both hands and drags it out.

As soon as he is clear of the vault's door, it surprises him by slamming shut, sealing him within the small exit tunnel in total darkness. He scrambles to light his flashlight and then looks around in the pitch-black darkness for controls to reopen either of the tunnel's steel doors, finding none. He is on the verge of panic when the exit door suddenly slides smoothly open, leaving him breathing a sigh of relief and coaxing his racing heartbeat back to normal.

The heavy case drops roughly from the escape passageway and makes a pair of scratch marks along the tunnel floor as he drags it back to the well of the North Tower. Realizing he is winging it with this impulsive plan to retrieve the Scroll, he is relieved to find a call button for the elevator. He presses it hopefully and waits.

Soon, he is rewarded with the sound of the elevator's movement high above. When it arrives at the bottom of the shaft, he pulls the large case on board; minutes later, he drags it into the Tower Lab.

JEFF UNLATCHES the case and carefully lifts the heavy scroll onto the large circular countertop that surrounds the room's central pedestal. The avatar waves an arm over it, triggering a set of laser scans that begin measuring its dimensions.

To Jeff's amazement, a pair of mechanized clamps suddenly materialized from nowhere, latching onto the scroll's golden handles. They slowly move apart to reveal several feet of the mysterious manuscript.

Jeff watches the clamps with a confused and surprised expression, touching their solid surface with his fingers: "How? ...These things are real ...they're not holograms!" He exclaims in disbelief. "How did you create them from thin air?"

"Not quite from thin air," BE answers. "My form generator simply manipulates matter at an atomic level... You may think of it like a 3D printer ...only on an atomic scale and without the printer."

"*Simply...*" Jeff repeats in disbelief, studying the amazing creations more closely. BE, meanwhile, has begun to scan the scroll's contents.

"Interesting," BE says as it pauses.

Jeff stops his examination of the tabletop creations to turn his attention back to the main event; he looks at the avatar curiously.

"The scroll appears to be written in an unknown language... one that is unlike any known language on earth."

Jeff looks at the scroll's odd script, written in vertical columns from bottom to top, looking as though the characters were stacked on top of one another. He stares down at the indecipherable text as he leans on the table and grumbles aloud in frustration. Leaning forward, he lays his hands on the scroll's open parchment and vents in a desperate voice: "There must be a way to translate you. We have to reveal your secrets!"

To his utter surprise and amazement, the scroll's text is suddenly transformed before his eyes. It has translated itself!

"It would appear that your request has initiated the desired response," BE acknowledges in a dramatic understatement.

Jeff pulls his hands off the scroll, afraid to touch it again for fear of reversing whatever has just occurred. "Is all of it translated? Can you read it now?" he stammers.

The avatar begins to roll the scroll forward as a laser scans the ancient parchment. Jeff watches in stunned astonishment as the letters not only rapidly change into English but also redraw repeatedly on the page, each column spawning what appear to be hundreds of columns in its place as the avatar quickly scans them all. By the time it reaches the end of the scroll, it has recorded the equivalent of thousands of pages of text.

Jeff watches the avatar curiously as it seems to be thinking, appearing still and with a serious expression.

"Wh-what does it say?" he asks carefully, "Did you find instructions for opening the portal?"

The avatar looks at him with an odd expression, as if he has just learned something that holds his full attention and is still trying to process it.

"The scroll must be kept from human eyes," BE finally warns as he looks up at Jeff. There is a grave urgency in his voice. "Its contents are evil in a way that I have never known. I have had to lock it away in a secure section of memory where it can remain safely isolated."

Jeff looks at the avatar in wonder, "Do you think it can influence *you?* ...could it really control even your programming?"

"It would appear that that is possible; its oracles are as quick to mutate as a virus; to a man, its deception would clearly be overwhelming," BE reveals. "Fortunately, your uncle gave me an impregnable prime directive, an unalterable benchmark for judging right and wrong. If he had not, it is doubtful that I would have been able to resist the Scroll's influence."

Jeff silently considers the avatar's words; they remind him of how he felt when he first read the Liberatricem Commemorans — a dark, desperate feeling. But that book was nothing compared to the Scroll; it was merely written by a man. In contrast, he recalls what Thaliard had written about the origin of the ancient scroll's mysterious spells: *By the word of the Dragon they were given...*

Images rush through Jeff's mind of the terrible dragon described in the *Book of the End*. He knows instinctively that this is the same dragon — they are one and the same. His realization sparks a healthy fear of the Scroll, prompting him to step away from the table. He looks at it nervously as he speaks to the avatar again.

"Were you able to find what we were seeking? Did you see a way to open the portal?" he asks anxiously.

"I believe I did," CHET confirms, "it is not words, but rather sounds that are the key. They must be verbalized exactly in order to work."

"How can we know their sound?" Jeff asks reasonably.

"The scroll conveyed to me the precise phonetic sequence ...I can teach it to you," BE assures him.

JEFF PAUSES, suddenly having second thoughts as he recalls Hunahpu's warning: *Doors can serve both sides.* "Is it safe to open a portal to such a place?"

"I was able to determine a means to direct the portal's location. If my calculations are correct, it will open directly into the fires of Tir Lai," BE explains. "The Dragon's artifacts will be drawn into it ...you must be certain that you are nowhere near the objects when it is opened."

Jeff hesitates as he understands BE's instruction: "Are you sure that's a good idea? Can the portal pull in anything else?"

"Opening into the fire is the safest place," BE argues, "...it is the surest way to prevent anything else from emerging .. Anything that may be seeking entry to our world."

Now Jeff is feeling even more concerned. "Emerging? What kind of thing?" he asks nervously. "What else does the Scroll say... does it describe what's on the other side?"

"What it describes is of no concern to you now; it will suffice to say that you would not want to meet its inhabitants, I assure you," BE answers ominously.

"In that case," Jeff says apprehensively, "I have just one other question: Once the portal is open ...how do we close it?"

⌘

20

HEARTS STRUGGLE

On their secluded Mediterranean island, the Maranish brothers have become aware of a deep stirring somewhere in the blackness of their souls.

"He has encountered the Ring," Eblis announces to his brother in an anxious voice as he enters the room.

"Yes, I felt it too," Chesed agrees. "We are bound to it still... the Ring has awakened and calls to us once more. There is also something else... something stronger."

"I sensed it as well," Eblis agrees. "What do you think it could be?"

"I know of one object... but it cannot be that. Yet, I wonder..." Chesed says in a suspicious voice. He turns from the windows where he has been standing to look at his brother. "How are the preparations progressing for our visit?"

"Very well... we will be ready for our departure before first light tomorrow," Eblis confirms.

"Good," Chesed says with a sinister smile. "I sense our venture will be even more rewarding than anticipated."

EUGENIA STANDS ALONE on the castle's open grounds, staring out at the ocean's distant horizon. Thoughts of the morning's events with Jeff swirl in her mind — especially one event in particular. She knew there had been a close friendship forming between them — maybe even a little attraction, she admits- but she can't believe that she kissed him — what was she thinking? But it is the way he kissed her back and her response to his kiss that troubles her most ... the memory of it makes her heart race and clouds her thoughts.

She shakes herself, annoyed at her own reaction. She has been careful for so long to avoid getting close to anyone ...except for her grandfather. She had long ago resigned herself to the fact that any entanglements only made her vulnerable or put those she cared about in danger. But she never expected *this* ...she never expected *him*.

It seems like a bad idea on so many levels. He's her boss, for one; what would it mean for her position and Board seat if they became... *involved*. Even the word sounded complicated.

She hears her phone chirp and looks at a text message from EB.

How are things in LH?

She considers telling him that Jeff has entered the Secret Vault, but realizes on second thought that that information had best be conveyed in person. Aside from that, she is not about to share her romantic struggles.

'When will U be back?'

...She replies, avoiding his question altogether.

Tomorrow evening.

'Good. Miss U.'

Same,

...he replies, then adds:

How is Hunahpu? I've been feeling a tug to
pray for him.

'I haven't seen him today ...but now that U
mention it, I've been feeling that too,' she
admits. 'I'll check & let U know.'

Thanks.

She lowers her phone and looks back toward the castle. Her eyes are drawn to the windows of Jeff's suite a few stories up; it looks like the kitchen lights are on. She decides to try calling Isabel.

"Hi, it's Eugenia," she says as Isabel answers. "I promised my Gran'da I'd check in on Hunahpu for him. Is he at home, by chance?" She listens as Isabel explains where he has gone. "Time alone... I understand. I won't disturb him," she answers respectfully, thanking her.

Eugenia decides that it couldn't hurt to pay a visit to the chapel herself; in addition to checking on Hunahpu, she can think of a few things of her own to pray about, as a matter of fact.

THE REGAL-LOOKING Gothic cathedral is completely silent as she enters; its peaceful atmosphere seems to cover her like a comfortable blanket. She walks softly up the aisle and stops to sit in one of the empty pews, taking a moment to pause and admire the chapel's beauty before bowing her head.

Almost instantly, a deep, stirring flood sweeps over her soul, making her eyes glassy with tears. It is a powerful moving of the Spirit that suddenly obscures all the other noise in her head. The deep burden it brings surprises her; it contains an unmistakable sense of sorrow and foreboding for Hunahpu, most definitely, but also a pleading cry for Jeff. The urgent prayer that flows from her heart for both of them is a cry for strength — as if both of them will soon be facing insurmountable dangers that will tax every ounce of fortitude they possess. The more she prays, the more overwhelming the burden becomes, making her double over with her head in her hands and then finally forcing her to her knees.

The shocking urgency of it fills her consciousness — she has no idea how long she prays this way, but when she finally climbs from her knees to sit again, her eyes and face are awash in tears. She wipes her face with her sleeve.

"May I?" she hears a kind voice ask as she looks up to see Hunahpu standing in the aisle beside her, holding a box of tissues. She accepts one gratefully and smiles as she slides over, inviting him to sit down beside her.

"I have always loved this chapel," Hunahpu says as he looks around nostalgically. "Cornelius truly put his soul into its construction."

"Cornelius built this?" She asks in surprise. "I always assumed that Barry had been the designer."

Hunahpu smiles as his eyes take in the gigantic auditorium; "I suppose most do — Barry was always building things," he admits. "No, it was Neil. After he turned over the reins of the corporation to Barry, he sank his life into this."

He smiles at Eugenia and adds, "He would be pleased to hear that you did not suspect it of him; he never wanted for it to be thought of as a monument to himself."

Genie nods with a smile that barely hides the deep sadness in her heart. They sit together silently for a long moment.

Hunahpu doesn't ask her why she is here in the chapel in the middle of the day or try to probe into what is troubling her. He seems to see past those questions as he looks at her for a brief moment.

He looks down at his folded hands as he speaks: "I have lived a long life," he observes with a grateful voice. "At times, it has been a hard life ...very hard." He pauses, and Genie sees his fists clench for a second as painful thoughts rush through his mind. "But it has been a good life," he adds as he takes a deep breath and releases it. He looks up straight ahead with a determined gaze as he continues: "When my time has come to move on from here ...to go to my true home... I will not eschew it."

He looks over at her, revealing a bit of the concern he truly struggles with: "Young Jeffrey, on the other hand, has merely begun his journey. His will be a difficult walk," he says the word "difficult" with tremendous emphasis and concern in his voice. "He will need a strong companion to accompany him on that journey," he adds, looking again into her face. "A very *special* partner. No ordinary companion will do for him; only one who is strong enough to walk that journey *with* him." His eyes convey the intent of his counsel, but he doesn't press the point, instead adding: "As you pray, pray that he will find such a partner."

She can't find the words to answer, but she knows he was talking about her and is secretly grateful for his implied tribute. His words about Jeff resonate within her — she feels the same way about Jeff's calling ...that it will be difficult. When the tension in her throat finally eases, she clears it as quietly as she can and then speaks softly.

"GRAN'DA SENDS HIS REGARDS; he called askin' about you," she informs him. "He was feelin' a burden to pray for you. Is everything all right?"

"Ah... EB is a very good friend. Thank you for letting me know," Hunahpu says appreciatively. "Our Father knows what we will need before we ask it of Him," he adds, referring to Jesus' words. "God's grace still amazes me, even after all these years. He makes us abide in the very dwelling place of the Most High — we dwell under the shadow of His great wings."

Hun's answer does not come across as trite or shallow; his calm assurance is strong and unwavering, carrying a force of conviction that feels to Genie as if it is a current of deep water that seems to wash over her soul. She nods back in agreement, thankful for his edifying reminder.

SHE LOOKS around at their ornate surroundings; "It really *is* a beautiful chapel, isn't it?" Her comment is more of an affirmation than a question. "Do you come here alone often?"

"No, actually," he answers honestly, "that has been an oversight of mine. It truly is beautiful."

"Well, now you can correct that," she answers encouragingly. "From now on, you can come here as often as you like."

Hunahpu looks around again silently as if he is taking in the sight for the last time. Then he seems to catch himself and looks back at Genie with a gracious smile, nodding yes, but not answering.

⌘

21

OPENING HELL'S DOOR

"You have almost gotten it..." BE encourages Jeff to practice repeating the pronunciation that the avatar has taught him. Jeff looks at the audio signature displayed on the large monitor in front of him, studying the places where his voice still does not match the pattern that BE provided.

"I guess they don't have Boston accents in Tir Lai. At least that's encouraging to know ...also probably surprising," Jeff jokes. BE looks at him stoically, obviously missing the joke.

"Once you have mastered this command for *closing* the portal, then we can begin with the one for opening it," the avatar presses ahead, ignoring Jeff's self-amused shrug.

Jeff nods acceptingly and clears his throat, then repeats the odd jumble of sounds while studying the screen intently. The peeks seem to match, but the timing is off this time.

"Don't focus quite so much on the screen," BE coaches. "Perhaps you should try it with your eyes closed."

Jeff feels a little strange about it but gives the avatar's suggestion a try, closing his eyes as he lets the sounds roll off his tongue. The computer chimes to confirm the match.

"Excellent!" BE commends him. "Now repeat it again...."

Jeff continues over and over, eyes closed, until he can flawlessly repeat the command as often as he likes.

"Very good, Jeffrey, well done, my boy," BE congratulates him, sounding more like a lifelong mentor than an AI program. "You are ready to learn the command for opening the portal."

As good as Jeff is feeling about his mastery of the first command, he feels suddenly uneasy about the next one. The cold reality of what he is about to open strikes him for the first time.

"Is the Scroll's case securely latched? The avatar asks.

"Yes, it's latched... but are you sure that's enough?" Jeff asks nervously. "Is it safe having it here at all when the portal opens?"

"Calculations of the portal's power are difficult to predict," BE admits. "Perhaps the scroll should be returned to the vault."

Jeff hesitates, "That won't be easy... the only way in is through Uncle Barrymore's study." He thinks for a moment... "I can take it back to the underground tunnel. The odds of anyone finding it there are pretty slim." He then looks at the large case, remembering how heavy it was, and glances back at the mechanized clamps that BE had created... "Say, do you think you could make something to carry it with?"

The avatar nods and closes its eyes for a second as Jeff watches a square platform appear on the countertop. The odd device looks a little like a bathroom scale, with a digital display at one end and a single handle in the middle. It is about an inch thick, with clamps extending downward a few inches on all four sides; Jeff can see that it is just the right size to fit onto one end of the Scroll's case as it stands on end.

"What's this?" Jeff says in confusion, "Am I supposed to lift it with this? You don't understand; I need something to carry it with... something that bears its weight."

"Take hold of its handle," BE instructs patiently.

Jeff reluctantly complies, determined to demonstrate to the avatar why it won't work. As soon as his hand grips it, however, Jeff feels the device lift into the air, holding its elevated position even as he tries pressing it back down.

"It's got AG propulsion — like a Dibjet!" Jeff exclaims.

"In a manner of speaking, yes," BE confirms, avoiding a detailed description of the differences. "Just pull it gently wherever you want it to go; rotate the handle slightly for vertical control."

Jeff pulls it closer and presses his entire weight onto it, lifting his feet off the floor, then lets go and watches it hover steadily in midair. "This is amazing!"

"It is merely a logical response to your request...."

...the avatar replies as if it doesn't understand why the device might be seen as the least bit amazing.

Jeff shakes his head unbelievingly as he hovers the device above one end of the Scroll's case and lowers it until the clamps attach with a series of clicks. The clamps double as a lock, preventing the case from being opened.

"As a safety precaution, the lift device is matched to your palm and fingerprints; it will not work for anyone else," CHET reveals.

"Thanks," Jeff says, wildly impressed. He rotates the handle and effortlessly lifts the heavy case a few inches off the floor, where it hovers as he lets go. "Well," he says hesitantly as he turns to look back at BE, "I guess I'll take this down now... I'll be right back." He is secretly dreading the next portal exercise more with each passing moment.

The case glides easily above the floor as he pushes it into the elevator. Jeff turns and slides the elevator's brass handle to the down position, but quickly notices that the case does not lower with the elevator — it hovers in place as the elevator descends, nearly hitting the ceiling! He urgently reverses the brass lever, rising back to the lab entrance. Then, with one hand on the case's lift device and the other on the elevator handle, he carefully lowers both of them in tandem, keeping a steady pace all the way to the bottom of the Tower's well. Once there, he moves the Scroll back to the tunnel opening and lowers it to the floor, leaving it there in the pitch darkness.

He has to will himself to return to the Lab, using every ounce of resolve he can muster. The higher the elevator rises, the more anxiety he feels. The feeling of Semjaza's dark attack — and the overwhelming onslaught he had faced in the Eljo invasion — all replay in his mind. He imagines what an alternate dimension... an entire universe of those dark creatures... could be like. He reaches into his pocket and grips the single seed he carries there.

The elevator stops at the lab entrance. Jeff coaxes himself forward and is soon standing in front of the avatar once again.

"It's in the tunnel," Jeff confirms, "hope it's far enough."

"Good," BE responds. It nods toward a set of headphones on the counter, "Put these on. It will prevent the portal from being accidentally triggered by anything other than your voice."

Accidentally triggered… the sound of that is the last thing Jeff wants to hear. He cautiously puts them on and then turns to the screen.

"I will replicate the pronunciation for you several times before you attempt it yourself," he hears BE say through the headphones.

Then the alien-sounding command begins to play, and its audio signature appears on the screen.

Jeff can't help thinking that it sounds like a rendition of Klingon from an old TV show… if he hadn't been so stressed, the thought of it might have struck him as humorous.

"Now, repeat the command exactly as you have heard it," BE instructs.

Jeff makes several attempts, each time missing sections of the phrase or botching its pronunciation. It is clear that his heart is not in it — in fact, he is terrified of getting it right.

"Your attempts reveal reluctance," BE interjects insightfully.

Jeff isn't surprised that the avatar can discern his intent just by hearing him.

"What if we can't close the portal after opening it? What if it creates a rift in the universe? How do we know it won't place the world in danger?" Jeff worries, rattling off just a few of the doubts that haunt him.

"The commands for closing and opening are from the same invocation within the Scroll," BE explains. "One is the proof of the other; if the one works to open the portal, then the other will work to close it. My calculations indicate that the interaction between the dimensions is strongly repulsive — causing them to naturally press away from one another. This is what causes the artifacts to be drawn in when in the presence of an open portal — the objects themselves are, in effect, repelled by our universe."

Jeff remembers from the ancient writings that the portal had obviously been opened before without endangering our dimension. Yet the idea still terrifies him.

The avatar looks at Jeff for a moment, perceiving the depth of his reluctance.

"There is no other way to destroy the Dragon's implements," BE points out soberly. "Must I remind you what is at stake if your quest fails?"

Jeff knows that it is impossible to argue with the avatar's logic. He closes his eyes and breathes a prayer for help, then steels himself, gathering what little courage he can find.

"Alright, repeat it again for me," he instructs BE.

Once again, the alien-sounding command can be heard through his headphones, and he studies its audio signature on the large screen, then repeats it — this time achieving a 90% match.

"Good, try it again," BE says, replaying the command for Jeff to hear.

Jeff's precision improves even further. BE asks him to repeat it again, but Jeff interrupts.

"I want to practice the command for closing it again first," he declares adamantly. "Verify that I can still say it."

"Very well," BE agrees, "ready for verification."

Jeff removes the headphones and closes his eyes in concentration, then recites the strange sequence of sounds that he mastered earlier.

The computer's chime confirms its match, and Jeff opens his eyes to see the '*100%*' measure flashing reassuringly on the screen.

Then, without another word to BE, Jeff closes his eyes again and speaks the new command in a loud and forceful voice.

THERE IS a sudden ***crack of thunder***, as loud as a lightning bolt striking the floor directly in front of him. Jeff's eyes shoot open, and he watches in spellbound terror as the tower's roof seems to split apart, bathing the lab in a red glow that looks like a scene from deep inside a violent volcano; its boiling magma is suspended impossibly upside-down over his head. The roar of its explosive fire is deafening, but even more hair-raising are the shrieks and wails he can hear coming through above the fire's din. Jeff's knees become weak, and his face turns pale with terror.

HE STAGGERS BACKWARD AS he tries to shout the command for the portal's closing at the top of his lungs, but cannot form the words through the fear in his voice. He trips and hits the wall, then slides to the floor, knocking over a chair on his way down; he is still staring upward with terror-filled eyes. After several failed attempts, BE shouts the words for him, and seconds later, the fearful portal is gone. Jeff sits staring at the lab's ceiling, which now appears untouched as if nothing at all has happened.

He is breathless. The portal had only been open for a few seconds, but it seemed to him like long minutes ...minutes in which he struggled to shout but couldn't get the words to come out, like a horrible nightmare.

BE asks him if he is all right, having already measured his vital signs, to conclude that there is nothing physically wrong with him besides an elevated heart rate and an adrenaline rush. Jeff doesn't hear the question, causing BE to repeat it...twice.

When he finally does respond, it is with a speechless look, directing his gaze down from the ceiling to look at BE. He slowly nods his head to affirm that he understands the question, ...and that he is okay.

"I think perhaps you had better take a break and get some rest," BE suggests in a sympathetic voice. "We can continue your preparations in the morning."

Jeff nods in agreement and slowly climbs to his feet, picking up the chair and setting it straight. His heart is still racing. He turns toward the door without a word, placing a hand on the wall to steady himself.

"That was very well done," BE says in a sincere voice.

Jeff stops and looks back with a dazed expression, giving the avatar a stunned-looking nod in acknowledgment, then he makes his way to the elevator.

⌘

22

FALLING FOR FEAR

J eff is standing in his suite's Library holding a crystal snifter when Isabel discovers him at home. It is a good thing she had been busy in the kitchen when he came downstairs — he had forgotten that she had seen him leave a few hours earlier out his front door.

"Oh, there you are...." Isabel says as she notices him, "I didn't hear you come in. Have you been home for long?"

"Ah... no... no, I just got in," he answers.

"Well, I can see you've had a hard day," she says insightfully as she takes a look at him. "Why don't you have that drink and relax? I'll let you know when dinner is ready."

Jeff puts the stopper back in the well-aged bottle of Luis XIII and sniffs the rich bouquet as he swirls it gently in his snifter. He remembers the last time he had enjoyed a glass from this bottle; it was on his second day here when he had been struggling to decode his uncle's first clue. So much has happened since then ...it seems like a lifetime ago.

He takes a sip and half-collapses into one of the comfortable

154 | THE DRAGON'S TAIL

leather armchairs, leaning his head back. He takes a deep breath and exhales, letting the tension begin to subside. The moment he closes his eyes, however, his mind fills again with an image of the horrifying portal and its terrible sounds. He shakes himself, trying to convince himself that the outcome could not have been better; he has proven that the portal exists and that he can control its opening and closing. A portal to another dimension! In purely scientific terms, it is a discovery of epic proportions! Unfortunately, he realizes that he can never tell anyone about it.

Worse still, he can't be absolutely certain that the ability to open and close it is enough. What if something, …anything, could, in fact, make it through from that dimension into ours? His only reassurance is in the fact that CHET had correctly calculated the location — the portal opens directly into the heart of Tir Lai's eternal fire. That should certainly limit unwanted visitors, he admits.

As he sits deep in thought, he hears ABBI greeting Hunahpu at the front door; a moment later, his great-grandfather enters the room. Jeff stands and welcomes him; the memory of the prior night's conversation is suddenly fresh in his mind, casting an unspoken awkwardness over their greeting.

"Can I get you a drink?" Jeff offers. Hunahpu politely declines.

The wizened old man studies Jeff's face for a second or two, then takes a seat. Jeff follows, sitting down beside him.

"I sense that you are still troubled," Hunahpu says, "…you struggle with what you must do."

Jeff looks at him suspiciously. "Do you know?" He asks carefully, "…what I have to do?"

"Only that it is the hardest thing you have ever faced," Hunahpu answers. "If it is hard for *you*, then it must be very hard."

Hunahpu pauses in thought, then continues as he takes stock of his own life. "It has always been a wonder to me that the most difficult tasks we face are those that test our will," he observes. "We can gladly spur ourselves to overcome any physical challenge, however difficult, yet when we face a challenge of the will, though it may be a task that a child could do, its conquering is a colossal feat. A test of the will is a test of the soul."

Jeff doesn't answer, but Hunahpu's point has hit home like a laser-guided missile. He sits staring at nothing in particular as his own battle of will swirls inside him.

"I sense that all is ready?" Hunahpu asks, surprising him.

Jeff looks up, wondering whether he should share anything about the challenge ...curious about what Hunahpu knows. "Y-yes," he answers carefully.

"Ah, then all that remains is to find the will to do it."

"It's not that easy," Jeff explains. "It's dangerous ...not only to me — if it were just me, then I'd risk my own safety without question; but it could destroy everyone here ...it might even threaten the entire world."

"I have no doubt of it," Hunahpu assures him. "If it were completely within your control, then it would be within your own power to do it. Remember, my son, the Quest is a lesson in faith ...it is a lesson in trust and obedience." Hunahpu leans forward and puts his hand on Jeff's arm: "Qam ruru munay Dyus, churi ...*You must yield to God's will, my son.*"

Jeff remembers those same words from the night before, recalling the topic of their discussion at that time... Hunahpu's premonition about his own life. He remembers what else Hunahpu told him then: *'To allow or not allow is neither yours nor mine to choose.'*

Isabel knocks gently on the door frame. "I'm terribly sorry to interrupt. Just wanted you to know that dinner is ready whenever you would like it."

They each thank her with a nod and rise.

JEFF IS quiet throughout dinner as he mulls over Hunahpu's words and replays their discussion from the night before one more time. It is hard to believe that that conversation took place only last night — so much has happened since then that it seems like ages have passed. The searing memory of the afternoon's terrifying experience with the portal is still vivid, relentlessly interrupting his thoughts …he can't shake it.

Isabel leaves the room, leaving Jeff and Hunahpu alone. He focuses on his great-grandfather sitting beside him, trying to block out the afternoon's memory.

"Have you shaken that feeling you described last night …about leaving?" Jeff asks him carefully.

Hunahpu lowers his gaze as he considers the question. "No, it has not changed," he answers simply.

"Does it have anything to do with my quest?" Jeff asks anxiously. "I couldn't bear it if I were to cause any harm to…I mean, if what I have to do is responsible for…."

Hunahpu cuts him off, "…Whatever happens, you must remember that it will be what God allows in His perfectly ordained timing. It is not your doing." Hunahpu speaks adamantly: "The importance of your quest is of far greater value than any one man!"

He leans forward and looks into Jeff's eyes intently as he continues, "Mine has been a long and full life. If God chooses to welcome me home this very night, I will not regret His timing; I am ready."

Jeff studies Hunahpu's eyes, seeing clearly the sincerity in his words. "Uncle Barrymore said something similar in his letter to me — on the night that he…." He struggles to finish the thought.

"He would be very proud to see what you have become," Hunahpu encourages, filling the poignant silence. "It is all that he hoped for and more."

Jeff sighs deeply, appreciating his Great Grandfather's words but not fully believing that he is worthy of them. He looks back at Hunahpu with a troubled expression; "I'm not sure I can do this without you. You're the reason… whatever I've been able to become has been because of you."

"I most definitely am not the reason," Hunahpu corrects gently. "You must stop looking to me and seek the true source of your strength!"

His great-grandfather's rebuke has been delivered in such a genuinely loving spirit that Jeff can't be offended, but it cuts him to the quick. Jeff sits silently, acknowledging that he is right.

Hunahpu places his hand on Jeff's forearm and bows his head, then begins to lead the two of them in an impromptu prayer.

Just outside the doorway, Isabel stops what she is doing and closes her eyes, secretly joining them.

RETURNING to his room an hour later, Jeff sits on his bed, exhausted. The stressful day has completely drained him, but he knows that his stress makes it impossible for him to rest; the incessant thoughts racing through his mind are jarring and rob him of sleep. He considers returning to the tower, but his last memory from there causes him to shudder. He thinks of changing into workout clothes and heading down to the gym, but quickly admits that he doesn't have the strength for it.

His mind works feverishly, seeking an answer to his dilemma — there has to be some other way of destroying the artifacts without endangering all of creation! His body is feeling sick, and his head has begun to feel like it is swimming in a swirling dizziness — it's like the dizziness he was feeling in Barrymore's secret vault. A memory flashes through his mind of the jolt he felt when he touched the Scepter — the sickness of it seems to shoot straight to his heart and continues upward, filling his mind with a disorienting fog.

His thoughts seem confused, as if he is hearing a dialogue with someone else. He wrestles to clear his head as an image of the Scroll fills his mind. Words seem to speak to him....

"*It reveals secrets....*" He hears the words spoken in his mind.

Yes, he agrees as he considers the thought, remembering that the avatar said it had shown what exists on the other side.

"There is another way... the scroll knows of it ... it knows another way to destroy the Ring and Scepter!"

The words again invade his mind, inviting him to consider the thought.

In his exhausted state, he admits that he might not be thinking clearly, but he is convinced of this much... the portal that opened today is dangerous — too dangerous. Hunahpu's disturbing premonitions have only reinforced Jeff's resolve to find an alternative — he *won't* be the cause of his Great Grandfather's death! He *can't* be!

It is beginning to seem to him that the Scroll itself is the only hope for another answer — it has to be found there — whatever alternative exists, the Scroll has to know what it is! Jeff's legs are moving even before his mind has registered this conclusion; he opens the secret tower entrance and is soon riding the elevator downward. Gnawing doubts about what he is doing haunt his conscience; the avatar's warning about it flashes to mind: *'...its oracles are as quick to mutate as a virus, to a man its deception is overpowering.'* Instead of heeding them, he pushes them to the back of his mind — he is driven instead by his fear of the terrifying portal and Hunahpu's premonition.

He finds the scroll's case sitting where he left it that afternoon and places his hand on the lift to raise it from the floor, allowing it to glide easily back to the elevator. He remembers to raise it in tandem with the elevator, although it takes him a few attempts to get the speed and timing correct; finally, he makes it back to his bedroom's entrance. The Lab would be a better environment for studying it, he admits, but he wants to avoid its unsettling memories ...as well as the avatar's notice. Somewhere in the back of his clouded mind, he can hear a warning that echoes like a ringing bell, telling him to leave the dangerous scroll alone.

His motions seem automatic as he watches himself open the elevator gate and move the case into the closet-sized alcove adjacent to his room. The warnings ringing inside him grow louder as his hands unlatch the lifting device, then carefully lay the case down, snapping open each latch. As the case splits open, the Scroll seems to glow with an eerie light in the small alcove's dimness. Jeff holds his breath nervously as he looks at the ancient compendium, hesitant to touch it.

HIS HEART IS BEATING WILDLY AS he finally stands and opens the secret entrance into his room. Turning to the scroll, he carefully lifts it from its case and carries it to his huge bed. To his amazement, its ancient text changes instantly into English as he unrolls it, this time without having to say a word.

Even though the words are in English, he isn't sure how to read them at first. It seems like a jumble of unrelated definitions, resembling a dictionary with entries out of order. He realizes that if it had been sorted at all, it was likely in the order of its original text, a detail that probably didn't matter much since he has no idea what he is looking for anyway.

He begins scanning the dense type, hoping to stumble across something that could help him destroy the artifacts. He is coming up empty on that point, but begins to notice that many of the spells contain titles for curing diseases, resolving conflicts, overcoming grief, or instilling joy and happiness. He is soon discovering explanations for scientific mysteries and secrets of the universe that he couldn't have hoped to discover on his own in a hundred lifetimes.

He comes across one to remove fear and anxiety and stops to read it twice, mouthing the words without saying them aloud. He suddenly feels an intense calm wash over him, carrying a tremendous sense of confidence; if he had been looking at himself in a mirror, he might also have noticed a veil of darkness sweeping over the surface of his eyes. In his distraction, he fails to notice that his initial interest in seeking a way to destroy the artifacts has begun to wane.

The scroll soon begins to reveal even more amazing scientific mysteries — strange, unknown elements and ways to derive new ones with fantastic properties. Jeff is shown ways to multiply seed output and even synthesize pure water from thin air — methods that could eradicate hunger and starvation worldwide!

He becomes engrossed in his reading, studying with fascination the scroll's descriptions of distant galaxies and methods for folding space — passing through alternate dimensions to span vast distances instantly. The scroll's knowledge seems limitless!

Jeff has already forgotten the avatar's warning about the scroll's abilities to persuade and deceive. He has become completely taken in by it, and soon every intention of destroying it has faded into a forgotten memory.

⌘

23

IRRESISTIBLE

A pair of dark ships makes preparations for launch from their docks on the Maranish brothers' fortress island. Even in the moonlight, the strange ships would stand out starkly against the pristine waters of the beautiful island's hidden bay if not for the cover of aerial camouflage that conceals them.

Far larger than Dibjets, the ships employ the same underwater propulsion and navigation systems as their smaller counterparts. These carry a far more ominous cargo; their holds are filled with Eljo troops, lying shoulder to shoulder on rows of long steel racks. Stacked in their corpse-filled pressure suits like a warehouse of hideous monsters.

On the command ship's bridge, Chesed and Eblis survey the ships' status and grin in approval.

"All is ready," Eblis announces, turning to his brother.

"Give the order," Chesed commands simply. His voice is like the sound of a snake eying its prey.

The ships break away from their docks and quickly sink beneath the waves as they move out to deeper waters.

JEFF BARELY NOTICES the light of a new sunrise filling his room. After reading all night, he is still mesmerized by the scroll, absorbing section after section as he pores over it. There are entries that offend his inner conscience, most surely, but he quickly skips over those, justifying his interest with the argument that the scroll contains so much that could be used for good.

It isn't until Genie calls his phone that he realizes what time it is. He has missed their training session.

"Where are ye?" she asks with genuine concern in her voice; "Isabel said ye haven't been down for breakfast this mornin'."

"I-I'm fine... I'm upstairs," he answers in a distracted voice, sounding unnaturally confused.

"Is anythin' wrong? Are y' feelin' alright?"

"Yeah... yes... sure," he answers dismissively. "I'm just doing some research."

"For yer quest?" she asks carefully.

Jeff pauses, he has to search his memory to recall what she is referring to; "Oh that," he says in a tone that reveals it had been the last thing on his mind, "I guess... yes."

Genie is growing more concerned by the moment. "Well, do y' want me t' wait. Are y' comin'?"

"W-wait? Coming?" he replies, clearly oblivious to the fact that he has missed their session. "I'm sorry ...I'm pretty busy now — have to go... I'll call you later," he adds as he drops the call.

GENIE LOOKS at her phone in disbelief, then quickly dials her grandfather. *"Shan'er,* I think there's somethin' wrong with Jeff... he missed our trainin' this mornin' ...he's actin' confused. It's not like him!"

EB can tell from the concern in her voice that something is seriously wrong. Eugenia is not someone to jump to conclusions, and he knows that she doesn't become emotional easily. "Maybe he's just overtired," he tries to reassure her, "he's been pushin' himself very hard the past few months."

"There's somethin' else," Genie confesses regretfully, "yesterday he opened the Secret Vault... we found the body of Seamus Gill there. There was a ventilation problem, and Jeff passed out... I'm worried about him — he's not actin' like himself!"

"The Vault!" EB exclaims, "Why did you let him?" His voice takes on a more urgent tone: "Let Hunahpu know what you've told me. He must check in on him at once," EB advises. "I'm gettin' ready t'leave here — I can be back in Loch Harnan by noon."

GENIE AGREES and promises to keep him updated, then quickly calls Jeff's suite, waiting for Isabel to answer. "Hi, Isabel... is Hunahpu there? Can I talk to him, please?"

"Yes, he's right here; what's wrong, my dear?" Isabel replies, sensing the concern in Genie's voice.

Hunahpu is on his feet beside her almost immediately, as if he has been expecting the call. He holds out his hand for the phone, and Isabel hands it to him without waiting for Genie's answer.

"What is it?" he asks urgently. Genie shares with him what she has just explained to her grandfather, and Hunahpu falls silent, as if a missing piece of information has suddenly fallen into place, solving a haunting puzzle in his mind. After a long pause, he speaks urgently to her: "You must pray for him, my dear... pray very hard — only God's power can intervene to reach him at this moment."

Genie is caught off guard by the urgency of his instruction; "Wh-why... what is it? What's wrong?"

"The Vault contained something more than just the Ring and Scepter... something else is stored there, very dark and powerful," Hunahpu explains. "If it has influenced him, then his very soul is in terrible danger."

"He never mentioned findin' anythin' else," Genie says in confusion. "Why would he keep it secret?"

"He was likely protecting you — I believe he knows what it is," Hunahpu explains.

Genie accepts Hunahpu's assurance that he will check on Jeff immediately, then hangs up the call and drops to her knees right where she stands in the gym; she begins to pray with a fervor she has seldom felt before.

HUNAHPU ASKS ISABEL TO PRAY, too, as he makes his way upstairs to Jeff's room. His first knock on Jeff's door brings no response, so he knocks again, louder. Finally, he hears Jeff's distracted voice from somewhere inside, far from the door.

"Yes? What? What is it?" His voice sounds annoyed at the interruption.

"Ñucaca canpa jatun - taitami cani" ...*It is your great-grandfather.*

"It's not a good time..." Jeff replies from a distance, not wanting to be disturbed, "I'll be down soon."

"I am afraid I must insist," Hunahpu says sternly. "I know about the Scroll."

There is silence as Jeff struggles with his conflicted thoughts and emotions; he feels like a child caught doing something wrong, even as he feels indignant about being challenged over it. Hunahpu waits for several long minutes, wondering whether Jeff will respond, and is just about to knock again when the door opens. Judging from Jeff's wrinkled clothes, unkempt hair, and tired eyes, Hunahpu discerns that he has been up all night. He can plainly see the darkness in Jeff's eyes, giving them a glassy, distant appearance and making him look as if a part of his subconscious mind is under a trance. Hunahpu accepts Jeff's invitation to enter the room and quickly looks around, but no trace of the golden scroll can be seen.

"You were unwise to read it," he says to Jeff in a firm rebuke.

"You're wrong about it," Jeff argues, "I was worried at first, too, but it isn't dangerous. It opened my eyes; there's so much it can teach us! You just have to read it to see for yourself."

"I will not!" Hunahpu objects, "And you must not either! It must be put away — if it were possible, it would have been destroyed long ago."

"That's where we're wrong!" Jeff contends. "It would be a mistake... it holds so many answers!" He speaks adamantly, but the conviction in his voice seems to be born more out of obsession than logic. "Why should it be different from any of the other books in the Secret Chamber? Uncle Barry said himself that *many* of them are dangerous ...that's why they could only be entrusted to those with a pure heart and motives," Jeff contends, "...and he said they could be used to help mankind. What makes any of those other books different from the Scroll?"

"Is it with a pure heart that you have secretly disobeyed the advice of your counselors and ignored your own judgment?" Hunahpu asks in a stinging indictment. "Are a man's motives pure when they defy his own conscience and cause him to turn his back on the spirit of truth? If even *you* cannot be trusted to do what is right in the presence of such an object, then what place does it deserve among us?"

Jeff feels a stab of conviction at Hunahpu's words, but quickly rationalizes his actions; it seems to him that the old man is overreacting. If he only understood what wonders the scroll contains, he would surely see Jeff's point of view. Jeff assures himself that everything he has done is for the good of those he loves... especially for Hunahpu! His motives are pure, in spite of how they might appear to others!

"I'm sorry that you can't see that what I'm doing is right," Jeff says unapologetically.

Hunahpu stands silently and searches Jeff's eyes intently for several long moments, then speaks in a quiet voice that barely masks the despair in his heart. "I fear that our final battle is nearly lost," he says sadly. "Who will stand against this evil if the Niergel's Mantle Bearer will not?"

Jeff stands, looking back speechlessly as Hunahpu hangs his head and turns to walk away.

"Wait! It's not like that. You don't understand ...I had to do it ...I did it for you!"

His Great-grandfather pauses and looks back: "You would do well to forget such excuses — you must not lay this charge upon others, least of all on me." He looks Jeff in the eye and speaks seriously, "There is very little time left now for you to complete your challenge," he warns. "You must choose quickly who you will serve …Return the scroll or destroy it while you still can."

⌘

24

ASTRAY FROM GRACE

J eff admits that Hunahpu's words have gotten to him, forcing him to take stock of his actions. In this brief moment of clarity, he knows that the only correct course is to complete his original mission — the artifacts have to be destroyed. After closing the bedroom door, he reopens the secret tower entrance with that mission in mind.

As soon as he sees the Scroll, however, his resolve melts like warmed snow; instead of securing it, he finds himself cradling it in his arms. *It couldn't hurt to read just one more of the mysterious oracles*, he thinks to himself. *Just one more look before destroying them.* He realizes the insincerity in his words, yet, in a classic denial of his own motives, he uses them nonetheless to justify his actions.

Just as before, he becomes quickly engrossed in the treacherous text. The words of the Scroll seem to wrap themselves around his mind and heart, drawing him in deeper and deeper, and before he knows it, several more hours have passed. The thought of destroying the ancient objects becomes more and more inconceivable ...he needs *more* time with them, he anxiously tells himself — they have to be

168 | THE DRAGON'S TAIL

studied! The answers they hold to the deepest mysteries of the universe are far too valuable to destroy!

IT IS THEN that a new idea strikes him: Cerdic had discovered the way to keep the Ring's power in check ...he built this entire castle for that purpose! If the castle's design could restrain the Ring, then why couldn't it be used to do the same for the Scepter and Scroll as well? The artifacts don't have to be destroyed, he argues to himself — they can be secured!

The fact that Barry's secret vault was already far more secure than Cerdic's capsule never enters Jeff's entranced mind. In fact, his thinking is uncharacteristically devoid of logic. In a clearer state of mind, he would have easily seen the truth, but his heart is not seeking truth. He is seduced by the idea of *keeping* the objects, even if it means willfully blinding his own eyes with this self-deception.

Besides, even if he wanted to speak the words that opened the portal, he can no longer remember them; they are forgotten — hidden away among the deeply repressed recesses of his subconscious mind.

IT IS NOW past ten thirty in the morning, and Jeff begins to hatch a plan for moving the artifacts to Cerdic's capsule. Working with the urgency of an obsessed man, he begins to piece together the moves and preparations needed, carefully recalling the blueprint of Cerdic's design. He thinks through the sequence in the old blueprints for opening the containment capsule and calculates that it should be large enough to hold all three objects.

Turning his attention then to the transfer itself, he realizes that he needs a way to access the main rotunda's capsule without anyone seeing him. He will need to get everyone out of the castle ...it will need to be evacuated; not only that, but somehow, the security cameras will also need to be disabled. Just as importantly, it has to be done without arousing suspicion.

After considering several options, he calculates that a reboot of the castle's surveillance systems, together with a well-timed evacuation, should give him just enough cover to access the capsule without being seen. A simple fire alarm wouldn't do, however. That would leave the security guards patrolling the castle; he needs to ensure that no one remains inside.

He remembers how everyone had been evacuated to the underground shelter when they were attacked; EB had simply issued an order to ABBI using *'emergency code Alpha.'* Jeff knows it will not be hard for the others to trace the order back to him, but he decides it is still the most viable plan. A cover story begins to take shape in his mind, adding to the web of deceit that he has already begun to weave.

ON THE BRIDGE of the approaching command ship, the evil duo stands side by side, examining their preparations.

"We will be approaching the hidden cavern in less than an hour," Eblis informs his brother.

"Excellent; prepare the landing party," Chesed commands with a satisfied grin.

Eblis reaches for the amulet around his neck, holding it in one hand as he presses the large ring on his other hand into it. His eyes close in concentration as his lips whisper a strange incantation, and the amulet begins to glow softly.

In both of the ships' holds, row after row of the dormant warriors suddenly stir from their deathly sleep and eerily rise from the cold steel slabs. They form long straight lines, standing silently at attention, shoulder to shoulder.

"Helmsman, switch to manual control," Chesed orders; "maintain maximum depth; we must not be detected."

GENIE HAS SPENT over an hour on her knees imploring Heaven on Jeff's behalf, then makes her way to his suite to check on him.

Hunahpu and Isabel are in the sitting room when she enters; their concerned expressions worry her as she sits down beside them.

"Did you speak to him?" she asks Hunahpu urgently.

"It is as I feared," he says gravely. "He will need our prayers more urgently than ever, I'm afraid."

Genie doesn't know anything about the Scroll, but the words from Hunahpu's disclosure ring in her mind. They resonate ominously in light of the evil that she already has personally experienced at the hands of the Eljo ...what could be more evil than that? Yet Hunahpu's words hinted that the Eljo were a small threat compared to what Jeff now faces.

"I should go see him ...to help him. I can talk to him!"

"Nothing, any of us, can say will sway him," Hunahpu explains sadly. "It will require a far stronger power to help him now."

"We can't just leave him like this!" she objects. "Isn't there *somethin'* we can do to help him ...to save him?"

"What he faces is a very treacherous evil," Hunahpu cautions. "It would be too dangerous for any of us to be exposed to its power."

"I'm not afraid o' danger," Genie declares honestly, "if there's a way t' fight it, then I have to try!"

"Indeed, you are fearless, my dear," Hunahpu commends her, "but this power cannot be defeated with blows or weapons. It is a bondage of the soul."

"With what then?!" she asks helplessly. "...How?"

"The battle is now Jeffrey's ...it is his alone."

Genie silently studies Hunahpu's face, seeking assurance in his eyes that Jeff will be okay. Hoping that the wise old man has some feeling ...some premonition ...that Jeff has a chance. "Is he strong enough?" she finally asks hopefully.

"It is not *strength* that he must find within himself, Hunahpu answers. "**He must find surrender ...complete and absolute surrender.**"

Genie understands. She watches the old man as he drops from his chair onto his knees, following him, as Isabel does the same. The three of them clasp hands as they kneel together and begin to pray.

EB wishes he had flown a Dibjet to London rather than taking a small corporate jet. The plane's pilots are doing their best to return quickly while following their flight path and obeying air traffic control directions. He has already emphasized to them that he is in an urgent hurry, but even if he had wanted to, he could not explain the real reason for his urgency. He fidgets in his seat and glances at his watch anxiously.

"Can we go any faster?" he asks, looking over the pilots' shoulders from his seat behind them.

"I'm afraid this is only a commercial plane, not a fighter jet," his pilot answers, trying to make a joke. He clears his throat awkwardly when EB doesn't register any hint of a smile, "...We should be there a few minutes early; we're ahead of schedule."

EB looks at his phone to see if Genie has sent him any messages; nothing yet. He sits staring out the side window, watching the British Isles slowly pass below them. His thoughts are filled with a jumble of fears and painful memories — about the Scroll and the toll it had taken years before, when their chief linguistic scientist had tried to examine it. The poor man had been a close friend ...EB was the one who found him after he had been driven mad and committed suicide. He closes his eyes and breathes an urgent prayer for Jeff, unaware that he is joining Genie and the others in prayer at that same moment.

Jeff checks his watch; it is nearly 11:30 AM.

HE REVIEWS HIS PLAN, going over it again in his head.

In his bedroom's secret nook, he kneels beside the open case, gently placing the Scroll inside and running his fingers over its golden surface in admiration. Once the case has been securely closed and is standing upright, he attaches the avatar's lifting device and guides the heavy case into the elevator. Moments later, he exits the elevator cabin into the darkened well beneath the tower, leaving the Scroll behind.

From there, he moves quickly through the underground tunnel toward the central domed chamber and wastes no time climbing up the stairs to the secret bathroom entrance — making sure as he exits the bathroom that the security camera above its door still points away, obscuring any view of his entry into the Hall. He climbs the Rotunda's large marble staircase silently, listening carefully for the sound of anyone approaching. To his relief, there is no sign of Hunahpu or Eugenia, allowing him to slip through the courtyard outside his own residence and duck quickly into the foyer of Barrymore's suite.

Once inside, he stops and breathes a sigh of relief at having made it this far undetected; his heart is beating wildly as he leans back against the door and catches his breath, finding the suite dark and empty, as he had hoped. Turning his attention to the suite's Study, he makes his way down the hall and is soon seated behind his uncle's desk, where he switches on the computer. It doesn't take him long to access the castle's surveillance system — EB had granted him Admin rights to it, along with most of the castle's other systems. With a few commands, he initiates a complete diagnostic of the system's servers, knowing that in exactly ten minutes, the process will lead to a full system-wide shutdown and restart, followed by a slow series of camera-by-camera diagnostics before initiating a second full restart. The entire process will keep the system offline for at least twenty minutes. He locks the user account while still logged in, preventing anyone else from aborting the program.

He checks his watch, registering the time: 11:41.

⌘

25

FALLEN DEFENSES

The dark ships glide slowly closer to the island's northern undersea cliff face, heading straight for the base of a plunging waterfall. In a single file, the ships cut into its turbulent wash without slowing, emerging on the other side in a deep, uncharted pool. Rising to the pool's surface, they come to a stop at a narrow beach.

"Quickly, warriors!" Chesed cries out over the ships' intercom, using the ancient Latin commands of a Roman officer: "Forma - Ad signa! Mandata captate!" (*Fall in! Await my command!*)

Swirls of filtered sunlight coming through the waterfall wash the scene in a surreal spectacle as the brothers step onto the hidden pool's sandy shore to inspect their grotesque troops. The scout who had earlier confirmed the passage's secrecy leads the way, entering a pitch-black tunnel in the surrounding rocky cliff; bright lights switch on around them as the brothers follow closely, with their eerie battalion entering behind them.

IT HAS TAKEN ONLY a few minutes for Jeff to let himself into Barry's hidden passage, and he soon stands in front of the vault's access panel, punching in the coded coordinates. The stone wall behind him seals, and the vault's door slowly begins to lift.

He looks at his watch impatiently as he waits for it to open: 11:44.

Jeff's eyes adjust painfully to the vault's bright white interior as he enters; he grabs the Scepter's narrow case by its shoulder strap, slinging it onto his back, and then retrieves the small reinforced box that holds the Ring, stuffing it into the cloth bag he is carrying. Moving to the vault's rear door, he presses his palm against its access panel, opening it, and then rushes through. It takes another full minute for the small tunnel's outside door to slide open, letting him exit into the underground passageway.

It's 11:47 when he reaches the elevator to retrieve the Scroll.

The avatar's lifting device allows it to glide easily as Jeff pulls it from the elevator cabin and then down the dark tunnel toward the center of the castle. He's moving in a near run when he reaches it, then he checks his watch again: 11:50. Pulling his O-P from his pocket, he speaks into it urgently:

"CHET ...CONNECT ME WITH ABBI ...HURRY!"
A second later, he hears ABBI's voice:
What is it, Sir? The computer attendant asks responsively.
"Alert all personnel to evacuate to the subterranean shelter imme-diately, *emergency code Alpha!*" he declares, mimicking the same words that EB had spoken on the day they were first attacked. Just as before, alert lights began to flash throughout the castle and a low siren begins to wail; Abbi's voice can be heard throughout the complex calmly instructing occupants to make their way to the emergency elevators.

At practically the same instant, the castles' surveillance systems go offline.

EUGENIA REACTS QUICKLY to the evacuation alarm, rushing from Jeff's suite as she contacts her security team.

"We've been hacked!" she warns as she hears about the loss of their surveillance systems. "Who ordered the evacuation?" she asks in alarm.

"We're still trying to determine that," they answer, obviously rattled by the surprising chain of events.

"Well, until we know more, proceed with the evacuation! Make sure everyone gets below!" she orders.

She suddenly thinks of Jeff, assuming that he is still in his room, and turns back to his suite to get him. Isabel is in the suite's hallway with a frantic look on her face.

"I knocked and knocked, but he doesn't answer …I think something terrible has happened to him!" she cries.

"I'll get Jeff," Eugenia promises, "Get down t' the shelter …don't wait for me!" She quickly looks around, searching the study, "Where is Hunahpu?" she asks Isabel with concern.

"I don't know …I think he left while I was upstairs," Isabel answers in a worried voice.

"Okay, that's fine …go ahead. I'll check here."

Genie makes her way up the stairs, checking rooms as she goes - there is no sign of Hunahpu. She knocks hard on Jeff's door and waits for an answer, then pounds harder still. When he still doesn't answer, she takes a step back and gives the locked door a swift kick that splinters the door-jamb, sending the door smashing into the wall as it violently swings open.

She searches the entire bedroom suite, finding no sign of him.

THE MALEVOLENT INVASION team cautiously approaches an ancient stone entry door, knowing that on the other side lies Leanan Sidhe's crypt. Eblis runs his fingers over the Latin engravings in the stone before turning his attention to the hidden keystones in the wall beside it — first locating and pressing on a round stone bearing the Niergel crest, then finding a square stone a few feet away, and finally the triangle; the heavy stone door rumbles as it slowly slides aside for the first time in a thousand years. The brothers wave forward a cohort of Eljo scouts, who enter first; one of them then returns to report that it is safe to enter. Within the crypt, scattered bones of the demon's long-dead victims glow eerily under the invading party's bright lights.

The crypt's secret door slowly closes behind them as they make their way up the ancient stone staircase and into the musty Vault of Archives. The brothers seem surprised to find its plush furnishings and extensive volumes. Chesed stops to examine the old logs that serve as the library's directory, then waves at the vault's contents dismissively and orders his troops to move on.

Eblis, meanwhile, is examining the ornate wooden door, matching it with his father's description. He looks to the wall on his left and finds the old torch mount — a relic of the vault's ancient past, then attempts to push it upward, but it remains frozen in place. He nods to the huge Eljo figure standing beside him and watches as it easily raises the jammed fixture, causing the door to slide open.

JEFF BEGINS to make his way up the secret staircase in no particular hurry; he is allowing time for the castle's evacuation. Finally, maneuvering the Scroll's large case through the bathroom opening — a feat that proves to be a bit of a challenge but is managed after several tries — he emerges into the private stall.

He checks his watch again: fifteen minutes remain for him to deposit the artifacts.

He pushes open the door of the stall and moves his dangerous cargo out into the Hall, and then into the open Rotunda. The controls for opening the capsule are just where the blueprints said they would be. He presses on a section of the marble chair rail, moving it inward an inch or so, then leans against the polished stone wall panel beside it, causing it to open with a click. The hinged panel reveals a small compartment — inside, Jeff finds a pair of chains wrapped through pulleys. Brushing away centuries of cobwebs, he pulls down on the chain nearest him and sees the round slab in the center of the Rotunda floor rise an equal distance. He is amazed at how easily it lifts, an obvious testament to the perfectly balanced counterweight system that the castle's builders designed. Using both hands, he begins to pull hand-over-hand until the cylindrical capsule's full height has been revealed.

HE WALKS TO IT QUICKLY, finds the latch, and pulls it open. Just as depicted in the blueprint, a pair of bars rises in the center of the capsule on which a shelf is mounted, where the Ring's wooden box once sat. Jeff pauses to study the capsule's interior, determining the best way of fitting the artifacts inside.

⌘

26

SURRENDER

E ugenia has no idea where Jeff has gone nor how he'd gotten out of his room unnoticed, but her worry has begun to give way to annoyance. While his closest friends have been worrying and praying for him all morning, he has had the nerve to slink off without even the decency to let them know if he is all right! Heading for his suite's front door, she pulls out her phone and hits speed dial, calling his number as she pushes the suite's door open.

To HER SURPRISE, she hears his phone's ringtone ...not through her handset, but in the Rotunda. The echo of it reverberates in the circular marble hall, making it hard to tell exactly where it is coming from. She holds her phone to her ear, waiting for him to answer as she creeps closer to the upper rotunda's thick marble railing, but is shocked to hear the call quickly disconnect instead. Now feeling more annoyed than ever, she quietly peeks downward through the thick marble spindles, careful to remain unnoticed. She can see him working on something in the center of the floor, but can't make out what it is.

She silently darts to the doorway of Cornelius' vacant suite and hides in its ornate arches where she can see him more clearly. Her eyes widen as he opens the large case and lifts its contents into the air. Its golden handles and pristine parchment appear to glow — it mesmerizes her as she stares at it, motionless.

JEFF CAREFULLY PLACES the Scroll into the open capsule, spreading it to wrap slightly around the upright bars at its center. Next, he pulls the scepter's case off his shoulder and places it into the capsule on the opposite side, admiring how well it fits with a satisfied grin. He finally reaches into the bag and pulls out the bulky case containing the ring, then reaches in again and takes out Cerdic's wooden ring box. Lying both boxes side-by-side on top of the capsule, he opens them and carefully lifts the Ring between his fingers.

It is more amazing than he ever imagined. Its bright golden surface and large stone are hypnotic in their beauty. He can feel its power pulsing through his fingers and rushing to his beating heart …it makes him feel vibrant and alive! More alive than he has ever felt before!

"*IT IS BEAUTIFUL, ISN'T IT*," the words echo through the Rotunda in a voice that reeks of slithering evil.

Jeff is jolted by a sudden, stabbing fear as a rush of emotion seizes him — a complex mix of anger, greed, and fear. He recognizes the voice; although he has never heard it before, he knows its nature — he recognizes its essence of pure evil. In his mind's seduced state, his first impulse is to seize the artifacts as his own; he instinctively tries to slide the Ring onto his finger — to use it against the sudden threat. As he turns to look up, however, he is quickly frozen in place by the terrifying sight above him.

High above the marble Rotunda floor, he sees Genie hanging in midair — a dark swirling mist is squeezing her by the throat as her feet kick, trying to reach the third-floor railing several feet below and behind her; she is gasping for air. Chesed stands behind her with a gloating expression while Eblis leads a swarm of Eljo monsters down the staircase to where Jeff stands.

"Let her go!" Jeff shouts threateningly as he holds the Ring poised at the end of his finger.

"GO AHEAD ...PUT IT ON," Chesed taunts, "KNOW THAT THE MOMENT YOU WEAR IT, YOUR REIGN AS MANTLE BEARER IS ENDED ...IT WILL BE MY GREAT PLEASURE TO WATCH YOUR DOWNFALL ...AND THE END OF THE NIERGEL."

IN HIS ENRAGED state of mind, Jeff doesn't care about the Niergel or his appointment as Mantle Bearer; he wants only to crush the gloating fiend standing above him and free Eugenia by force. He holds the Ring to his finger and tries to push it on, but for some reason, he can't ...his hands refuse!

Eblis smirks at Jeff's futile effort as he walks toward him, but then stops short — something seems to hold him back, as though an invisible wall stands between them. The Eljo forces encircle Jeff but cannot approach his position.

Jeff suddenly realizes that something is protecting him. Wondering if it is Cerdic's wooden box — the box that was carved from the Shepherd's Staff — he picks it up and waves it closer to them. Eblis snarls and grips the pendant around his neck, making it glow more brightly, but the Eljo troops remain immobile.

Jeff looks up at Genie again — the Smokey tendrils that hold her are allowing her short gasps of air, enough to keep her conscious, but she is slowly losing consciousness. She holds herself still, realizing that any sudden movements could cause her to snap her own neck.

"LET HER GO!" Jeff repeats, holding the wooden box up toward Chesed.

Chesed lifts his bony hands and slowly claps in a mocking gesture. "RELEASE HER?," he taunts, "...I RATHER LIKE HER, ACTUALLY.

SHE COULD BE A DELIGHTFUL ADDITION TO MY BAND OF WARRIORS — NOT ALIVE, OF COURSE." His cold eyes stare down at Jeff cruelly as he continues, *"HAND OVER THE RING AND SCEPTER, AND I WILL CONSIDER SPARING HER LIFE.*

He moves his head to the side, catching a glimpse inside the open capsule as he slowly rubs his hands together in delighted anticipation. *"IF THERE WAS SOMETHING ELSE FOR WHICH TO TRADE, HOWEVER,"* he adds in a sly voice, *"...SOMETHING EVEN MORE VALUABLE ...WELL, THAT COULD BE AN EXCHANGE WORTH MAKING."*

JEFF CAN SEE Genie's eyes rolling back, and her movements are becoming weaker and increasingly jerky — he knows she doesn't have much time.

"Release her ...let her breathe, and we'll talk about it," Jeff shouts, trying to buy time.

"YOUR SENTIMENT IS YOUR FAILING — IT MAKES YOU WEAK." Chesed raises a hand toward Genie, and the grip on her throat tightens even further, squeezing the life out of her.

"NO! STOP! PLEASE ...DON'T KILL HER! ALRIGHT! ...Alright! I'll hand them over. Just let her down."

Jeff places the Ring on top of the capsule and raises his empty hand, showing that he isn't holding it. "You can come take it ...take all of it." He looks behind him, "I'll back away," he says, carrying Cerdic's box with him, "...set her down over there." He points to the opposite side of the Rotunda, near the wall, as he makes his way toward the spot.

The Eljo hordes split apart as Jeff moves — as if a force surrounding him is pushing them back. Genie's limp, unconscious body is lowered to the place he requested, still dangling by her neck. Jeff reaches there just in time to catch her as she is dropped the remaining few feet, like a discarded rag.

. . .

CHESED, meanwhile, lifts his arms out to his sides as a black mist engulfs him, carrying him over the railing and gently lowering him three stories to the floor below. The fire in his eyes reflects his lust for power as he takes hold of the Ring and immediately slides it onto his finger. He closes his eyes, and his head tilts backward as a great rush runs through him; then he holds his ringed hand toward the capsule, causing the Scepter to break free from its case and fly to him.

It surprises Jeff to see the Scepter fly in the same way that the Shepherd's Staff had. Chesed presents the Scepter to Eblis with a gloating smile. *"MY BROTHER, BASK IN OUR VICTORY!"* he expounds as Eblis takes the Scepter. *"TODAY WE ARE RETURNED TO OUR RIGHTFUL PLACE ...AS GUARDIANS OF THE MYSTERIES — SERVANTS OF OUR LORD SEMJAZA, SON OF THE DRAGON!"*

Chesed then reaches into the capsule and lifts the Scroll triumphantly as the enormity of the horrible truth dawns on Jeff... it's over — he has *failed*. He looks down at Genie's unconscious body in his arms as absolute hopelessness overwhelms him. He is powerless to stop them, and there is nothing anyone else can do — none of them can fight the Eljo. Because of him, the Maranish brothers now have not only the Ring and Scepter but the Scroll of the gods as well! There will be no stopping them!

Jeff carefully lays Genie down on the floor and bravely stands as he sees the brothers turn to face him. He knows what is coming next as Eblis raises the Scepter toward him — he is about to face the same fate that his parents suffered. But he hardly cares — he is haunted by the sense of complete and utter failure; he has betrayed everyone who trusted in him, ...everything they fought for, ...and soon they all will suffer the same fate that he now faces.

A single tear fills his eye and rolls down his cheek as he closes his eyes and awaits the inevitable, deadly blast. Just as he does, a vivid memory rushes through his mind. He recalls something Colby Abbott said in Sunday's sermon — it jars him soberly....

When you find yourself in that same condition — and most certainly you will one day- tell your Savior of the grief that distracts you, of the

woe that overwhelms you. Confess your sins, acknowledge your
inability to rescue yourself, and cast yourself immediately upon the
gracious promise of the loving God!

Jeff feels tears escape his eyes as he silently breathes a prayer, begging for forgiveness. It is a prayer of genuine contrition, a prayer of repentance, …a prayer of complete and absolute *surrender*.

SOMETHING strange suddenly surges within him, catching him by surprise. He feels an odd anticipation — it is an *unexpected* confidence, …an irrational boldness that seems to fill him at this unlikeliest of moments. He opens his tear-filled eyes to see a tormented and frustrated look on the evil brothers' faces. Their attack on him has failed — the Ring and Scepter appear powerless to harm him. He remembers Huahpu's words the day they learned how Arubija had become immune to the Ring's power, wondering how anyone could compel God to provide such protection: '...*He has already made His choice.*'

SUDDENLY, **Hunahpu's voice** echoes in the cavernous Rotunda as he urgently shouts to Jeff.

"CHURI! — QAMPA K'ASPI!" ...*My Son! — Your Staff!*

JEFF LOOKS UPWARD with shock to see his great-grandfather standing on the stairs above him and tossing the Shepherd's Staff into the air. Jeff reaches for it, catching it as it flies instantly into his hand.

Before he can stop them, however, Jeff sees a flash of light from Chesed's Scepter and looks back to Hunahpu, screaming — "NOOOOOOOOOOOOOO!" as his great-grandfather is engulfed in a brilliant flash and crumbles onto the staircase as a pile of ash.

· · ·

THE SHOCK of Hunahpu's death fills Jeff's soul with an inexpressible fury — it suddenly ignites within him like an inferno, causing the words that have been suppressed in his subconscious mind to erupt from his lips. He lifts the Shepherd's Staff in front of him with both hands and shouts the ancient words at the top of his lungs in perfect enunciation and with the authority of a man possessed with Heaven itself!

The thunder crack that splits the air shakes the entire castle as an enormous lightning bolt shoots upward from the tip of the Staff and through the skylight, splitting into three as it strikes the tops of all three towers. With a deafening roar, the hellish portal splits the air above them, completely filling the ceiling of the huge Rotunda above their heads — so large that the heat of its boiling magma and raging fire nearly burns Jeff's skin. Its hot red glow reflects off the visors of a hundred armor-clad Eljo warriors as they begin being pulled upward, thrashing frantically as they are sucked toward the opening. Their host corpses disintegrate as they cross the portal threshold, and Jeff can hear the painful screeches of the misty black creatures as they are pulled into its raging fire.

Chesed and Eblis at first cling to the Scepter and Scroll, but then try desperately to release them as they find themselves being pulled into the air behind their Eljo slaves. They thrash and kick wildly in an attempt to free themselves, but are quickly pulled higher toward the terrifying portal. Jeff watches the horrific sight as both men's hideous bodies are consumed in the portal crossing, leaving only the ancient objects themselves to be pulled into the molten fires of Tir Lai.

Jeff finally shouts the command for the portal's closing and collapses to his knees, planting the Staff on the floor in front of him and clinging to it for support. Nothing remains of the evil brothers or their invading force. The ancient artifacts are gone — destroyed once and for all in the eternal fires that forged them.

HE TURNS BACK TOWARD GENIE, kneeling as he scoops her into his arms. Through tears, he sees EB running toward them and looks into his old friend's face, weighed down by his crushing shame and remorse. With the fog gone from his mind, his reawakened conscience accuses him loudly... his own shameful disobedience and deceit caused this tragedy. He looks at Genie lying limp and badly injured, ...and is also stabbed with the realization that his beloved great-grandfather is gone.

EB checks on his granddaughter and then quickly turns to Jeff.

"...*Hunahpu*..." Jeff says mournfully as his eyes cloud with more tears.

"I saw what happened...." EB interrupts to save Jeff from the pain of saying more, "...I saw it all."

Jeff bows his head in grief, and EB places a hand reassuringly on his shoulder. The flood of pain that washes over Jeff is more than he can bear; he breaks down and weeps bitterly.

⌘

27

BROKEN

J eff has been sitting beside Genie's hospital bed for hours. EB sits on the opposite side of her bed, holding her hand. The nearby monitors are reassuringly reporting strong vital signs despite her injuries. Her neck and throat are badly bruised and swollen, including a partially crushed esophagus, and this time, her recently healed collarbone has been broken. Yet, miraculously, she has no other injuries. Jeff closes his eyes and breathes a prayer for her recovery, grateful that her injuries are not more serious.

"Hey...," he suddenly hears her say in a hoarse voice.

He opens his tired eyes to see her groggy, half-asleep gaze looking over at him.

"Hey," he answers, his own voice reflecting a range of emotions that he can't begin to describe.

She takes in her surroundings, realizing where she is. She looks back and forth between her grandfather and Jeff.

"I'm sorry ...I was a bloody fool t' get caught like that..." she begins...

"You did nothing wrong!" Jeff says, standing to his feet. "It wasn't your fault..." he looks down at the floor, ashamed to look her in the eye — his heart is awash with regret, "...it was mine."

She looks into his eyes, reading the depth of his pain. "What is it? What happened?" she asks quietly.

Jeff fights back a swell of emotion as he hides his tears and turns quickly, then leaves the room.

GENIE LOOKS at her grandfather with a shake of her head, signaling that she doesn't understand.

EB squints his eyes as he braces himself to say the words he deeply eschews; his grief is heartrending as he softly explains: "They killed Hunahpu."

Genie raises a hand to her mouth in disbelief, and her eyes quickly well with tears. As deeply as she grieves the loss of their dear friend, that grief is exceeded by the sorrow she feels for Jeff; her heart breaks for him.

She finally looks toward the door after struggling for a few moments to regain control; "Oh dear God... poor Jeff...."

EB nods silently. "He watched it happen but couldn't prevent it — he blames himself."

"That must have been so hard for him...." Genie says with a genuinely wounded heart.

After a silent pause, she looks back at EB; "What happened? How?"

"It was the Scepter," EB simply explains with deep sadness.

Genie closes her eyes with a look of anguish. "I can't imagine what that must have been like for Jeff," she confesses, glancing back toward the door where he had gone out. "Dear Lord... oh Jeff."

After a sullen silence, she lifts her gaze back to EB curiously; "The last thing I remember was bein' choked... I guess I blacked out." Her hand finds her forehead as she pieces together her fractured memories. "We were hopelessly outnumbered ...I thought we were done for sure." With a perplexed gaze at her grandfather, she looks for the missing piece. "What stopped them?"

"Jeff did. It was the most astonishin' thing I've ever seen; I never would believe it if I hadn't witnessed it with my own eyes." He thinks for a moment about how to describe what he saw, then simply says: "No description could do it justice; you'll have a chance to see it fer yerself — the cameras came back on in time to record it."

Genie shakes her head. "But there were so many of them; how did they get in? They surprised me from behind — from inside Cornelius' suite," she reveals, trying to understand the puzzle.

EB nods. "Aye, we pieced that together from footprints in the suite's main hallway. The tracks led to the Vault of Archives; there must be a secret tunnel there that we didn't know about. It's a pity that the security cameras were offline." He pauses for a moment as he considers whether to reveal Jeff's involvement in that detail, but decides against it. "We're undertakin' a search of the island perimeter to locate their ship."

Genie starts to get up, but grabs her neck in pain as soon as she tries to lift her head, realizing how swollen it is.

"Ye need to sit tight, Lassie," EB chides her, "Ye've got a good team — let 'em do what Ye've trained 'em t' do."

She looks at her grandfather in frustration and nods reluctantly, knowing he is right.

AFTER LEAVING THE HOSPITAL, Jeff wanders out onto the castle grounds and makes his way to the bench where he had often found Hunahpu sitting. He remembers in hindsight how his great-grandfather had been spending more and more time on this bench, especially in the last few weeks. In all that time, it had somehow escaped Jeff's notice that the small monument a short distance away marks a set of flat stones with names engraved in their polished granite surfaces; it took EB's pointing it out to him. The names are of Jeff's mother and father, *Jeffrey and Katrina Sutherland-Hastleworth*, along with an older stone engraved twenty years earlier — bearing the name of Jeff's grand-mother, Lydia. Beside Lydia's is another stone engraved with Cornelius' name.

Beneath each stone, EB had explained, is a sealed capsule containing their ashes, which had been carefully collected from the spot where each of them died. The ashes of Katrina's father, Aeden, had been buried beside his predeceased wife.

Surrounded by floral wreaths, the sealed titanium capsule containing Hunahpu's ashes stands prominently on a small stand in front of the granite stones. Jeff kneels, lifts it, then settles on the bench, holding it in his hands. He is feeling wracked with guilt.

"You tried to warn me," he confesses, speaking to his memory of the kind old man, "but I wouldn't listen." A fresh tear runs down Jeff's cheek. "I'm so sorry... I'm so, so sorry..." more tears follow, forcing him to wipe his eyes and then to lean forward as his body briefly shakes with sobs. When the brief outpouring has subsided, he sits up again, lifting his eyes to the horizon. He remembers watching Hunahpu stare in the same way countless times, but never truly understood its attraction until now.

A FRIENDLY VOICE catches his ear; Eusebios Christos is standing just behind him. Jeff glances back to see the kind-hearted missionary staring contemplatively out over the sea.

"Such a wonder of God's creation, isn't it?" he asks Jeff rhetorically. "The sea is truly a beautiful thing — she gives her bounties to man — a sight to behold. But she takes life too; who can stand against her when her fury is aroused?" He looks down at Jeff and back at the sea as he silently walks around the bench, sitting down beside him. "Yet she still knows the voice of the one who calmed her when he walked among us."

Jeff nods politely and follows his gaze, admiring the view, though he doesn't fully follow his point.

"That voice still speaks," Dr. Christos continues, "no matter how severe the storm that rages, His voice still calms the troubled sea; He is still its Master."

Jeff considers those words as he looks down at the capsule in his hands; "It's ironic, ...I spent all my life until recently denying that God even existed — insisting that life and death were just the results of random, meaningless probabilities. But now..." he pauses gripping the capsule tightly, "...now that I truly know Him ...I'm wrestling with His choices."

He turns to Christos with a pleading look; "Hunahpu didn't deserve what happened. Of everyone, he was the one who deserved it the least!" Jeff's knuckles are turning white as he struggles with the thought, "God chose to protect *me* ...the one who *failed* and *denied* Him. But He let Hunahpu die."

"You're looking for fairness," Christos notes, "God has never promised fairness." His comment draws Jeff's gaze with a look of confusion. "You are perhaps confusing fairness with justice," Christos explains, "God is Just, that is true, yet He is also merciful. That mercy led Him to the Cross so His Justice could be satisfied." Christos leans forward as he speaks softly, "Christ took *our* punishment ...was that fair?"

He straightens and looks out over the sea again as he sighs, "This is a broken world ...I have seen the evil that men can do." Looking back at Jeff again, he continues, "While we remain here, it is our duty to fight against such evil. It is a fight! And it is not a fair fight!"

Jeff looks down, his heart deeply troubled by the inescapable shame and remorse that haunt him. "What if we are the one who is evil?" he asks Christos. "How can a man fight himself?

"Ah, my friend," Christos says, comfortably assuming his lifelong role as a Pastor. "Evil is bound in the heart of every man ...we are a cursed race. That's why it took an act of God as drastic as the Cross; His breaking of the curse has paid our debt, but it has not yet purged our cursed nature from us. Not here, not yet."

"But if our evil remains, how are we any better than them?" Jeff asks doubtfully.

"We are not better; we are only sons. His adoption of us was without merit on our part, and our standing is because of what we *are* and not what we have done; what matters is **what He has made us** ... we are heirs of His promise ...we are His sons." His voice reveals an intensity in his spirit that belies the gentleness of his words. He sits quietly for a moment as they both watch the glistening sea caps. When he speaks again, it is more with the familiar tone of a friend than the exhortation of a preacher.

"It was with the greatest joy that I learned of your salvation; Hunahpu was thrilled to tell me of it." He looks at Jeff reassuringly, "Your faith is still young, God's work in you will take time, but it *will* change you. You cannot help but be changed when walking in His presence."

"I just hope that I can manage to stay there …in His presence," Jeff says honestly.

"You cannot hope to leave it," Christos corrects him, "He is with you always; never forget this."

Jeff continues to struggle; "I just feel so …guilty," he confides, feeling more comfortable sharing his deepest torments. "It was all my fault; I was trying to hide the artifacts — I knew it was wrong...I was deliberately disobeying what I knew was right. If I hadn't done that, Chesed and Eblis would never have had the Scepter …and Hunahpu would still be alive. I don't deserve to lead anyone; I don't deserve to be the mantle bearer."

Christos listens quietly, then speaks in an understanding voice.

"All these are thoughts about yourself. You will never find comfort and assurance by looking within yourself. Remember, it is not your *own* merit that saves you — it is Christ's; likewise, it is not your *hold* of Christ that saves you — it is Christ; it is not even your faith that does the saving — it is Christ and Christ alone. It is the truth of what *He* is, and not what *we* are, that gives rest to our souls."

He looks at the capsule in Jeff's hands and places his own hand on top of Jeff's; "Hunahpu is now rejoicing in the company of beloved friends and his dear Savior. He lived his days and has earned his well-deserved reward. It is hard, but we must rejoice with him …we must let him go."

⌘

28

AFTERMATH

H ours later, EB reenters Genie's hospital room with news.
"We've discovered a hidden cavern behind the falls on
the northern shore — a sonar scan revealed it. Two Eljo
ships have been found inside, along with a tunnel that appears to lead
to the Crypt."

"Our team didn't open it, did they?" Genie asks with alarm.

"No, certainly not," he assures her. "If nothin' else, though, I dare
say the Maranish brothers were a darin' pair."

"And don't forget treacherously cruel and maniacally evil," Genie
adds.

"Indeed, the world is far better off without them; there is no doubt
of it," EB agrees.

"I take it the ships are empty?"

"That would appear to be the case. We'll study them where they
are until we know more; no sense takin' the risk of bringin' them into
the sub-level hangar."

"They are submarines? That explains how they arrived without bein' detected," Genie deduces. "We'll need to enhance our under-water defenses."

"Brandish is already working on it," EB informs her, "...he is talking about underwater microphones and sonar arrays, along with plans for a barrier to prevent anyone else from gettin' into that hidden cavern."

"Usin' an Anti-Gravity Curtain?" she asks.

"That would do, I suppose. Although it may be difficult to explain to tourists the sight of a waterfall flowin' upward." He smiles as she rolls her eyes at him.

THEY ARE INTERRUPTED by a knock at the door and turn to see Jeff and Isabel.

"Doctor Lebenberg has placed you on a puree diet," Jeff explains. "I don't mean to disparage our hospital food, but I thought you might appreciate some of Isabel's cooking."

Genie sits with her mouth agape as an entourage of waiters in formal uniforms follows them into the room, quickly covering her bed table with a linen tablecloth and setting it with a place setting of silver and crystal. Others arrange a table and chairs beside her bed and set them formally to match. To finish the room's transformation, a pair of candlesticks is added to the tables as the lights are dimmed, bathing the atmosphere in a warm glow.

Jeff invites EB to have a seat as he pulls out the chair beside him, and then Covered dishes are served to each of them. The waiters lift the silver covers from their plates to reveal whipped potato and spinach soufflés with veal pâté.

Bradford, the head waiter, waves toward Isabel as he announces the menu, adding: "For dessert, our chef has prepared homemade raspberry sherbet and her specialty, chocolate mousse."

Genie smiles at Jeff, anticipating the chance to finally finish the dessert that was interrupted several weeks prior.

EB accepts Jeff's invitation to ask a blessing for the meal; the room grows quiet as he remembers Hunahpu's faithful life and sacrifice, as well as the amazing deliverance that has been provided to them. Genie sees Jeff wipe a tear from his cheek as the prayer finishes.

It seems as though EB is in an unusual hurry — he finishes his meal in record time. The moment he is done, he rises from his seat and whispers something to Isabel.

"I'm afraid I need to be on my way for a prior appointment, he suddenly announces to everyone, excusing himself. My compliments on a truly marvelous meal, as usual."

"I'll accompany you, if you don't mind," Isabel suggests unexpectedly, "I have some cleaning up to do in the kitchen." Turning to Jeff, she smiles warmly and adds, "Bradford can assist with anything you need."

JEFF LOOKS at Genie as they both recognize what is happening. He can't help but be reminded of the antics EB and Hunahpu used to play when they were encouraging the two of them to spend time together. After they have left the room, Jeff looks up awkwardly from his lonely seat at the table, seeing Genie perched in her bed a foot or two above him. Without hesitation, he lifts his plate and places it on one end of her bedside table, carefully arranging things to make space. She smiles at him as she watches him take a bite standing up.

In seemingly no time, Bradford arrives with a stool for him to sit on; Jeff thanks him, then offers a toast, lifting his water glass. "To the best wait staff a hospital ever had," he says as Genie clinks her glass against his with an amused nod.

Bradford skillfully seems to disappear as the two of them share in conversation.

"Gran'da told me a little about what happened this afternoon; I confess that much of it is still a blur," she shares. "Are you okay?"

Jeff nods yes and sits quietly for a moment, swept up in his thoughts; he finally answers. "I remember Hunahpu telling me that his sharp memory had been both a blessing and a curse to him — I know exactly what he meant now. I remember every detail of what happened; it's as if I've watched it replay a hundred times in slow motion."

He looks at Genie uncomfortably with a serious look that reveals his deep regret; "I'm sorry, …it was my fault that you got hurt; I put you at terrible risk — you were nearly killed."

"You didn't put me at risk," she counters, "I don't recall *you* being the one hangin' me in mid-air. If anything, I'm the one who owes you an apology." She pauses uncomfortably and then continues, "I was … well …I was spyin' on you; it was wrong, I know. If I had had my wits, I should never have allowed myself to be taken by surprise like that."

"I figured that …the spying part, I mean," Jeff concedes. "You were right to do it; what I was doing was wrong. I deserved to be stopped."

"You didn't exactly invite those creeps here — it was a bloody invasion!" Genie argues. "You couldn't have known that would happen."

"That's the trouble," Jeff admits humbly, "…what would have happened if they didn't? I might have gotten away with keeping the artifacts …and remained enslaved by them — it would have meant failing the Quest and losing my place as mantle bearer. Maybe even the end of the Niergel!"

Genie considers that silently, realizing he is right, and he hadn't even mentioned that he would have lost his job at Hastleworth and forced the dissolution of the company. She keeps these thoughts to herself and breathes a silent prayer of thanks for the obvious answer to their prayers. After a short silence, she looks at Jeff with a sense of wonder and speaks quietly:

"What if it was God's plan all along — the whole thing? It's like He orchestrated it to have the Maranish brothers here; that's what broke the artifacts' spell on you and caused their destruction!"

The thought has an undeniable ring of truth, but it is not especially comforting to Jeff — it just makes him feel even worse that God had to take measures as drastic as those in order to wake him up.

"You may be right," he concedes, "I just hope I'm never the cause for Him to have to do anything like that again!"

"Somethin' tells me you've learned the lesson pretty well," she says in encouragement. "You certainly won't forget it.

"Speaking of not forgetting," she adds with a smile, changing the subject, "...I think I'm ready for that chocolate mousse now."

THE REST of the week passes quickly as a full investigation into the attack and its surrounding events is conducted. Jeff cooperates fully, sharing as much as he can without revealing the castle's deeper secrets. He admits to initiating the evacuation order and confesses to interfering with the surveillance system. As it turns out, the evacuation was deemed a brilliant move that prevented a greater loss of life. The surveillance incident is referred to the Board for their determination.

The Board members will begin arriving on Monday for Hunahpu's Tuesday Memorial service; it will be one week to the day from his tragic death.

⌘

29

BITTERSWEET

Jeff wakes early on Tuesday morning; truthfully, he barely slept. It's hard to believe a week has passed since the tragic events. The days have passed quickly as the investigation has kept him fully occupied.

Today is Hunahpu's Memorial Service — the thought of it lingers on Jeff's mind in a mix of sorrow and dread. He ignores his bedside clock, which shows he still has an hour before the alarm, and makes his way to the bathroom to get ready.

His activities have alerted ABBI that he is up early. Jeff is pleased, but no longer surprised, to find coffee waiting for him downstairs in a freshly brewed pot. He pours a cup of the strong dark roast and sips it black.

Glancing at the kitchen table, he notices his uncle's Bible; he has become accustomed to reading it there the past few mornings. Sliding into a seat, he opens it to the bookmark where he'd left off last.

He can't help recalling how he had been seated in the same spot early on the morning of his uncle Barry's Memorial service months earlier; he had gotten up early that day for Hunahpu's arrival. He thinks of the times he spent with his great-grandfather since then, replaying dozens of their conversations in his mind — especially one of their last, the night he shared with Jeff that he would be leaving soon.

Jeff releases a deep sigh as he stares out the kitchen's west-facing windows at the endless darkness of the early morning sky and the blackness of the colorless ocean. The familiar glow of orange light from the approaching sunrise gradually reflects off thousands of whitecaps; he loves the way the scene contrasts with the dark purple western sky.

His mind drifts to what Christos said to him about letting Hunahpu go. The words have become a solid anchor to him during the past week of raging turmoil.

WHILE HE CONTEMPLATES THESE THOUGHTS, his doorbell rings, and ABBI announces that EB is at the door. Jeff quickly invites him in, greeting him in the hallway with a hug.

"I suspected that you might be up early," EB says as he greets him. "I must confess that I didn't sleep much last night m'self."

He is dressed formally in a black suit and a pair of his signature high gloss shoes; Jeff puts on the teakettle and invites him to have a seat at the table. EB glances at the open Bible as he sits.

"I see you're readin' in the Psalms," he notes approvingly, "I always find comfort there as well."

Jeff nods as he carries a covered plate of Isabel's blueberry muffins to the table and lifts the glass cover off them, sliding a pair of plates in front of each of their places. He grabs one of the muffins and cracks it open as he sits down but doesn't take a bite. He doesn't seem to have much of an appetite.

"I'm glad to see Genie is feeling better," Jeff notes with genuine relief.

EB looks at him as if he intends to say something, but then reconsiders. "She is a hearty woman, like her grandmother," he says instead.

"I can certainly vouch for that," Jeff admits. "Since she's been out of the Infirmary, she hasn't taken a moment's rest. Between adding underwater defenses and piecing together a recap of the invasion, plus dinner together every night — not that I'm complaining, of course." Jeff's fondness for her is written clearly on his face as he speaks about her; EB can't help smiling as he recognizes it.

JEFF IS quiet for a moment and then speaks introspectively, "I can't help wondering if it might be a good thing if the Board were to vote against granting me permanent status," he suggests unexpectedly.

"What on earth are you sayin', Lad?" EB responds in surprise.

"Oh, I could still find something to do for the company, I'm sure," he explains, "maybe something at more of a peer level with Genie and the others."

It suddenly dawns on EB what Jeff is getting at; he considers it for a moment quietly and then follows the changing subject. "Did I ever mention that Gretchen was my subordinate when she first joined the company?"

His comment piques Jeff's curiosity, as EB knew it would. "No, I don't think you ever did. Was that in your undercover work?"

"Aye, we worked quite closely together — I trusted her implicitly, as she did me; that was extraordinarily helpful for both of us and valuable to the company, I might add. At least, that's what Barry always said, and I wholeheartedly agreed."

"Were you married at the time?" Jeff queries with increased interest.

"Not at first, but we knew we had feelin's for one another; it was no secret, to be honest. Workin' together so closely might have sped things along, in fact. The more time we spent together, the more we wanted — I'm sure you can imagine how that goes."

"The company, ...the Board, didn't have any objection?" Jeff probes. "Aren't there policies against fraternizing with subordinates and that sort of thing?"

"Certainly, harassment would not be tolerated, but there is no prohibition against mutual affection."

"Well, what about concerns of favoritism?"

"In some positions, that could become an issue, certainly," EB concedes, "but if it is the CEO position you are referrin' to, then there would be more than sufficient scrutiny to prevent anythin' improper."

Jeff is slightly taken aback when EB mentions the CEO position; he had somehow believed he was keeping his true question sufficiently concealed. EB smiles at his reaction.

"It is not a good idea for a man to wait too long to make his intentions known," he advises Jeff candidly. "His intended may not wait around forever, y'know."

Jeff's face reddens. He considers denying the fact but quickly concedes to himself that he and Genie do, in fact, have feelings for each other. It suddenly seems apparent that everyone except the two of them had already recognized that fact ...or maybe just one of them, himself.

ABBI ANNOUNCES ISABEL'S ARRIVAL, and Jeff checks his watch; it's six o'clock already. Isabel has gotten into the habit of having breakfast ready at six-thirty because of Jeff's seven o'clock workouts, and the habit has become the norm. When she arrives, she is surprised to see both men seated in the kitchen. In an instant, there is a steaming cup of tea sitting in front of EB, as if by magic. Jeff starts to get up to pour himself another cup of coffee, but is stopped short by Isabel standing beside him with the pot already in her hand.

By seven o'clock, they are pushing back from the table after a delicious breakfast. EB smiles as he walks down the hall beside Jeff, placing a hand on his young friend's shoulder in a pat.

"I will say this," he confides, "a girl like Eugenia could use a good housekeeper to supplement her cookin' skills." From behind them, Isabel beams a delighted smile as she understands the thinly veiled meaning of the men's conversation.

EXITING THE SUITE, Jeff takes in the impressive sight of the castle's circular domed heart with its white marble balconies and twin staircases, noticing once more how the large stained glass dome catches the morning sunlight and bathes the space in multicolored hues. The Rotunda's welcoming design and white marble stand in stark contrast to Jeff's memory of what occurred here just a week ago.

They make their way to the Great Hall, where the other Board members are already assembling. Many of them had stayed the night to avoid traveling at daybreak. A long table down the center of the Hall has been set with a breakfast buffet where guests can help themselves.

General Zobrist greets them with condolences and accompanies them as they walk. Berenger is just emerging from the elevator as they approach it — he greets the others with hugs.

"Ol' Hunahpu will be dearly missed," he says to them, offering his sympathies.

Eugenia approaches as they are speaking, and the men greet her with a kiss on the cheek. Jeff is the last in line — she looks at him warmly as he kisses her cheek and then returns his greeting with a quiet "good morning." He can't help but be impressed by how well she appears to be recovering. Her conservative business suit and turtleneck hide the majority of her injuries. She is still nursing her broken collarbone with her left arm in a sling, but she conceals it cleverly inside her jacket.

"It was at a terrible price," Berenger says, acknowledging Eugenia's injuries and looking at the rest of them, "but we've gained a great deal of intelligence from their stranded ships."

He quietly provides an update on his engineering team's analysis. "We have eliminated any doubt that they were built using our designs," he confirms. "With only minor exceptions, they are a mirror copy. Our engineers are working with Brandish to exploit this to the greatest extent possible."

"Excellent; perhaps we can meet at Jeff's to discuss it in detail after the Board meeting," EB suggests. "It would be, well ...inappropriate to raise the topic with the full Board present." Jeff and the others quickly agree.

"Speaking of inappropriate conversations, where *is* Blandus?" Jeff asks.

"He sent word that he would not be attendin' the Memorial; he plans to arrive in time for the Board meetin' at one o'clock," EB explains.

"I'll station a detail outside to welcome him and his guards when they arrive," Zo offers.

"Good thinking," EB agrees.

THE ELEVATOR OPENS AGAIN, and a delegation from Peru emerges. Jeff recognizes several of its members from his Uncle Barry's Memorial service — he quickly excuses himself and goes to meet them.

"Ripuy Kaypi Wasinchik Allinpuni Ñoqa ka-ni," ...*Thank you for traveling; welcome to our house,* Jeff says as he greets them. He can see that several of them have been crying recently; the look of their pain hits Jeff hard — as much as he's been struggling to cope, he still blames himself for what happened.

"Kausayninchejqa llakiymanta, ñak'ariymanta junt'a," ...*It is a sorrowful time.* He adds in sympathy, his own eyes becoming clouded with moisture. Each of them hugs him, offering him words of comfort that touch Jeff deeply under the circumstances. An elderly woman lifts something from her bag and offers it to Jeff: a Quechua translation of the Bible.

"This belonged to your Grandmother, Lydia," the woman explains.

Jeff feels a tear run down his cheek as he accepts the gift, then hugs the woman gratefully. She smiles back at him and bows her head politely, and then rejoins the others in her group.

"Qan muna-nki Puriy Mikuy Ruraykapuway," ...*please, you must be hungry,* he offers, inviting them to have something to eat.

. . .

As JEFF LOOKS around at the growing crowd, the weight of Hunahpu's loss begins to hit him harder. He slips into an empty alcove just off the Hall, out of sight of the others, and drops down into a chair, unable to stop the sudden fountain of tears that has ambushed him by surprise. While he silently cries, he feels an arm wrap across his shoulders and recognizes Genie's embrace as she sits down beside him and leans her head against him.

"Ye can't blame yerself," she says as he self-consciously wipes his face and lifts his head.

"He warned me," Jeff confesses, drying his eyes. "He even told me that he knew he was going to die. I could have prevented it. How can I face everyone here knowing I'm responsible?"

"Ye don't know that," Genie argues. "If Chesed and Eblis hadn't found what they wanted in the Rotunda, they would have searched the castle for it — dozens of people could've been killed! Even you. God had a reason for allowin' what happened.

"What y' did was wrong and definitely stupid," she continues bluntly, "but look what God did in spite of it — the artifacts were destroyed, and the Maranish brothers are dead, along with their Eljo army, and we have their captured ships. I saw the security footage of what happened — it was a miracle! ...an amazing victory! I know Hunahpu would have wanted his death to count for somethin' — what could be greater than that?"

Jeff looks at her appreciatively as he regains his composure. "EB is right ...he called you a hearty woman; said you were like your grandmother that way."

Genie pauses in surprise at the comment. "Hearty? What, like a Shepherd's Pie or somethin'?" she asks jokingly.

"I thought maybe that was a Scottish expression," Jeff says in self-defense.

"Maybe in, like, 1910," she retorts with a smile.

She grows quiet again and looks at him closely. "Anyway, ... thanks." Her voice is softer as she brushes his hair gently with her fingers. She looks intently into his eyes, their faces nearly touching ... her glance falls to his lips, and in an instant, their lips touch. The passion in her kiss seems to engulf him, making his heart race and his spirit soar as the thrill of it momentarily replaces every other thought.

She looks into his eyes when it ends; "Ye're goin' to do great ...the strength y' need is there inside ya — it's so strong I can feel it," she whispers.

"You can, eh?"

She slowly nods with a confident smile.

"Is it a *hearty* feeling?"

She gently pushes him away; "Stop it!" she chides with a smile. Then she hands him a handkerchief to dry his eyes and face, finally giving him her approval that he looks presentable enough to return to the Hall.

Genie's encouragement has been exactly what he needed. The memory of her words and touch ...especially her kiss, somehow fills him with a calm assurance and unassailable confidence.

As GENIE WATCHES the transformation in him, she finds herself remembering Hunahpu's words in the chapel: *'No ordinary companion will do for him; only one who is strong enough to walk that journey with him.'*

"...Or *hearty* enough," she says under her breath with a self-amused smile. It feels bittersweet, ...she truly misses the kind old man.

⌘

30

MEMORIAL

The large Chapel is filled to capacity once again as Jeff and the other Board members make their way down the aisle to their reserved places in the first two rows. Jeff takes his expected place on the center aisle in the front row, the last to be seated. He can see the camera crews on the balcony and down along the side walls, knowing that the service is being simulcast to the other sites, especially Peru.

He holds his Grandmother's Bible in his hands, cherishing it.

Dr. Christos climbs to his feet from off to one side of the platform; Jeff has come to expect him there, kneeling among the choir pews. His liturgical robe and sash flow regally as he makes his way across the platform to the main lectern.

He opens with a scripture reading...

> *"...He shall wipe away every tear from their eyes;*
> *and death shall be no more;*
> *neither shall there be mourning, nor crying, nor pain, any*
>   *more:*

the first things are passed away.

Revelation Twenty-One, verse Four."

"May God add His blessing to the reading of His word."

"AMEN..." the congregation replies. The sound of their united voices thunders in the large cathedral — sending a familiar thrill through Jeff as he joins in saying it.

"Our hearts are saddened to gather again so soon to bid farewell to another dear friend, Hun Hunahpu Itzamna."

As CHRISTOS' words continue. Jeff's thoughts are filled with memories of his great-grandfather's talks. He had never known another man who possessed more genuine wisdom than Hunahpu and guesses that he never will.

For the first time since Hunahpu's tragic death, Jeff feels his heart filled with gratefulness rather than mourning; he feels thankful for the time they were able to have together, realizing what a miracle it is that he was able to know him at all. He considers his Great Grandfather's lifespan — more than seven hundred years, and realizes that it had been a difficult life, with more pain than Jeff can imagine enduring.

He recalls something that Hunahpu said to him after his uncle Barry's death; it was on the day Jeff was appointed CEO: *'A long life can become burdensome; there may come a day when the desire for a meaningful death overtakes even the wish for a meaningful life.'* Jeff understands that in his explanation of Barry's motives, Hunahpu revealed his own desire. *'A meaningful death,'* Jeff mulls over the words in his mind. Eugenia echoed the same: *'Hunahpu wanted his death to count for something.'*

. . .

SEVERAL BOARD MEMBERS share their remembrances of Hunahpu in their eulogies, as does one member of the delegation from Peru. EB is one of the last to speak, sharing a touching tribute to his dear friend. Christos calls on Jeff, last of all.

Jeff stands behind the dais and clears his throat quietly before beginning; Genie looks up at him supportively and reaches for her Grandfather's hand, holding it tightly as Jeff prepares to speak.

"I SUPPOSE that if we stayed here all week, we could barely begin to share the stories of Hunahpu's life," Jeff begins, "...a man who touched so many lives so profoundly." He pauses and looks toward Heaven, "Those will have to wait until we see him again. I, for one, look forward to being regaled with more of his *wonderful* stories."

Jeff draws a deep breath and lets it out, focusing on maintaining composure. "*Awki* ...that is a Quechua word for Grandfather... was a mentor and a friend to me — the wisest man I have ever known. If it had not been for his gentle guidance, I wouldn't be standing here as a believer today. That is a gift for which I will be eternally grateful to him.

"I remember the way he often said goodbye to me with the phrase, *Diosman Qayllaykuy* — a Quechua expression that my Grandmother used to say — it means, *draw near to God*. He not only said that, but he also lived it ...his life was a living example of how to do it. I came to realize that his wisdom came from that nearness. He explained it to me one day by saying, ' *A man cannot come to wisdom in the same way that he comes to knowledge. Instead, in order to approach wisdom, he must set aside what he thinks of as knowledge and come to seek and know the mind and will of God.* '

"He taught me that listening to your heart is infinitely more powerful than only considering what is in your head." Jeff looks out over the audience and scans the huge cathedral, noticing some of the stained glass windows still being repaired from the earlier Eljo's attacks.

"We have faced some difficult times in the past few months, as all of you know. I suppose I've struggled as hard as anyone, certainly harder than anything I've ever faced in my life before. But Hunahpu never seemed to struggle — he somehow always knew the correct path and always seemed to know what was coming next.

"I recall a particularly low point for me when I had struggled to the point of exhaustion. I will never forget his words as he looked at me dangling at the end of my rope, out of answers. He simply said: '*Good. You have come to the end of your own path, ...now you can begin.*' The profound wisdom of that advice was a great example of the way he could put his finger on the root of an issue. He had an inner compass that never wavered.

"Now it is his time to end one path and begin another." Jeff lifts his Grandmother's Bible, which he still holds in his hands, and opens it. He turns to Christos with a nod as he continues. "Dr. Christos opened our service with a beautiful reading from Revelation chapter twenty-one. I'd like to end by reading that passage in Awki's native tongue:

Chantapis Diosqa, imaschus waqachiwasqanchejta chinkachillanqataj, nisunman nanayta, llakiytawan

"The literal translation is: *...God will not merely dry off our tears; he will wipe them out completely by removing the causes of unwanted tears — all suffering and sorrow.*"

"In a fitting foreshadowing of that glorious promise, Hanahpu's final selfless act of sacrifice put an end to what might have been the dawn of unimaginable suffering for countless people. But that was just one of the endless list of things he did that earned his well-deserved reward. He is now free forever from suffering and sorrow, and we rejoice with him for that." Christos nods gratefully as he recognizes the advice that he himself had given Jeff days earlier.

Jeff looks again toward Heaven; "*Huq p'unchaykama,*" he says, adding a translation of the simple blessing that his Grandmother, Maria, had said at his parents' funeral, "*...until another day.*"

. . .

THE SOUNDS of the Choir and huge pipe organ can be heard through the Chapel's large open doors as Jeff and EB stand outside in a receiving line, along with several members of the Peruvian delegation.

Eugenia is one of the first to approach them, using her free arm to hug her Grandfather as she kisses him. She moves to Jeff, looking at him with a pleased smile; he ignores her apparent congratulations and holds out his arms instead for a hug, wrapping her in them for a quick squeeze before kissing her on the cheek. She holds him close for a moment longer and places a return kiss on his lips before backing away with a blushing glow.

Jeff glances over at EB, who is watching with a wide smile. *"What?"* he asks his older friend with a shrug that feigns ignorance. Genie looks back at her Grandfather and pats his cheek with a knowing grin. General Zobrist is the next in line. He nods professionally as he politely ignores the affectionate display in front of him and shakes EB's hand.

JUST AS ZO finishes greeting the rest of the receiving party, his phone chirps, drawing his attention. Eugenia's phone chirps as well. Both of them turn and look up to see Blandus' black helicopter fly past them overhead, heading for the landing pad about a mile away. Eugenia nods to Zo and places an earbud in her ear, and seconds later, she is coordinating the movements of her team to prepare for Blandus' arrival. The two of them begin walking toward the castle as a team of others wearing earbuds quickly join them.

Jeff also glances up from the reception line and watches the helicopter fly overhead, following it as it moves away into the distance — an uneasy feeling has suddenly come over him — he senses an unwelcome presence that he uncomfortably recognizes.

⌘

31

MALEFIC CREW

As the last of the Memorial attendees files past, Jeff excuses himself and walks briskly back to the castle, leaving EB to escort the Peruvian team. Upon entering the castle, Jeff quickly greets several groups who are offering condolences, carefully explaining that he is in a hurry as he thanks them. He breaks into a slight jog toward the Rotunda stairs and makes his way quickly to his suite. Rushing into his room, he pushes open the still-splintered door and moves directly to the dish of seeds on his nightstand, dumping the entire contents into his jacket pocket. Without pausing, he turns and exits the room.

He hesitates at Hunahpu's door. The room's emptiness feels unsettling as he stops for a moment and steps through the open doorway. It occurs to him that his Great Grandfather had always known to pray for him whenever a threat arose ...Hunahpu somehow always saw threats coming before anyone else. In the quiet of the room, Jeff suddenly realizes that he himself now seems to be the one who can see something coming.

. . .

WHILE HE IS CONSIDERING the thought, he hears the castle's door alarm announcing that a weapon has been detected; Jeff knows that means Blandus and his bodyguards have arrived. He wastes no time returning downstairs, arriving in time to see Blandus standing at the door while two of his guards submit to pat-downs. The foreboding that Jeff feels grows stronger as he approaches them.

"How many guards are there?" he whispers to Zo as he draws near.

Zo turns his back to Blandus and his men, quietly answering that there are eight altogether — two here and six more out in the foyer.

"Is that all? Have you seen them?" Jeff asks suspiciously.

"Yes …why?" Zo answers curiously.

Jeff doesn't answer; instead, he walks straight past Blandus toward the door. He is squeezing one of the seeds in his fist as he feels it begin to vibrate, confirming the danger he has been sensing. Pulling the door open, he steps through aggressively, expecting to see the hideous sight of Eljo pressure suites, but instead finds only the usual team of tough-looking mercenaries in black suits. In fact, this time, they aren't even insisting on holding their weapons — all of them have chosen to give them up, stepping past Jeff one by one as they are carefully scanned and searched. The last of them looks at him with a cold gaze as he starts to pass; it makes Jeff shudder uncomfortably. By all accounts, the man has normal vital signs and is very much alive; however, Jeff is certain that something is dangerously wrong.

Before the man reaches the door, Jeff puts his hand on him and leans close, whispering a familiar refrain: "*Per Vergam Dei…*" The seed in his hand sends a surge up one arm and down the other, causing a bright flash to be seen in the man's eyes. The bodyguard stops and staggers forward for a few steps, then looks around, appearing disoriented.

Jeff pats him on the back and opens the door for him, then follows the man inside. He immediately encounters Blandus looking considerably more stern-faced than he had on his prior visit.

"Is there anything wrong?" Blandus asks coldly. "Have my guards passed your inspection?"

Jeff offers Blandus his hand to shake. "Please excuse the heightened level of caution," Jeff explains. "We've had a number of ...incidents... in recent months, and we can't be too careful. We wouldn't want any harm to come to you or our other guests."

Blandus' expression remains stoic. If anything, he has been practicing his steely demeanor since he was last here. "Yes, I do recall hearing that you've had some trouble of late," he remarks coldly. However, you needn't worry about us; I can assure you that my guards and I can take care of ourselves."

"That's good to know," Jeff says with just enough innuendo to leave Blandus guessing whether his comment was meant as reassurance or a warning that his security team would be watching them closely. He suspects it was the latter.

Blandus' eyes narrow suspiciously as he continues. "In any event, as you can see, my men have chosen to disarm in a gesture of good faith. In light of recent tensions, we thought it best."

"Thank you," Jeff says, looking him in the eye. "Your men are welcome here; you have nothing to fear from anyone in Loch Harnan."

Blandus nods without smiling. "In return for our good faith gesture, I was hoping they might be allowed to accompany me to the office suite for the Board meeting."

Jeff considers the request — it obviously looks like a thinly veiled attack plan, especially in light of Jeff's encounter in the foyer. On the other hand, if the threat is what he suspects, it might be best to have them where he can personally keep a close eye on them.

"Perhaps that can be arranged; I'll ask EB to put it to a vote," Jeff offers.

Blandus nods again, with a sly smile this time, as Jeff excuses himself and walks away.

FINDING EB STANDING WITH EUGENIA, ZO, and Berenger, Jeff explains Blandus' request. Several of them object to the idea at first, but Jeff quiets them with a gesture to get their attention.

"This could be an opportunity in our favor," he quietly explains. "If there is any trouble, it would violate the Florence protocol."

EB considers it for a moment. "Jeff is right," he agrees. "The Florence protocol was included in the bylaws by Cornelius because of the parties' distrust of one another. It stipulates that any act of violence enacted by, or on behalf of, one board member against another will result in the immediate loss of that party's Board seat."

"Spread the word to the others," Jeff instructs. "We'll invite Blandus' guards to join us."

"Are you sure that's wise?" Zo asks in surprise.

"I didn't say we had to invite them alone," Jeff adds with a smile, "I'm sure Genie can muster an equal number of qualified agents to provide security. How can he object? Just remember, any aggression has to come from them."

"I'm on it," Genie agrees immediately as she steps away and taps her commlink.

"Right then," Zo says, folding his huge arms. "This should be a rather interesting Board meeting."

EB AND JEFF are the last to enter the large Boardroom, noting the Board members seated around the table, as well as Blandus' contingent of eight guards standing along the wall behind him; they are matched by an equal number of Hastleworth guards standing along the wall behind Jeff's seat. Blandus has a smug look on his face.

EB brings the meeting to order. "In our first order of business, we have a motion by Mr. Sutherland to grant Mr. Alfos' request for his security detail to be present for today's meeting. In return, Mr. Sutherland requests an equal number of his own security personnel. Is there a second for the motion?"

"I second," Blandos says quickly in a smooth, confident voice. The guards behind him stand coldly at attention, their eyes scanning the Board members' faces closely.

"All in favor, say, Aye," EB requests, calling the vote. A number of Ayes are recorded.

"All opposed say nay," Dr. Christos replies, " Nay.

"I'm sorry," Christos says to Jeff, "personal convictions prevent me."

Jeff nods reassuringly to him, letting him know it is ok.

"The Ayes have it," EB announces with a gavel strike. "The security personnel may remain for today's session only."

Jeff has been studying Blandus' reaction and the faces of his guards carefully. He notices that several of the guards' eyes flicked to all black several times during the vote, especially when Christos voted nay. They appeared to stand down as the vote passed. Jeff has the sense that they had been prepared to attack immediately if it had gone against them.

EB PAUSES and looks toward Huanhpu's vacant seat; the other members' eyes follow sadly. "Let the record show that the seat formerly held by Hun Hunahpu Itzamna sits vacant due to his recent passing. As a matter of protocol, the Board is required to initiate a search for a replacement member to be elected as soon as practical. Barring any objections, the minutes will show that said search has been authorized." The room is silent for a moment, giving any member a chance to object. EB strikes his gavel: "No objections have been received."

"The next order of business is a review of certain circumstances in connection with last week's attack by Eljo forces," EB announces.

JEFF WATCHES BLANDUS' guards — all except one bear angry scowls on their faces as the attack is mentioned. The one exception, the man Jeff encountered in the foyer, looks back at the others with trepidation. Jeff casually slips his hand into his jacket pocket and takes hold of another seed, squeezing it in his fist. He focuses his eyes on one of Blandus' guards — one whose eyes he has seen flicker several times.

'*The power of the Staff is in the one who wields it,*' he thinks to himself silently, remembering how Semjaza had been repelled without Jeff saying a word out loud — he had only been able to think the words.

"*Per Vergam Dei...*" he repeats silently to himself with his eyes fixed on the guard. Instantly, there is a subtle flash of white light in the man's eyes, and he holds his forehead, catching his balance. Then he looks around, appearing as disoriented as the first man had looked back in the foyer.

IT IS clear that the Board members are unaware of what has just transpired. "Please turn your attention to the monitors in front of you," EB requests. "The footage you see is a compilation from the castle's surveillance cameras just before twelve o'clock last Tuesday afternoon."

They are watching a recording of the security monitors on the day of the attack. It contains a grid of video frames containing views from individual video feeds. As they watch, the series of separate video feeds begin to go offline, turning each panel to solid blue with a message in white lettering that indicates 'No Signal.' EB pauses the recording to explain:

"All of the castle's security cameras remained offline, as you see, for approximately fifteen minutes." He fast-forwards, then resumes playback.

The video panels begin flashing from blue back to live video as different areas of the castle come back online. Everyone's attention is drawn to a set of images of the Rotunda, which has become filled with Eljo invaders. Eugenia can be seen from several angles hanging by her throat high above the floor. The feeds have no audio, but Jeff is clearly arguing with Chesed and holding the Eljo invaders at bay. Blandus leans in close, studying the security footage with keen interest.

JEFF TAKES hold of another seed in his pocket and quickly focuses on the next of Blandus' guards, in whom he had seen the unsettling flicker of blackened eyes. As he issues the silent plea, he sees the guard's eyes flash white and watches him stagger like the others, catching his balance and looking up, clearly disoriented.

THE VIDEO FEED continues to play. The attack on Hunahpu has thankfully been edited out; Jeff isn't sure he could bear to watch it happen again. Shown without sound, Jeff's use of the Staff and the opening of the Portal are clearly visible. The feed shows the open portal in terrifying detail, including the way it consumes the Eljo forces and then the Maranish brothers. Blandus flinches angrily as he watches it. Jeff notices several more of the guards' eyes shift to all-black as they watch the scene angrily and clench their fists.

JEFF TAKES advantage of the distraction to target two more of the remaining guards, squeezing a pair of seeds in his hand. A pair of flashes in quick succession leaves the two of them looking dizzy and disoriented. Three guards remain.

"THE GAP in surveillance was caused by a system diagnostic and restart, which Jeff has admitted initiating." EB continues to explain. "Our security experts have concluded that it constituted a routine maintenance event which, although poorly timed, resulted in no permanent damage. Their recommendation to the Board, should you accept it, is to adjure in the strongest possible terms that this not be repeated, with no further action necessary."

"Jeffrey, I must request that you abstain from this vote," EB instructs, then he opens the floor to debate.

"This is an outrage!" Blandus immediately objects. "Tampering with the company's surveillance systems is a most serious offense. This is but a slap on the wrist! I must insist that Mr. Sutherland immediately step down as CEO!"

· · ·

JEFF IS NOT PAYING attention to Blandus' words; his focus is on the last three guards. He squeezes another pair of seeds in his hand and does his best to concentrate, waiting for an opportunity.

"THE CASTLE'S surveillance systems are private assets," Eugenia speaks up, countering Blandus' argument, "they are not company systems."

"That makes no difference!" Blandus goes on. "How can he be trusted as an officer of the company if he exercises such errors in judgment?"

Zo immediately speaks up, "Are you angry that he reset the cameras? Or is it because he obliterated your invasion force?"

"How dare you!" Blandus growls, standing to his feet.

AS JEFF FINDS his next opportunity, a new flash shakes one more of the guards. The disoriented guard stumbles backward against the wall, holding his head.

EB IS POUNDING HIS GAVEL, calling for order. As the room quiets, he speaks to Blandus, "Should you desire it, Mr. Alphos, you have the floor for two minutes."

Blandus' face is set in a cold and cruel expression that takes the others in the room aback. They have always known him to be arrogant and unfeeling, but have never seen him show such apparent rage and hatred. He leans both hands on the table, looks the other board members in the eye, and then focuses his gaze on Jeff. His voice is steady and calculating as he continues to stare at him.

"My constituents are demanding that this, ...newcomer... be removed immediately."

"Nonsense!" Zo exclaims.

"Under what pretense?" Adalwin Brinker asks skeptically.

EB taps his gavel, reminding the room that Blandus' time has not expired.

"We raise the charges of blatant dereliction of duty," Blandus continues, "willful disregard for the company's welfare, and placing his own interests above his responsibilities as CEO. Where has he been for these past three months? Off chasing superstitious myths while the company is left floundering without a leader!"

JEFF IS NOT PARTICULARLY concerned about Blandus' rant, but his direct stare is making it difficult to focus his own gaze on the remaining guards without giving away what he is doing. He squeezes two seeds in his hand and looks back at Blandus calmly.

EB STRIKES HIS GAVEL, announcing that Blandus' two minutes have expired. Blandus sits down slowly with a smug look as he continues to stare at Jeff.

"Mr. Sutherland," EB says following parliamentary procedure, "These charges have been brought against you by a duly appointed Board member. Do you wish to respond?"

Jeff accepts and rises to his feet.

"I WILL CONFESS that there have been times in the past three months when I felt that this role was beyond me; there have even been times when I wished I could have walked away from it. The day that Angus was killed was one of those days," he says, looking back at EB, who lowers his head soberly, "...nearly losing Eugenia during the Eljo's invasion was another," he adds as he glances at her, seeing her eyes moisten with tears, "...and Hunahpu's death most certainly was.

"But in all of those times, I never lost faith in the *people* who make up this company or in the mission that they stand for. In that respect, I adamantly deny the charge that I have ever disregarded the company's welfare or been derelict in my duty to it ...or to them. The company's leadership is right here, all around this table, and not just in my seat. It is far from being adrift, as I see it.

"Regarding the pursuit of self-interest, I don't feel that I need to defend or justify myself or my actions — those of you here who know me can judge those for yourselves. The past three months have been extraordinary beyond belief; they have changed me in ways I never imagined possible.

"As to the charge of chasing superstitious myths…," he places his hand on the monitor screen, drawing the others' attention to a frozen image of the open portal as it is consuming a hundred black ghosts, along with Chesed and Eblis, "…it appears, rather, that they are *supernatural realities* …and it is *they* that have been chasing *us. …Until now.*" He leans his hands on the table and looks Blandus in the eyes, "…, But now we are prepared to begin chasing *them*."

BLANDUS'S FACE grows even harder, and his gaze fixes on Jeff with pure hatred, but he soon catches himself and sits back in his seat, as his expression changes to a smug-looking smile.

Everyone else in the room looks at Jeff with varying degrees of awe-stricken wonder. After a silent pause, EB clears his throat and endeavors to get the meeting back on track.

"Thank you, Jeff, …Mr. Sutherland," EB says as Jeff takes his seat. He looks at the others, "Is there a motion to vote on the charges that have been raised?"

Blandus lifts his forearm with two fingers raised to indicate yes.

"The motion has been raised. Is there a second?"

The room remains silent as the Board members look at one another.

"The motion has not been seconded," EB announces, striking his gavel.

⌘

DESPERATE MEASURES

J eff regrets being drawn into the exchange with Blandus; it has only made it harder for him to remain unnoticed as he attempts to dispatch whatever Eljo evil still possesses the remaining guards.

He barely hears EB's words as he calls for a vote....

"Now, to close the matter of the surveillance incident. You have heard our security experts' recommendation. What say ye?"

"I move that we accept the recommendation!" Zo bellows in a booming voice.

His motion to accept quickly passes with nine in favor and Blandus voting in opposition; Jeff abstains.

EB looks at Jeff with a warm smile as he introduces the next agenda item. "It is with very great pleasure that I confirm Jeff's successful completion of his Challenge; let me be the first to officially congratulate you on this momentous achievement!" The Board members break into applause — at least all except one of the Board members.

Jeff nods uncomfortably as all eyes focus on him. This really isn't helping his effort to save them from the Eljo-possessed guards.

"As you know," EB continues, "as a result of his quest's completion, he is now eligible for confirmation as the official CEO and permanent Board membership. This must be officially authorized by a simple majority vote.

"All in favor…."

Ten Ayes are recorded. Not surprisingly, Blandus is opposed.

"AND NOW, for the vote that we have waited three months to undertake… Chairmanship of the Board." A copy of the company bylaws appears on their monitors, with the pertinent section highlighted. EB reads aloud as the others follow on their screens:

"*Selection of a new Chairman must be made by a vote of no fewer than ten full members, representing one hundred percent of the company's shares. Furthermore, the vote shall be determined by a count of voted shares, rather than the number of members' votes.*"

"I should inform the Board that Hunahpu left his shares to his great-grandson, Jeffrey," EB explains. "Therefore, 100 percent of the company's shares are indeed represented in this room."

JEFF TAKES ADVANTAGE OF THE MEMBERS' momentary distraction to target the remaining guards. He squeezes the pair of seeds that he still holds in his hand, but is only able to see the face of one of the remaining guards. He quickly decides to take care of that one while he has the chance, watching as a flash of white light leaves the guard, who looks dizzy and disoriented.

EB CONTINUES, "As the largest shareholder and a permanent Board member, Mr. Sutherland will be participating in the vote for

Chairman along with the rest of us. In addition to his shares, each of you holds 1% of the shares, with the remaining 20% represented by Blandus Alphos.

"Mister Alphos, have you conferred with the shares' owners regarding their vote in this matter?"

"I have," Blandus replies. "They have authorized me to nominate a candidate on their behalf."

Everyone rolls their eyes, guessing that he will be nominating himself without a doubt.

"Very well," EB acknowledges, "Who is your nominee?"

"Dreyken Sidero," Blandus replies.

A gasp can be heard throughout the room as everyone wonders how the Borgia could think that Dreyken had the slightest chance of consideration.

JEFF, meanwhile, is still trying to get a bead on the last of the guards, but he is standing directly behind Blandus, who, from Jeff's vantage point, blocks the guard's face completely.

"YOUR NOMINATION IS DULY RECOGNIZED and noted," EB confirms. He then steps to the side of the lectern and hands his gavel to Eugenia, surprising the others.

"I yield the Chair to Eugenia so that I may speak on my own behalf," he declares. Eugenia nods to him to go on. "As you all know, Barrymore was a close personal friend and mentor to me for most of my life. I always felt that I would never know a more capable or noble man than he was. And so it is with a great deal of conviction and personal joy that I nominate a man who has proved himself to be every bit Barry's equal in those respects. Please allow me the privilege of nominating Jeffrey Thomas Sutherland-Hastleworth for Chairman of the Board."

The room is once again flooded with applause, as this time, the

Hastleworth agents also join the Board members in expressing their approval of EB's nomination.

JEFF NODS gratefully to his older friend but is more focused on waiting for Blandus to shift so he can get a clear look at the remaining guard. Blandus, however, is sitting as still as a stone statue, and just as cold-looking.

EB ASKS to retake the gavel, and Eugenia quickly accedes, returning him to his place as the meeting chairman.

"Are there any further nominations?" The room remains silent.

EB strikes his gavel, "Nominations are complete. There are two nominees for Chairman of the Hastleworth Board. A quorum of at least ten Board members must be present; the candidate with the highest number of shares voted 'yea' will be the winner."

"Let me remind our shareholders," EB says carefully - clearly speaking for Jeff's benefit, "that the results will be determined based on the number of shares you control."

JEFF IS STILL STRUGGLING to see the remaining guard; he carefully shifts in his chair, moving closer to Hunahpu's empty seat in an attempt to see past Blandus, but his rival board member meets his gaze and stares at him suspiciously.

"FOR THE CHAIRMANSHIP," EB begins, "the first nominee is Dreyken Sidero."

"All in favor..."

"Aye," Blandus says in a loud voice.

"Those opposed..." Everyone else responds, nay.

"Let the record show that Dreyken Sidero has earned a twenty percent share," EB notes.

"The second nominee is Jeffrey Sutherland."

"All in favor…"

JUST AS EB is saying this, Hartwin Odem suddenly reaches for his throat, clearly choking. Jeff notices a smoky black tendril slowly wrapping around his neck, but can't see where it is coming from. He somehow has the presence of mind to shout, "**Aye**!" registering his vote before jumping from his seat. Several others have risen as well and are rushing to help Hartwin, while Blandus sits with a gloating smirk on his face as he watches the commotion that interrupts their voting.

From his standing position, Jeff can see the remaining guard; his eyes have turned completely black as long stringy tendrils of smoke flow from his fingertips toward his choking victim. Jeff clenches the seed still in his hand, and his stare burrows into the Eljo guard, instantly shattering the black mist in a bright flash. Rather than staggering in a disoriented daze, however, this guard collapses to the floor.

Hartwin draws a long gasp of air and sits up straight, signaling that he is able to breathe again.

Doctor Abayomi leaves Hartwin and rushes to the fallen guard to check on him. Blandus immediately stands and orders his guards to stop him, but they don't move, looking at the scene with dazed, confused expressions.

"I'm a medical doctor!" Imhotep explains urgently to them as he kneels beside the fallen man. The moment he touches him, he knows something is very wrong. "This man has been dead for some time!" he exclaims after a short examination. He notices a wound behind the guard's ear; "He's been shot, …He was murdered!"

BLANDUS SUDDENLY REACTS IN RAGE, jumping onto the doctor and choking him as he orders his guards to attack the others. "KILL THEM! KILL THEM ALL!" he shouts.

It takes half a dozen Hastleworth agents to pull Blandus off the doctor while his guards raise their hands in surrender and back against the wall. "We don't even know how we got here!" one of them confesses as he readily surrenders.

As Blandus is being restrained, he begins to growl and writhe grotesquely — his eyes suddenly turn completely black, and a deep, monstrous voice emerges, "*All of you will die!*"

At once, a thick black mist rushes from his mouth and eyes, rising into the air as it gathers above him; then it strikes the table and explodes outward, catching the Board members in the chest and stealing their breath.

Jeff sees one of its black wispy tentacles racing toward him but meets it with his fist, still squeezing one of the Staff's seeds; he pounds it onto the table with a loud cry: "*PER VERGAM DEI! ...IN THE POWER OF CHRIST!*"

The brilliant light erupting from his hand illuminates the room like a flash grenade, instantly obliterating the Eljo monster and leaving only wisps of black smoke dissipating in the air.

The Board members are coughing and gasping for breath, but they are all alright.

"I'm really gettin' t' hate those things!" Eugenia exclaims angrily as she climbs from her chair and bends over to catch her breath.

———————

SEVERAL MORE OF her agents entered the room in response to the emergency call button she had triggered. They cuff Blandus and the other guards and lead them out of the Boardroom. Blandus is yelling objections and insisting that his superiors be notified.

"Sidero has won!" he yells, "you didn't have ten votes!"

Eugenia gives instructions for her team to pull a hood over his head.

"Take them to the holdin' cells until we figure out what to do with 'em," she instructs.

The dead guard is taken to the castle's morgue, and a forensics team combs the room for any other evidence.

AN HOUR PASSES before they are able to resume the Board meeting, now down to ten members.

"A full review will be made of Mr. Alfos' outburst and physical attacks," EB explains. "It does appear that the Florence protocol was violated. The result of which will likely be the loss of the Borgia's Board seat, pending their appeal, of course.

"The company's bylaws state, and I quote, that: *'a quorum, once established at a meeting, shall not be broken.'* Therefore, the meeting is still in session.

"The vote for chairman was not fully concluded prior to our ... interruption. The bylaws make no specific provision for an interrupted vote. If there are no objections, we will continue from the point at which the interruption occurred." The Board members glance around the room at one another, nodding in agreement with EB's recommendation.

"Very well," EB continues. "The voting began with twenty percent of the company's shares voted for Dreyken Sidero. Voting for the next nominee had already begun, and one vote in favor was recorded. A repeat vote is not permitted by the bylaws. Nonetheless, since a full quorum of eleven voters had already been a part of the vote in progress, the record will show one vote in favor, with seventy-one percent of the company's shares having been voted in favor of Mr. Sutherland." As EB says this, the rest of the Board members breathe a palpable sigh of relief.

"We have only to complete the vote then," EB declares: "All opposed...?"

"Let the record show that no opposed votes have been recorded." He strikes his gavel.

"By a majority vote of seventy-one percent, and with a quorum of voters present, **Jeffrey Sutherland is elected as Chairman.**"

The room erupts in applause.

JEFF BARELY HEARS the applause as he looks down at the worn armrests of his leather chair, which had been occupied for so long by his uncle Barry. He can't help but become suddenly emotional as the weight of it hits him. The shoes he had already begun to fill were a giant's.

A thousand thoughts run through his mind at once as a flurry of events from the past three months replay in his head. He finally realizes that EB is inviting him to the lectern to say a word, and it takes several moments for him to respond. He stands and shakes EB's hand, wrapping his arm around his dear friend's shoulders and embracing him, then steps to the lectern and glances down at the two empty chairs beside him as he gathers his thoughts.

"IT MIGHT SOUND UNORIGINAL, but the only words that come to mind are: 'Thank You.' Not simply for this honor, but for everything that all of you have meant to me over the past few months, ...the way that you have embraced and supported me since I arrived here."

Jeff looks at EB, "EB, ...you've been a friend unlike any I've ever known, ...as solid as a rock and a trustworthy counselor to me, thank you."

Jeff's eyes turn to Eugenia, "Genie, your help to me these past months has been completely selfless; with your own heavy load of responsibilities, you gave so much of yourself to our training sessions. Not to mention placing your own life in harm's way." Genie glances down humbly as everyone looks at her and nods in agreement at the sight of her arm in a sling. "...How can I ever repay you for that?" he adds quietly.

He then looks back to Hunahpu's empty chair, and his eyes become misty, letting a single tear escape and roll down his cheek. The room waits silently as he regains his composure. "Hunahpu was much more than a teacher and mentor to me; he was *family*, as you all know. Our days together over the past few months were a rare and precious gift. The lessons he taught me, ...especially the ones that led me to the Lord, were a gift so great that my gratitude can never be sufficiently expressed. He was the wisest man I will ever know and also the most selfless."

Jeff chokes back his emotion as he pauses. "...His last act of generosity was his most selfless of all; in that profound moment, he saved far more than *my* life, ...and it has changed me forevermore.

"Agradiseyki Awki *...my deepest thanks to you, Grandfather,*" he quietly says to the empty chair, wiping the tear from his cheek. His private expression is left untranslated.

HIS EYE IS DRAWN to the chair beside Hunahpu's — now his own. "How can I ever express enough thanks for all that my uncle Barry did for me? In making my rescue possible," he nods to EB gratefully, "and for all that he prepared in advance to help me. I couldn't possibly have reached this point without him."

A heartfelt round of applause erupts in honor of Barry's memory. As it ends, Jeff quiets the room with a gesture of his hand as he looks at everyone with a humbled expression. "There's something I'd like to do if you'll permit me," he says, "I'd like very much to pray for all of you."

With that, Jeff closes his eyes and begins to pray, fighting back a tremendous swell of emotion as he lifts each person in the room to God's throne, one by one, beginning with EB and continuing around to Zo. His words seem to flow from a deep reservoir of spiritual feeling, ...a place beyond himself, as he prays for each of them and the mission still ahead, ... for God's help and safety in the coming days.

There is not a person in the room who does not recognize it; ... it occurs to all of them that Jeff has received a new gift — perhaps his most powerful of all. He is revealing a spirit of intercession — much like the one that belonged to his great-grandfather.

. . .

WHEN HE FINISHES, he is surprised to find Christos standing beside him. The elder missionary places his hand on Jeff and invites the others to come to gather around; then, with the laying on of their hands, all of them, with one mind, commend him to the work that lies ahead, ...from this day forward it will be his life's work.

⌘

33

A NEW DAY

T he sunset has turned the western horizon into a spectacular
display of yellow, red, and orange-colored sky. Jeff and
Genie sit together on the garden bench, watching the spectacle of colors, interspersed with purple and blue and streaked with
wisps of white clouds, as the orange fireball slowly sinks into the
ocean.

The events of the day swirl in both of their minds. Genie replays
Blandus' bizarre and desperate attack in the Board meeting, while Jeff
can't stop thinking of something much more extraordinary — the way
she kissed him before the Memorial service.

He reaches over uncertainly and offers his hand for her to hold —
she quickly accepts it.

"Thanks again for your encouragement this morning," he says. He
sees her eyes drift briefly to his lips as she smiles.

"You're welcome," she says in a tone that seems to communicate
much more than just the common expression. "Told you that you'd do
great today."

Jeff sighs as he considers the day, with a flurry of other memories flashing through his mind. "You're probably used to all this — you've lived here most of your life, ...there's really never a dull moment in Loch Harnan, is there?"

"Well, I think that your experiences here have been more excitin' than most, but I've certainly had my share of excitement lately," she agrees.

"That's for sure," he commiserates, "...any *more* excitement is likely to have killed you!"

"Well, I'm glad to still be here," she answers softly with a smug-looking smile.

"That makes two of us," he replies quietly, looking her in the eyes.

He is reminded of something that EB said at breakfast:

> 'It is not a good idea for a man to wait too long to make his intentions known.'

He suddenly feels his heart beating faster as he considers it. 'His intentions,' ...the words seem to reverberate in his mind. He knows that he does, in fact, have intentions, ...he admits that he has known it for months without allowing himself to face the fact. He takes a deep breath and quietly stares at the ocean while pondering it. The sun has nearly disappeared beneath the horizon, and its light casts a golden glow over everything it touches.

Genie sits quietly beside him. She can tell that he is struggling and has a pretty good idea of what he is struggling with. The truth is that she has struggled with her feelings, too, ...for a long time. But not anymore — she came to terms with her feelings a while ago. Waiting for him, it turned out, was even harder. Without a word, she leans against his shoulder and releases a deep sigh of her own; "It's beautiful, isn't it?" she says quietly.

Jeff feels himself lean into her a little as he welcomes her nestling. "Yeah, ...really beautiful," he answers in a half-whisper.

They sit together like that until long after the sun has disappeared and a star-filled sky has replaced the streaks of golden sunlight. Their casual conversation recounts the past few months' events, especially the last week, as Jeff confesses how much his time here has changed his thinking on so many things.

It has honestly changed everything, he admits silently to himself. Most of all, he realizes that it has changed his feelings about finally settling down …about sharing his life with someone. He can definitely see Genie being that person — if she is interested. For now, neither of them dares to move for fear of interrupting the moment; they are both trying to make it last for as long as possible.

Finally, Genie lifts her head and brushes aside her long hair, looking over at him. He takes the opportunity to stretch his arm over her shoulders and looks her in the eyes as she stares up at him in the moonlight. Her glance falls to his lips again, and he soon meets hers with a soft kiss. Her reaction leaves no doubt in his mind that she is as interested as he is — she leans her head back as he takes her in his arms and kisses her again.

He looks into her eyes and brushes back her hair with his fingertips.

"Now/Now what/what?" they both ask simultaneously. They look at each other in surprise and laugh together.

"Well, we've already done the *just friends'* thing," Genie offers, cutting directly to the point. "I guess that just leaves *'enemies'* or *'lovers.'*

"Hmmm," Jeff ponders, "I definitely wouldn't want you as an enemy — I've seen you fight."

"I guess it's lovers, then," she says softly.

Her words draw Jeff to her like a powerful magnet. He leans forward and kisses her again as she wraps her one good arm around his neck and returns his kiss with unmistakable feeling.

The two of them are walking on air when they slowly make their way back to the castle. It's after ten o'clock, and the main lobby and Great Hall are deserted as they enter. Jeff invites her to his suite for coffee, but Genie decides that it might be a good idea to slow things down a little.

"You can walk me back to my door if you'd like," she suggests instead. He agrees, realizing that she is right. When they kiss good-night in front of her door, Jeff feels his heart ache; the way she looks at him as she says goodnight makes him forget how to walk for a moment. He checks to see if his feet are touching the floor before starting back to his suite, wearing a broad smile.

Wednesday Morning...

BLANDUS BOARDS HIS HELICOPTER, looking forlorn. He and his Eljo-free crew of bodyguards know what awaits them back at the Borgia's headquarters. In his disastrous performance, he has lost the Borgia's Board seat and has been permanently banned from all Hastleworth facilities and Loch Harnan. To make matters worse for him, the group of Eljo that Jeff destroyed had been in the vanguard of the most elite Estonian troop; Koletis would not be pleased.

Genie and Zo stand stone-faced as they watch the chopper lift off, escorted by a half dozen dibjet fighters.

"That's the last we'll see of him — and good riddance!" Zo says as they watch them fly away. He turns his head toward Genie with a friendly smile. "It's a new day — that it is."

Genie remains characteristically stoic, hiding her smile, but he can easily discern the joy in her eyes. 'It is definitely a new day,' she happily thinks to herself, privately admitting that her thoughts are focused on Jeff rather than Blandus.

LATER THAT AFTERNOON, Genie checks her watch as she prepares to set off on a rare midweek trail run, kneeling for a moment to tighten her shoelaces. The simple task is a struggle for her, seeing that she still has one arm in a sling.

The sound of Jeff's voice surprises her.

"Hey, I'm glad I caught you. Mind if I join you today?"

"Think y' can keep up?" she answers with a smile. She looks down at her loosened shoelace in frustration. "Since ye're here, can y' tighten this lace for me?"

"I don't know," Jeff jokes, "looks like a ploy to get me to kneel at your feet."

"It's likely to be the only time yer not chasin' after me," she teases.

"I think I like the sound of that," Jeff says with a grin as he kneels and steals a kiss. He finishes tying her laces and quickly joins her as she trots off.

"So, what are y' plannin' t' do now that yer Quest is over with?" Genie asks as they jog together.

"Not sure. I suppose I should get to know the company a little better. I'll probably spend more time at the London office. I'm sure EB would appreciate a break."

"It's been ages since I visited the Sydney or Hong Kong offices myself," Genie admits. "I suppose a trip is in order."

HER COMMENT SPARKS a plan in Jeff's mind… a global tour sounds like a great idea.

⌘

34

OVERTURE

Jeff soon unveils his plan for them to tour the company's global facilities together.

"EB and Adalwin will be accompanying us," he explains to Genie, referring to Adalwin Brinker, the company's President.

"Us?" Genie challenges.

"Well, yes. I can't go on a world tour without my head of security. It's a dangerous world, after all."

"It sounds like ye're orderin' me to go… I suppose I have no choice then."

Jeff strokes his chin thoughtfully… "Hmm, that hadn't occurred to me; I guess I *could* order you, couldn't I. But I suppose a polite invitation may be better." He takes her hand, lifting it to his lips as he bows his head.

"Madame, voudriez-vous m'accorder l'honneur de votre belle présence?" (*Madam, would you grant me the honor of your beautiful presence?*)

Genie can't hide her smile as she curtsies. "Oui, oui, monsieur. Ce serait un honneur." (*It would be an honor.*)

THEIR FIRST STOP is the London office, where Jeff spends two days meeting with the management team. EB and Adalwin excuse themselves from dinner the first evening, leaving Jeff and Genie to dine alone at Oxo Tower, overlooking the Thames — a restaurant that Adalwin has enthusiastically recommended. They receive a warm personal welcome from the head chef and are seated at the restaurant's best table. (Adalwin later smiles as he claims to have no idea how that happened to have been arranged.) After dinner, the two of them spent the evening strolling along the Thames.

That was a much better date than they would find at their next stop, in Berenger's underground bunker. Nonetheless, Jeff and Genie both love that visit, albeit for different reasons. Genie is briefed on the engineering team's latest Aerotech and Intelligence advances, while Jeff gets to examine DNA from the Eljo pilots' captured corpses.

FOR THE REST of their trip to Sydney and Tokyo, Berenger insists that they take the company's newest Dibjet rather than a corporate plane. Aside from being much faster (capable of speeds up to 30,000 KPH in low Earth orbit), it is also outfitted with its own energy shield and a mobile version of Brandish's laser cannon. Adalwin feels out of place as the only one on board who isn't qualified to fly the thing, but finds the abundance of pilots comforting.

Jeff has to admit he is enjoying his free evenings with Genie much more than his daytime meetings. He still is not accustomed to being treated like royalty — to be perfectly honest, it makes him feel like a rare species of zoo animal. His times with Genie, in contrast, give him a chance to truly relax.

EB and Adalwin keep finding excuses to miss dinner each evening, and the chief chefs at some of the finest restaurants in Sydney and Tokyo keep coincidentally appearing to greet them wherever Jeff and Genie dine.

AFTER A TWO-WEEK TOUR, they finally deliver Adalwin back to London. Genie waits on board the Dibjet for the final leg back to CNAL, surprised to hear EB inform her that he is staying in London for a few more days. There seems to be an unusual amount of activity outside the craft as it is serviced, but she is too weary from their travels to take much notice. She dozes off as their ship departs London with Jeff at the controls.

IT IS several hours later when Eugenia awakes and notices that they have been traveling longer than she expected — as a matter of fact, they are in orbit! From the cabin window, she can see they are flying somewhere over New England, with the entire American continent visible ahead.

"What are we doing? Where are we?" she exclaims in surprise.

Jeff looks back over his shoulder at her with an apologetic expression. "Sorry, you looked exhausted, and I didn't want to wake you. I need to take one more short excursion."

"Excursion?" she says as she looks through the windshield at the astonishing view of the earth below them. "Where to, exactly?"

"It's just a quick jaunt to explore some family history," he explains, "Thought you wouldn't mind coming along; hope it's okay."

"Sure, …that's fine," she agrees, sounding surprised as well as distracted by the mesmerizing view.

It doesn't take much longer at their speed for her to begin noticing that they are starting a descent toward the northern plains of North America.

"Roger that…" Jeff says into his headset to air traffic control. He repeats his location and airspeed to the controller, along with the latitude and longitude of their destination, as Genie looks on curiously. She can see mountains in the distance and realizes that they are getting nearer. As she watches the scene carefully, they descend to several thousand feet, and her heart races a little faster; she has seen this landscape before. Her excitement finally reaches a screaming pitch as Jeff nears a forested mountain vista and hovers beside a pristine mountain lake, then sets the Dibjet down in a small clearing.

GENIE LOOKS at him with an unbelieving expression as a surge of emotion wells up within her: "How'd y' know? How'd y' find it?" she says as a wide grin fills her face.

"EB told me," Jeff reveals as he watches her expression.

Genie slaps the button to open the hatch control and rushes outside, running to the edge of the small hillside where they have landed; it overlooks Diamond Lake in the foothills of the Rockies, ... she recognizes the place — they are in Montana, and this is the same lake where her father taught her to fish. She studies her surroundings in disbelief — in fact, this is the exact spot where her father had pitched their camp! She holds a hand over her mouth as she looks back at Jeff, only to see him walking toward her with two fishing poles in his hands, already rigged with fly fishing lures.

She doesn't speak but grabs a pole with a playful smile and takes off running toward the lake; Jeff chases her. The water is ice-cold as they rush into it, wearing their sneakers. Genie checks her line and quickly lets fly a cast that sails 100 feet, then begins slowly reeling it back; she repeats the process with a grin from ear to ear.

Jeff isn't as coordinated — it takes several tries for him to get it right, and even then, he can't place it as far out as she can. He is still trying to get the hang of it when Genie reels in her first catch — a giant Northern Pike. Jeff looks at the beast of a fish in disbelief as she offers him a high-five. It's big enough to feed a dozen people! Genie removes her hook and releases it back into the lake.

Jeff casts again and immediately feels something bite; "I have one!" he exclaims proudly. It splashes wildly in the water as he reels it in, finally lifting it into the air to reveal a bream about six inches long. Genie stifles a laugh as she sees how small it is.

"Better be sendin' that one back t'grow up a bit," she jabs.

Her next catch is a beauty of a largemouth bass. Eventually, Jeff reels in a twelve-inch bluegill. They begin catching more and more as the late-day sun seems to bring the fish to the surface, looking for their dinner. They fish for the rest of the afternoon, keeping their best catches for cooking over a campfire.

JEFF GETS a fire going while Genie is cleaning the fish. Soon, they are seated in camping chairs by a warm fire as Genie flips her handiwork in an iron skillet. Jeff adds a little olive oil and seasoning, revealing that he has come prepared, and produces a bottle of red wine with crystal glasses, toasting their day as they sip it and admire the breathtaking view.

The air grows cooler as night falls, making the fire that much more inviting. Jeff drapes a blanket over Genie's shoulders, and she snuggles it around her neck, then leans her head against him with a satisfied sigh. He hugs her close as they admire the amazing blizzard of stars that has filled the vast open sky.

After enjoying the serene quiet together for a long while, Jeff suddenly stands to his feet, drawing Genie's eyes curiously. She watches him wrap a blanket over his shoulders in the cool air, looking like a cape as it settles over him, and then feels a swell of anticipation as he drops mysteriously to one knee. Light from the campfire illuminates their faces as she looks at him curiously, suddenly feeling a flurry of butterflies inside.

He speaks softly, wrestling with nervous tension of his own.

"The past few months have been the most amazing of my life," he begins honestly. They both recognize that that's clearly not an exaggeration. "I have to admit... when I met you for the first time, I knew that my life had changed forever, and it wasn't because of the castle or my heritage or even those ludicrous Eljo! ...it was because of you."

Genie feels tears welling up in her eyes as she listens. The tightness in Jeff's throat grows as he watches the emotion reflected on her face. He quickly clears his throat and does his best to lighten the mood....

"...From the first time you flipped me over your shoulder, I knew you were a different kind of woman."

Genie raises a hand to her lips and laughs nervously. She wants to make a joke about his lack of fighting skills back then, but decides not to interrupt him, listening intently.

"Those first training sessions were pretty tough. I have to confess that it was only the thought of being with *you* that kept me coming back... to be honest, I could hardly wait most mornings.

"Since then, you've been not just a trainer and coach, but also a protective partner. You've risked your life for me more than once! Even more than that, you've been my friend and my inspiration, ... you've honestly become my heart's passion."

A tear runs down her cheek, and she brushes it off.

"I know now that I can't bear the thought of living a day without you."

Genie stares into his eyes, seeing the deep sincerity in his heart reflected there. Jeff reaches out his left hand for her to hold as he continues....

"Genie, it would be my greatest joy to spend life together with you...."

"...as your husband," his right hand emerges from under the blanket, holding a diamond ring; he presents it to her as he continues...

"...Will you marry me?"

For a moment, Genie can't speak; she just nods as a surprising rush of tears begins to flow down her cheeks. For once, she doesn't try to hide them as she watches him push the ring onto her finger and breaks into a wide grin.

They jump to their feet, and she throws her arms around him as she gasps the only words that come to mind: "YES ...YES ...oh... yes, I will!"

THEIR KISS IS like a fireworks display of vivid color as they hold each other tightly. Jeff feels like shouting for joy as he looks into her face, then squeezes her and spins her around. The laughter that erupts from both of them springs spontaneously from a place deep in their souls.

They both know unquestionably that whether they live another day or a thousand years, this moment is the happiest of their lives!

⌘

35

THE STAGE IS SET

A leaded crystal drinking glass shatters as it smashes against the wall, leaving the wall's thick oak paneling wet with its contents and the scent of forty-year-old Cognac. Blandus cowers in fear as he stands before the man who has thrown it.

"The extent of your failure is breathtaking!" Dreyken Sidero shouts at him. "Not only have you failed in your plan to seize control of the Board — a plan that you assured me would succeed — but you have lost our seat entirely! More than that, you led nine members of the elite guard to their destruction, including the supreme leader's closest general! You know the punishment for failure — Koletis will not be merciful."

"PLEASE! I beg you!" Blandus pleads, "...hide me! Save me from him!"

"And put at risk my own life and those of our colleagues? Do you think Koletis would simply forgive such an act?" Dreyken waves to the men holding Blandus. "Get him out of my sight!"

Blandus screams for mercy as he is dragged from the room. Dreyken looks out his window with a sullen expression as the screams slowly fade into the distance. The past few months' events do not bode well for him or his organization. It had been a mistake to trust the Maranish brothers — their own greed for power had been their downfall. Now Dreyken knows that this spectacular disaster will surely cause Koletis to doubt the Borgia's usefulness.

"THERE IS a call from Estonia for you, Sir, on line one…" he hears his secretary say over the intercom. Dreyken draws a deep breath and steels himself. "Put him through," he acknowledges as he moves to his massive desk and takes a seat, lifting the phone to his ear.

"Good evening, Sir," he says carefully.

The voice on the other end of the line speaks in a calm, smooth tone, without a hint of anger or disapproval. Still, it is not a kind voice; Dreyken knows better than to mistake it for that.

"It would appear that we have had a setback," the voice says in a matter-of-fact tone. Dreyken zeroes in on the word 'we.'

"Mr. Alphos is on his way to you," Dreyken says sternly, not wishing to show any hint of weakness. There is silence on the other end of the line; Dreyken takes it as approval. "What will you do with him?" he finally asks.

"He will die, of course," the voice states coldly, "but that is no longer a concern of yours."

"Of course," Dreyken agrees.

"It would seem that we have a new nemesis," the voice continues, "…a man so young, and yet he has accomplished more in a few short months than his predecessors had achieved in a thousand years. How do you suppose that is possible?"

Dreyken swallows uncomfortably, "I don't know, Sir."

Another long pause makes him straighten in his chair and flinch nervously. He cannot help but acknowledge the unspoken charge this silence conveys: if their attack in Boston had succeeded, all would be different. It had been Dreyken's decision to divert their forces from Jeff to pursue Barrymore on that fateful night.

"What are your orders, Sir?" he finally asks, breaking the unbearable silence.

"You are to do nothing," the voice says calmly, but the subtle threat it carries can be clearly heard behind the words. "The time is near now; the next move will be mine."

A CLICK SIGNALS that the call has ended. Dreyken leans back and loosens his collar uncomfortably, using the back of his sleeve to mop the beads of sweat that are forming on his forehead. He has an idea of what is coming, …the world will never be the same.

⌘

The End

THANK YOU FOR READING!

PLEASE TAKE A MOMENT TO LEAVE A REVIEW.

(Scan the QR code below)

Join the mailing list for updates on new releases and special offers at: arkharbor.press and click on Contact.

Continue the Adventure in Book Five:
Niergel Chronicles
The White Castle

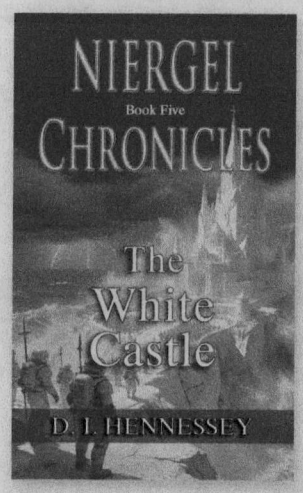

Niergel Chronicles - The White Castle

AUTHOR'S NOTE

Separating Fact from Fiction

The Niergel Chronicles is clearly fiction, but also contains many interwoven elements of truth. The distinctions below are listed for any reader who may not be familiar with the Bible or what Christians actually believe.

CLEARLY FICTION:

'Hastleworth Enterprises' is, of course, a fictional company; any resemblance to real companies is entirely unintended and coincidental.

The Bible's account of Noah's Flood is not fictional. Everything else about the story of Arubija, his family, and their survival of Noah's flood is fictional.

There really is no secret Niergel organization.

'The Borgia Syndicate' is a fictional creation and is not meant to resemble or portray any real persons or organizations with or without similar names.

Leanan Sidhe (*pr. Lan han Shee*) is a fictional character from Irish folklore, one of Ireland's mythological vampires. The fictional demon was said to appear as a beautiful woman who could inspire poets and musicians, sharing with them intelligence, creativity, and magic – but at the price of their lives.

The depiction of smoky Eljo creatures is fictional. The Elioud race (Eljo) are described in the Book of Enoch, which is not in the Bible. They are said to be the children of the Nephilim, the offspring of fallen angels.

The Bible does make reference to the Nephilim, saying simply that: "The Nephilim were in the earth in those days, ... when the sons of God came unto the daughters of men, and they bare children to them," Gen 6:4. Scholars commonly believe that *"the sons of god"* were the fallen angels described in the New Testament book of Jude: *"And angels that kept not their own principality but left their proper habitation, he hath kept in everlasting bonds under darkness unto the judgment of the great day."* Jude 1:6.

The Cylch o Awydd (The Ring of Desire) is fictional. Magical objects like Eternal Rings, Scepters, and Scrolls illustrate the deceptive ways in which we can be persuaded to defy God or rely on human reason. Not realizing that our reasoning can easily be manipulated by our soul's true enemies.

The Shepherd's Staff is fictional. Its attributes are a metaphor for the way God can choose ordinary people and use them to accomplish remarkable things.

The alternate dimension of 'Tir Lai' is a fictional place.

The secret Estonian organization and references to Koletis (The Beast) are fictional creations of the author. The Bible does speak of coming end-times events in which a powerful world leader, known as the Beast or Antichrist, will lead the world into a great final battle called Armageddon.

DEFINITELY NOT FICTION:

The story of Jeff's journey is a reflection of the real search that every man and woman confronts sooner or later. Jeff eventually realizes that his greatest discoveries are revelations about himself, especially his one greatest need. Which, it turns out, is for a personal connection with his creator.

BOOKS BY

D. I. HENNESSEY

Books in the Within & Without Time Series:

Book 1: Within and Without Time

Book 2: The Traveler

Book 3: The Secret Door

Book 4: Evil Ascendant - Deliverance

Book 5: The Time of His Choosing

Book 6: A Mission Rarely Given

Book 7: An Unexpected Hour

Books in the Niergel Chronicles Series:

Book 1: Niergel Chronicles - Last Hope

Book 2: Niergel Chronicles - Quest

Book 3: Niergel Chronicles - The Tenth Mantle Bearer

Book 4: Niergel Chronicles - The Dragon's Tail

Book 5: Niergel Chronicles - The White Castle

Available on Amazon

Within and Without Time Series:

"www.amazon.com/gp/product/B09DFDM364"

Niergel Chronicles Series:

"https://www.amazon.com/dp/B0BCHSRZ56"

NOTES

1. IMPOSSIBLE VICTORY

1. Come Staff of God!

14. APPROACHING STORM

1. Matthew 14:28-31.
2. Parts of Abbott's sermon are inspired by: C.H. Spurgeon, Sermon #3562, "Peter walking on the Sea," MAY 3, 1917.

30. MEMORIAL

1. Dr. Garry Koch

www.ingramcontent.com/pod-product-compliance
Lightning Source LLC
Chambersburg PA
CBHW072214170626
46813CB00003B/937